I0678341

Chasing Dreams

by

JoMarie DeGioia

PUBLISHED BY:

Bailey Park Publishing

ISBN: 978-1-944181-30-7

Chasing Dreams

Book One of the Cloud Canyon Series

by

JoMarie DeGioia

Chapter 1

Cloud Canyon, California

Laurel Tanner leaned forward and squeezed the steering wheel. Her convertible VW Beetle strained up the mountain. Trees taller than she'd ever seen loomed on both sides of the winding road. Craggy rock walls were so close on her right that she could almost count the cracks between the stones. The Beetle climbed higher. The scenery was breathtaking. Rugged, stark, beautiful. She barely noticed it, though. The Sierra Nevada were just bumps standing between her and her dream.

The wind whipped through her hair but she wouldn't put the top up. The air might be whisper-thin up here but, with every mile she put between herself and San Francisco, she could feel herself starting to breathe a little bit easier.

She sniffed and wiped her cheek with the heel of her hand. Stiffening, she blotted her wet palm on her shorts. She wouldn't cry for Brad, that jerk. He wasn't worth it. Nope. The only person deserving her tears was dead and gone.

"Mom, I should have listened to you."

Oh, what a fool she'd been. Well, her mother hadn't

raised her to make the same mistake twice. Brad might have had all the power in their relationship, but now? Now that he'd ended it? She was the one making the decisions. It was just too bad her mother hadn't lived to see it.

Laurel was twenty-six years old, after all. She would just put Brad out of her mind like she put San Francisco in her rearview mirror and get on with her life. That's what she would do. Get to Reno and earn enough money to come back and open her own gallery, thank you very much. She would have the space to create the art she wanted to, and Brad could stuff his belittling opinions right up his backside.

She let the hum of the road beneath her tires soothe her frazzled nerves. She might not be the only one on the road this afternoon, but the traffic here was nothing compared to the Bay area. In fact, the road had grown more narrow and twisting over the past fifteen miles or so. Now a double yellow line divided the two lanes. Her chest tightened. Was this even the same highway?

She glanced in the rearview mirror. She couldn't see any cars behind her. Nope. Just more road disappearing around the bend. She peered through the windshield. No cars were visible in front of her, either. In fact, it seemed like it had been miles since she'd passed another car.

She spied a sign on her right, and it appeared postage-stamp small considering the huge number printed on it. She was now at five thousand feet. *Yikes.* She blew out a breath and looked down at her water bottle. She reached for it and gave it a shake. Empty. When she lifted her head again a flash of brown caught her eye. A deer loomed in front of her, a big guy with wide antlers. Her heart stopped as she drew closer. She pulled the wheel sharply to the right just an instant before the impact barreled through her body. With its tires squealing and brakes screaming, her sweet little car fought to stay on the road. It lost the battle.

As minutes passed, her heartbeat resumed and slowly returned to normal. Her car no longer made its usual purring sound. No, the only sound coming from the engine now was a low hiss. She fumbled for the key on the steering column and managed to crank it to the off position. She left it dangling in the ignition.

At least the airbag hadn't gone off. She'd heard those things could do a lot of damage to a person. Wait. Was that a good thing or not? With her eyes still squeezed shut, she took a mental inventory of her body.

Nothing seemed to be broken. She gingerly lifted her head off the steering wheel and glanced over to her right. Oh, that rock wall was close. The car's cute rounded fender was crumpled up toward the windshield. Her eyes stung with fresh tears. At least these tears had nothing whatsoever to do with Brad.

She banged her hand on the wheel. "Damn it!"

She opened her door and stepped out of the car. There was no wounded deer on the road. No blood either, that she could see. Maybe she hadn't killed it, then.

She slammed the door shut. "Thank God for small favors."

She slowly walked over to the guardrail bordering the woods and sat down. She couldn't look at her car. She just couldn't. Her future had been in front of her. There was nothing but heartache behind her, and God only knew she couldn't go back there anyway. She had no prospects in San Francisco. Brad had seen to that. She had no way to get to Reno. And now she added a wounded deer to the mix. Could this day get any worse?

* * *

The squeal of rubber tires broke through the birdsong in the woods and Jack Butler braced for the sound of impact. He soon heard it. Scraping, screaming metal against unyielding rock. It had to be some fool tourist who wandered out onto Old Mill Road instead of staying on US 80. *Great.* His first chance for a solitary hike in over a week and now he had to stop and go see what the hell happened.

He shifted his backpack to one shoulder and made his way toward the road. He spotted a small blue convertible smashed up against a rock outcropping about thirty yards away, but couldn't see any passengers from his vantage point.

He pulled his radio out of his pack and pressed the button "Hey, Bo. Over." he called.

"Hey," Bo's voice squawked back. "What's up? Over."

"There's a wreck on Old Mill Road." Jack paused, throwing a glance in the other direction to gauge the approximate location. "About ten miles south of Cloud Canyon. Over."

Bo's bark of laughter reached him over the static. "I

thought you were off-duty today. Over"

Jack cursed softly. "Yeah, me too. Just send the truck? Over."

"Will do," Bo called back. "But it's gonna be a while, Cuz. Pete's out with the flatbed. Over."

"Okay." Jack walked toward the wreck. "I'll radio the EMTs if they're needed and stay with the wreck. Over."

"Cool," Bo returned. "Bo, over and out."

Jack put the radio back and cupped a hand around his mouth. "Hello! Do you need help?"

He didn't get an answer. He came up to the car and could see there was no one inside. The right fender was a mess from where it had kissed the rock wall. He stepped around the wreck and saw who he assumed was the driver sitting on the guardrail a few feet away. *Whoa.* Maybe he should have expected a female to be driving the wimpy little car. He couldn't have dreamed up this particular female, though.

A white cotton tank hugged the girl's breasts and khaki shorts rode high on her sleek thighs. Her hair was a mess of blond curls falling halfway down her back. A punch of desire struck his belly. He let his gaze follow her bare legs down to her sandaled feet. Her toenails were painted pink. Sweet and sexy.

He forced his attention back to her face. She stared at the ground. He placed her age somewhere in her mid-twenties. She looked a little pale, and any desire he felt swiftly took a backseat to responsibility. His Ranger training returned in a rush.

"Miss?" he asked.

She pushed her hair back from her face with one shaking hand and turned toward him. She gazed up at him for a long moment. Her eyes were a deep hazel green, like the woods behind her. They were tilted slightly at the corners and framed by long lashes. She had gorgeous eyes.

"Are you all right?" he asked.

"What?" The girl seemed to shake herself. "I... Yes."

He ran his gaze over her again. He didn't see any visible injuries, so he could guess what was wrong with her. Dehydration. Tourists didn't realize how dry the air was at this altitude. It could do a number on responsiveness, which could explain the single-car accident. She certainly appeared a little dazed right now. Besides, it wasn't like the rock wall jumped out in front of her.

He shrugged off his pack, unzipped it and reached inside. Damn. The only bottle with any water left was one he'd already opened. At least he'd only taken a sip.

"The tow truck will be a while. I'm sorry." He unscrewed the cap and wiped the top of the bottle on his shirttail. "Here." He handed her the bottle. "I think you're dehydrated."

She blinked up at him and ran her tongue over her lips. Her full, pink lips. "No. I just finished a bottle not long ago."

Jack shook his head. "You could use more water."

She shrugged and grasped the bottle, then raised it to her mouth. Man, he could watch her drink all day. Her lips grew wet against the same spot his mouth had been minutes before. His heart jumped as desire struck him again. Hard.

She handed him back the bottle. "Thank you." Suddenly she jumped up, her eyes wide. "Oh, the deer! I... I hit a deer. Before I hit the rocks, I mean. Before I hit the rocks I hit a deer."

Jack stepped around the her car again and saw a fist-sized dent in the left fender. "I'm sure the deer is fine, miss.

The dent isn't even—"

"I have to make sure he's okay." She ran past him, across the road and into the woods.

"Wait! Shit." Jack put the empty water bottle back in his pack and followed after her. "Wait, miss!"

He caught up to her a few yards in. She stood frozen beside a thick tree, the shade and sun fighting over her. She looked helpless, her pretty mouth turned down in a pout. Damn it. He'd always been a sucker for a damsel in distress.

When she made a move to run off again, he gently grasped her arms to hold her still. She stopped again and stared up at him for a long moment, those beautiful eyes of hers shining. He released her and shook his head.

"The damage to your car isn't from the deer," he told her.

She shook her head and turned from him. "This is just too much." Her voice was barely a whisper.

"What?"

She began to pace, her gaze on the ground. Her fingers tangled in that amazing hair. "Mom, she's…" She sniffled. "And Brad, that son-of-a-." She began to mutter more words he couldn't catch.

She turned in circles and he glimpsed tears on her cheeks. Was more than dehydration causing her disorientation?

"If I hurt that deer?" Her voice rose in pitch. "Oh, I can't take this!"

"Stop." He grabbed her again, feeling her body tremble in his hold. "Please. You have to be still."

She stared up at him again. "What?"

"I'm trained in First Aid, miss. I have to see if you're hurt."

She rolled her eyes. "Oh, I'm beyond."

He couldn't guess what that meant. He gently felt her skull, finding no bumps beneath that springy silky hair of hers. "You don't seem to have a head injury."

"Maybe I should have it examined anyway."

"Why? Are you in pain?"

"No. Nothing that would show on a CAT scan, I'm sure." She waved a hand. "Go on."

He moved his hands to her neck and gently tilted her head upward. He began to feel her neck and, thankfully, she didn't flinch. No whiplash, then. Her skin was smooth and warm beneath his fingers, though. He fought the urge to stroke her cheek.

She reached up and wrapped her hands around his wrists. "Thank you, but I'm fine."

He stared at those delicate hands. Oh, man. He bet she could feel his pulse racing at the touch of her skin to his. He had to distract himself. The deer. That should do it.

"The deer, miss," he said. "Was he a big guy?"

She nodded. "Huge."

He gave her a smile. "A Mule Deer, most likely. His brush with your little car is probably a distant memory for him already. In fact, he's most likely off looking for Mrs. Deer right now."

Hope flared in her eyes and her lips parted. "Are you sure?"

"I know these woods pretty well."

She blinked up at him then and laughed, low in her throat. His mouth went dry and he dropped his hands from her. That sound she'd made. That laugh. It was dark and rich and sexy as hell.

"You know these woods, huh?" She swiped at the tear on her cheek and gave him a small smile.

He'd thought her pretty before, but when she smiled like that at him? She was amazing.

"I never met a real mountain man before," she said.

She came closer. The desire she'd aroused earlier flickered again. His chest tightened and his blood pounded low.

She leaned back and stared up at him, her brows arched over those remarkable eyes. "He never looked at me like that. Not ever."

"Who?" He could hear the roughness in his voice.

She shook her head, her smile growing wider. "You look at me like I'm the only woman in the world."

Her words struck him, and suddenly it seemed as though she was. *Easy, Jack.*

She tucked her face up against his throat and he froze. He held his breath as she nuzzled him.

"You smell so good." She stood up on her toes. "I wonder how you taste."

Before he could think of something to say to that, she wrapped her arms around his neck and kissed him. He started to pull back, he truly did, but she tasted like honey and heat. God help him, he wanted more.

16

Groaning, he deepened the kiss. His tongue delved into her, tasting and teasing. She was so sweet.

She lifted her lips a breath away from his. "Oh, can you kiss!"

She kissed his jaw, flicking her tongue against his skin. She brought her mouth to his neck and nipped him with her teeth. He moaned, rough and low.

"I've never kissed a mountain man." She urged him back toward a fallen tree behind him. "Sit."

He happily bowed to her command, amazed that he hadn't tripped over the damn tree.

She straightened then, her brow furrowed. He was never one to take advantage of a woman and he wasn't going to start now. He made a move to stand.

"No." She bit her lip, then climbed onto his lap. "For once I'm going to have what I want."

For once *he* wanted that too. To just live in the moment and feel. To scratch the itch that had started the minute he'd seen her perched on that guardrail.

She straddled him as he kissed her throat, then pulled back and cupped his cheek. Her eyes were dark as she gazed at him. "I sure like kissing you, mountain man."

He pulled in a breath, trying to gather his control. "I have a name."

"No." She shook her head. "No names."

That didn't seem right to him either, though he was tempted to look around for cameras. Here he was, Jack Butler. Forest Ranger. Sitting in the woods and kissing a beautiful girl. He could imagine his cousin Bo's shit-eating grin if he ever found out about this.

The smell of the crushed Jefferson Pine needles reached him as his boots shifted on the forest floor, pine and lemon mixing with the sweet scent of her. He could feel every inch of her body against him as she pulled him closer.

Then she placed a hand in the middle of his chest. It was just a tiny gesture but it was enough to tighten his pleasure-starved limbs and still his racing heart.

Taking his hands from her, he shook his head. "We can't do this," he said, guessing what she meant.

She nodded, then blew out a breath. Her agreement doused his desire like a dunk in the springs.

Then she smiled up at him. "But gosh, that was some kiss."

That was an understatement. He'd felt what was between them. He dropped another kiss on her soft mouth, he couldn't resist she was so sweet, and pulled away from her. "Yeah."

Her cheeks were flushed now, rosy and pink as she lowered her lashes. Was she blushing?

"I've never done that before," she said. "I mean, making out with someone I just met."

Well, he'd never done anything this wild, and certainly not with a pretty stranger.

"That makes two of us." He helped her to her feet. "The tow truck will probably be here in a few minutes."

He stood and rubbed his hand over his face. What had he been thinking? Okay, he hadn't been thinking at all. Just feeling. For once in his life he'd just let go. He smiled to himself. Well, a little bit anyway.

"I'll walk you back." He waved her ahead of him. Her hips wiggled with every step. This girl was trouble.

But he was damned if he didn't want to finish what they'd started.

Chapter 2

Laurel couldn't look at her mountain man as she walked back to the car. She'd jumped a stranger, for goodness sake! But she'd wanted to kiss this stranger. This man who'd so sweetly offered her his bottle of water and then kissed her like he was thirsty for her.

He was amazing, really. And gorgeous. He had wide shoulders in that soft flannel shirt. Long, strong legs in his faded jeans. And she couldn't have imagined a more handsome face. Chiseled, with eyes a shade of blue she'd never seen before.

She couldn't ignore how good he'd made her feel, either. Sure, they'd stopped long before making what would no doubt have been an enormous mistake not to mention a first for her. An anonymous hook-up? Never.

Still, she'd never felt so free as she had for those few minutes back there. Like she was a part of him as she let herself go. She'd never felt anything like the kind of passion in this guy's kisses. And this kind of connection? She'd never experienced that in her life.

She stretched her arms over her head and took a deep breath. This was just what she'd needed. Energy surged through her body. What amazing luck, tripping over the handsome mountain man. Ready and willing and hers for the kissing. Maybe her luck would hold when she got to Reno. Maybe she could finally get on with her life.

Reality in the form of her squished car put a damper on her euphoria. She let out a breath.

He faced her. "Are you all right?"

Laurel ran her gaze over him. His shirt was half tucked into his jeans and his hair was a mess of dark brown waves. She could see the mark on his neck where she'd nipped him. His neck was strong and his skin was smooth. Warm and delicious. Ooh.

Her cheeks flaming hot, she nodded. "I'm fine."

She wouldn't be embarrassed. Not today. So she wasn't very experienced with men. So this was a complete aberration. She never had to face him again or what they'd done in the woods. For a second, just a split second, she wished they could do it again. More kisses. And a whole lot more than kisses.

He stared at her, his brows arched, and the silence stretched wide between them. Her every sense was pulled taut, hyperaware. Her ears picked up birdsong, and the wind in the trees. Her nose caught the scents of the woods and the man in front of her. This was way too much. Way too strong. Was he as affected as she was?

He opened his mouth to say something and she braced herself for some more awkward small talk. A loud horn sounded, followed by a rumbling engine that could only belong to a big truck. It was a flatbed tow truck, she was relieved to see. She and her car could get on their way. Exactly where to, she would worry about after she made good her escape.

The truck rolled to a stop in front of her car and the driver's side door opened. A man stepped down, almost as big as her mountain man, and grinned at her one aberration. "Hey, Jack!"

She jerked out of her reverie. Crap! So much for anonymity.

"Hey, Bo," her mountain man, Jack, said. "This is…" He looked at her expectantly.

"Laurel," she provided.

"Laurel," Jack said. Her name sounded sexy coming from his mouth. "This is my cousin Bo."

His cousin. Jack's cousin. Well, that explained why

they had the same incredible blue-gray eyes.

"Hello," she said.

"Uh, her car is pretty wrecked," Jack went on. "I'd give her a ride, but I was on a hike and the Jeep is parked down at the trail head."

"No problem," Bo said. "I know you're off-duty. I'll give the lady a ride into town."

She blinked. Off-duty? She looked at Jack again. He looked too rugged to be a cop.

Jack thanked Bo and studied her as Bo put her car up on the truck. Was he still thinking about it, too? How well their lips fit together?

"Thank you. Jack," she said.

He didn't say anything more, just kept looking at her with those intense eyes of his. She hurried away from him, climbed into the passenger seat of the tow truck and closed the door. She squeezed her eyes shut. So much for not being embarrassed.

Her one fling. Her one time to just be in the moment. Well, at least she would never have to see handsome Jack again.

* * *

Bo finished securing the car on the flatbed and sauntered over to Jack. "What's going on, Cuz?"

Jack's cheeks flamed. "I don't know what you're talking about."

Bo jerked his head toward the cab of the truck. "She's a hottie. And there was more than Ranger good-doin' between you two when I drove up."

Jack dragged his gaze away from his cousin and ran his fingers through his hair. "You're imagining things."

"Okay, I'm imagining things." Bo chuckled deep in his throat. "And that's not a hickey on your neck."

Jack lifted a hand to his neck. "Damn your tracker eyes."

Bo shrugged and walked back to the truck. "See you tonight."

Jack froze. Ah, shit. Tuesday night dinner at his aunt's house. With the whole family.

Jack watched as Bo drove off in the tow truck, taking the girl with him. Laurel was her name. Laurel. The girl who came out of nowhere to spoil his hike and make his day. Hell, his year. Laurel who was the sexiest girl he'd ever kissed in his life.

No names. That was what she'd wanted. A smile curved his mouth. Well, that was shot to Hell. He'd never see her again, though. What did it matter? It was what it was, and he knew he would never forget it. He turned and went back into the woods.

"Bo, you better keep your big mouth shut tonight at dinner," he grumbled.

* * *

Laurel stared ahead as the tow truck driver, Bo, sang along with the country music on the radio. Something about lost love or lost dogs. At least he was on key.

"We'll take a quick look at the car when we get it to the shop in Cloud Canyon," Bo said. "It looks pretty bad, though."

Laurel nodded absently. Her mind was still back in the woods. Still on her mountain man. Jack. So what if she knew his name now? So she was riding along with one of his relatives? It didn't change a thing.

She glanced out the window as they passed through what must be the center of Cloud Canyon. It resembled a colorful version of a frontier town. The strips of stores and restaurants had façades which made them look like they were individual buildings. There were storefronts on the ground level, and what she guessed were offices or apartments on the second. She spotted a hardware store, a few boutiques, a café and several antique stores. Everything appeared to be on a slant, probably because the roads tilted up and down.

There were a lot of cars parked in the shopping district. That made sense to her. The town was directly on the route toward Lake Tahoe. One store had handmade items for sale, stubby tree trunks carved into bears and moose. Another had Native American art and dream-catchers. The store next to that one featured thick sheepskin rugs in browns and tans which spilled over racks set on the sidewalk.

After the truck rocked steeply side to side, it turned into the garage parking lot and finally leveled out. Blowing out a breath, Laurel opened her door and stepped down onto the sidewalk.

"It'll just take a couple of minutes to get the car down," Bo said. "Then you can take your stuff out and go to the waiting area."

Laurel nodded. "Thanks."

Her poor squished Beetle soon sat on the pavement. While Bo popped open the trunk she walked over to the car. The fender and hood looked worse from this viewpoint and she cringed. She didn't even try to open the door. She just reached in to get her purse off the floor.

Bo rolled her suitcase over to the sidewalk. "Is that everything?"

"Yes, thanks," she said.

Sadly, she'd only taken what she thought she'd need for a short stay in Reno. Everything else she had was still back in the San Francisco apartment she'd shared with her mother. It was a good thing that the rent was paid through next month, since it looked like this little trip might take longer than she'd expected.

She extended the handle of her suitcase and headed toward the sign marked "Customer Waiting Area."

The room had orange vinyl chairs, stacks of rumpled magazines and a small TV in one corner. There was a coffee maker in the opposite corner, and the carafe held an inch and a half of the blackest coffee she'd ever seen. Yuck. She rolled the suitcase over to one of the chairs and sat.

At least she was alone with her thoughts for the moment. Not that she wanted to think about how much money Bo would need to get her back on her way.

She felt a wave of dizziness swell over her body. The smells of burnt coffee and motor oil permeated the waiting area, churning her stomach. She closed her eyes and leaned her head back, trying to imagine the scent of the woods and clean air. And hot handsome mountain man. Mmm, Jack.

"Laurel?"

Her eyes snapped open and she found Bo staring down at her. "W-what?"

He smiled, instantly reminding her of Jack. "You fell asleep," he said. "We looked at the car. If you'll come into the office we can go over the preliminary estimate."

"Preliminary estimate." She offered him a small smile. "That sounds ominous."

She gathered her things and followed him out of the waiting area.

Bo sat down behind a cluttered desk and waved her into the chair across from him. "This is a very rough estimate. The damage to the engine is repairable, but the parts are expensive."

She braced herself. "How much are we talking?"

"At least fifteen hundred to get it running again."

"Oh, no." She stared at a spot on the floor and tried not to pass out. How could she pay for a room in Reno with what little she would have left after the repairs? She had to meet with casino and gallery owners to try to get them to commission her work. She had close to zero contacts in San Francisco despite working in her mother's store for all those years. More than that, how would she ever be able to open her own gallery now?

Bo's chair creaked and she watched as he stood and crossed to a little refrigerator in the corner of his office.

"Here." He pulled out a bottle of water and cracked off the twist top. "You're probably dehydrated."

She blinked, flashing back to earlier that day. But this bottle was full and unopened, and that one had tasted like Jack.

"Thanks." She took the bottle and drank deeply.

A look of relief crossed Bo's face, then he sat back down. "The air up here is pretty thin, and if you're not used to it? Well, it can make you a little goofy."

"Yeah, don't I know it." She drank more of the water.

"Thanks, again."

"Now, don't worry about the body work."

She raised her brows in question.

"I'll take care of it." He shrugged. "It's a hobby of mine."

She shook her head. "I can't let you do that."

"Sure you can. Besides, it'll be fun turning that crumpled mess back into a cute little bug."

She managed another smile. "It is a mess."

He stood up again. "Where are you staying?"

"Reno."

"Huh?"

She waved a hand. "Never mind. I don't know where I'm staying. I have to save my money to pay you, actually."

Bo scratched his chin, which she now saw was covered with the same brown stubble as Jack's. Gosh, she had to put Jack out of her mind!

"The rooms at the Treetop Inn aren't too pricey," he said.

"How much is 'not too pricey?'"

Bo was quiet for a moment. "My cousin Chloe runs a café in town. We passed it on the way here."

Her stomach growled at the thought, but what did that have to do with a place to stay? Her heart stilled. Yikes, was he asking her out? She'd just jumped his cousin in the woods not an hour ago! Could things get any more awkward?

"She needs some help since Tiffany ran off with an out-of-towner," he said. "If you need to make some quick money, that is."

She nearly smacked herself. That's what she got for making assumptions. "Waiting tables?"

He shrugged. "I guess."

She thought for a moment. Why not? She'd done it in San Francisco for a couple of summers. "Thanks. That would be great. How do I get to Chloe's café?"

"Let me finish up and I'll take you there."

About a half an hour later they drove up to the café in Bo's pickup truck. Cars were parked in front of the place, but she didn't see any customers inside through the wide front window. "Breakfast and Lunch" was painted in white script letters across that window, which was framed with navy blue trim. The rest of the exterior was painted cream and had wine-colored shutters.

The Cloud Café was sandwiched between a boutique and a beauty salon in a stretch of six storefronts. The sidewalk slanted in front of the building, giving the illusion that the entire place was leaning to one side. Laurel was seized by a sense of vertigo and held on to the door handle to keep herself upright.

Bo parked his pickup a few spaces ahead of the café. Laurel cautiously opened her door and stepped out. She straightened and tried to focus. Looking at the building straight on helped her get her bearings.

She turned to him. "Thanks again."

"No problem." He grabbed her suitcase from the back of the pickup and wheeled it over to her. "Let me introduce you to Chloe."

A bell above the door jingled to announce their arrival and they stepped inside. Laurel stood her suitcase up on its feet and looked around the place. It was charming, and filled with an eclectic mix of mismatched chairs and tables with folk art and antique signs on the walls. The smell of cinnamon was in the air, along with the faint scent of lemon polish.

"Hey, Chloe!" Bo called.

Bo's cousin stepped out from what Laurel guessed was the kitchen.

"Hey yourself," Chloe said with a smile.

Chloe had thick wavy brown hair tied back in a low ponytail and big blue-gray eyes. Laurel's stomach dipped. This pretty woman could only be Jack's sister. *Way to put two and two together, Laurel.*

Bo stepped closer to his cousin. "Chloe, let me introduce you to Laurel…" He looked at Laurel for clarification.

"Tanner." Laurel held her hand out to Chloe. "It's very nice to meet you."

Chloe shook her hand, her eyes bright. "Chloe Butler. Bo said you might be able to help me out for a few days?"

"Yes. I'll be glad to make some tips, that's for sure."

"Great." Chloe waved a hand toward the dark wood table closest to Laurel. "Please sit." She picked up a pitcher of iced tea off the oak counter. "A couple of glasses, dear cousin?"

Bo grabbed two tall glasses from the shelves behind the counter and placed them on the table. "I gotta get going. Can I talk to you for a minute, Chloe?"

Chloe nodded. Laurel poured tea into the glasses as Jack's sister stepped outside with Bo. More Butlers. She now knew way more about Jack than she'd ever thought to, or at least more than she'd planned when she'd kissed him.

She picked up her glass and drank deeply. At least the tea was good. Strong and sweet. She flashed on that moment when Jack had kissed her. Strong and sweet like Jack. She shook her head.

"I'm just not built for a fling," she murmured.

* * *

"What's up?" Chloe asked Bo.

Bo grinned and shook his head. "You won't believe it, but that brother of yours found himself in a bit of trouble today."

"With Laurel?" She snorted. "No. Jack just isn't the impulsive type."

Bo shrugged. "I don't know about that. I tell you, if I'd found her stranded in the woods—"

"Spare me." Chloe held up one hand. "Now what about Jack and this girl?"

"There's something between them. I don't know what happened but Jack deserves a chance to see if anything develops."

Chloe eyed him, then nodded. "True enough. When I think about what that witch of an ex-wife of his put him through, I see red. Where's Laurel staying?"

"That's another thing. From what little she told me, I'd guess she's really low on cash."

Chloe thought for a moment. "I've been looking for someone to take the apartment upstairs. It's a shame it's been sitting there empty."

Bo grinned. "That's what I was thinking."

Chloe glanced at Laurel through the glass. The girl was pretty, and right now she looked dog tired. "Do you think she would take it?"

"Doesn't hurt to offer."

She looked back at Bo. "How long is she staying?"

He winked. "Depends how long it takes me to fix her car."

"You're such a busybody, Bo."

"Hey, anytime you want my help fixin' you up just holler."

"No thanks!" She laughed. "Okay, okay. I'll ask her to take the place."

Chapter 3

Laurel turned her head as the bell jingled above the door.

"I'll see you and Josh at my Mom's at seven?" Bo asked.

"Yep," Chloe said.

Laurel smiled. "Thank you again, Bo."

Bo nodded. "I'll be in touch about the car."

He left and Chloe sat down to face Laurel. The woman stared at her for a long moment, as if trying to place her. Finally, she picked up the glass of tea Laurel had poured for her. "I'm glad you'll be helping me out in the café. How about staying in the little apartment upstairs?"

She blinked in response and Chloe laughed lightly. "You'll get used to us Butlers, Laurel. We tend to jump in with both feet. Aside from my brother, that is."

Laurel said nothing to that.

"Bo told me you might be having some money problems?" Chloe asked.

Laurel stilled, then gave a short nod.

"Bo has a mouth on him," Chloe explained.

Laurel prayed Bo never learned about her and Jack in

the woods, then. "The truth is, I would love the opportunity to work for you. But an apartment? I don't know. I'll only be here long enough for Bo to fix my car."

"Bo's mom owns this strip," Chloe said. "I only pay rent on the café and no one's used the apartment in months. It's just sitting empty."

Bo's mother? Jeez, more of Jack's family? Laurel chewed her lower lip. Bo had told her it would cost at least fifteen hundred dollars to fix her car. That would leave her with less than seven hundred dollars. Not much of a stake, and rooms in Reno were pricey. The few gallery owners she'd spoken with were willing to look at her portfolio, though it was just sketches, really, and heading there was taking a chance. Well, she'd taken a chance on Jack this afternoon and had been more than rewarded. Her lips still tingled with the memory of his kiss. But a job and a place to stay in Cloud Canyon? It seemed surreal.

She would be a fool to turn down Chloe's generous offer, though.

"That would be wonderful, actually. Thank you, Chloe." She took another long drink of her iced tea. "Mmm, this is good."

They were both quiet for a long moment.

"Bo said Jack came to your rescue," Chloe said.

"Yes." Laurel's cheeks grew hot and she took another sip of tea. "I guess Jack called Bo's garage."

She put down the glass. When she glanced at Chloe again the other woman's brows were drawn together.

"And then my big brother deserted you? That doesn't sound like Jack."

Laurel didn't want to think about how she'd run from him into the safety of Bo's truck. How she'd been unable to face his deep gaze a moment longer. How could she tell his sister that?

"He didn't desert me. Not at all." She rubbed her forehead. "I'm, sorry. I've had one heck of a day."

Chloe gently touched her hand and Laurel relaxed a little. "I won't pry. Just let me lock up and I'll show you the apartment."

Laurel nodded her relief as the subject of Jack was blessedly dropped.

* * *

Jack knocked on his aunt's front door and shifted from foot to foot. He'd showered and changed into chinos and a golf shirt after coming home from his hike, but he couldn't get Laurel's scent out of his mind. Hot and sweet. And God, the way she'd clung to him.

He rubbed his hand over his face. This was what happened when you let too much time pass between women.

"Come in, Jack," Chloe said.

Jack stared at his sister for a moment. He hadn't even noticed the door had opened. "Hey. Are the rest of them inside?"

"Yep," Chloe said. "We're just waiting on you."

Jack edged passed his sister and stepped inside the familiar home. He'd grown up running between this house and his mother's, just over on the next block. It was furnished as sparsely with sleek modern stuff as his mother's was crowded with antiques. The sisters-in-law were very alike, though. Warm and affectionate. Nosy and interfering. He loved them both.

He walked into the dining room and found all eyes on him. Bo sat at the table, wearing a smirk. If he found out that Bo had told them about Laurel he would smack that expression off his gloating face.

Jack adjusted his collar to make sure that tell-tale hickey was hidden. Bo might be a tracker, but Jack's mother was no slouch in the eagle-eye department herself.

"Cousin Jack," Bo said. "Nice of you to join us."

"Yeah, like I had a— Hi, Mom."

Jack's mother eyed him, her brows raised. Then she smiled with clear pleasure. "Hello, Jack. Come give your mother a kiss."

He walked around to where she sat beside Chloe's son Josh and pecked her cheek. Josh's arms went around his neck and Jack lifted the four-year-old and held him close. "Good to see you, little man."

Josh giggled as Jack plopped him back into his seat. Jack kissed his Aunt Beth's cheek and sat himself across from Bo. A wooden bowl of his aunt's famous fruit-and-greens salad sat in the middle of the table, along with a big bread basket. His stomach growled and he reached over and grabbed a warm roll.

"What's new?" his aunt asked.

Jack stilled for a moment, then spread butter on his roll. "Nothing much."

Out of the corner of his eye he saw Bo and Chloe

exchange a knowing look. He took a bite of bread and chewed. *Here it comes.*

"Jack's been a busy boy," Bo said.

"Really?" His mother spooned salad into his bowl. "I thought you were off today."

Jack swallowed. "I was."

"Don't you usually go up into the mountains on your days off, Jack?" his aunt asked.

"Yeah." He stabbed some greens with his fork. "I did."

"But what about the girl?" Chloe asked.

He froze with his fork in midair. *What girl, Chloe?* As if he didn't know. Damn Bo, anyway. His mom and aunt watched him, their eyes bright.

"I found a stranded motorist out on Old Mill Road and called Bo," Jack said. "That's all."

Bo didn't add anything to Jack's story. Nope. The fool just grinned.

Jack glared at him. "What?"

"Well, you didn't ask about her car," Bo said. "You would think you'd be interested, seeing as how you're the one who found her."

Jack narrowed his eyes in his cousin's direction. "Cars are your business, Cuz."

"Chloe says she's pretty," Aunt Beth said.

He shot his sister a look. "How do you know? Where did you see her?"

Chloe speared a sliced strawberry from her own salad and swirled her fork in the air. "Laurel works for me, Jack. As of this afternoon."

"She's working for you?" He must have heard her wrong. "What?"

"She needs to make some money to pay Cousin Bo's outrageous prices."

"Hey, I told her I would do her body work for free."

"For free?" Jack's mother said, winking at his aunt. "She must be very pretty."

"She is," Jack said before he could stop himself.

Chloe arched a brow and turned to their mother. "She's going to stay in the apartment for a while."

"Your apartment?" Jack asked.

Chloe blinked at him. "Gee, Jack. You're not the only one in this family willing to lend a helping hand to a stranger in need."

Jack wouldn't say another word. Nope. He just chewed on his mouthful of greens. Laurel was working at Chloe's? Hell, she was staying in the apartment above the café?

"She told me she'd had one heck of a day," Chloe added.

Jack stared at the table as he ate. She'd had one heck of a day, huh? At least she was spared this interrogation. When he looked up, his sister was staring at him again.

"What?" he snapped again.

She threw her napkin at him. "Lighten up, Bro," she laughed. "You'd think you were the one who'd had one heck of a day."

Bo barked a laugh and Jack just shook his head. Great. The only woman he'd ever fooled around with in the woods was now working for his sister.

His mind worked as he deflected more questions from his family with grunts and nods. What exactly had Bo told Chloe this afternoon? He didn't really know anything. Yeah, he'd seen that hickey. The tender spot on his neck gave a twitch at the thought. Chloe couldn't know much more than that, though. Unless Laurel had told her. Would she? He didn't think so, but he didn't really know her. Well, that wasn't exactly true.

He knew how she kissed. He knew how she smelled. He knew how she felt in his arms.

He wouldn't give his family any of those details, though. He'd suspected Laurel could be trouble from the first moment he'd seen her. How would he avoid her now? Now that he would run into her at the café every day?

Suddenly, he wanted to see her. Maybe finish what they'd started in the woods before his damn conscience had set him back on the straight and narrow. He let out a breath and drained his glass of iced tea. There was a bigger question plaguing him, though.

How the hell would he hide his attraction to Laurel from his eagle-eyed sister?

* * *

Laurel checked her appearance in the faintly-pocked mirror standing in the corner of the bedroom the next morning. She ran her fingers through her hair and noticed that the dry air in the Sierra Nevada had an amazing effect. Her hair was glossy and curly instead of frizzy and out of control. She grabbed a ponytail holder out of her toiletry

bag on the bedside table and tied her hair back in a low
ponytail like Chloe Butler had worn yesterday.

Chloe's small apartment was more than fine for the
time-being. It was quite cozy, and resembled rooms at a
bed and breakfast more than an apartment above a business.
Of course, the mouth-watering scents of bacon and coffee
drifting up from downstairs added to the illusion. Chloe had
made her a delicious sandwich last night, and Laurel looked
forward to sampling more of the café's food sometime this
morning.

She perched on the edge of the mattress set on the
narrow iron bed and bent down to tie her Keds. Topping a
pair of white Capri pants she wore one of her mother's tie-
dyed creations, a filmy sleeveless camisole in shades of
blue and green and trimmed with tiny bugle beads below
her breasts. It was a little too dressy for waiting tables, but
she needed to have her mother close today.

Up until the minute she'd fallen asleep last night and
immediately upon waking this morning, she hadn't been
able to forget the events of yesterday. Brad's hateful words
of the morning. Packing in a rush to get the heck out of
there. That poor deer jumping in front of her car before she

smacked into that rock wall. The only good memories involved the hot mountain man who'd come to her rescue. Jack Butler.

Had she really thrown herself at him? Yep. She could blame her behavior on Brad or on the deer, on the circumstance or the thin air. But the truth was she'd wanted to kiss him. It was that simple. And that complicated, as she worked for his sister for the time-being.

She stood and straightened the faded quilt on the bed. She'd slept like the dead last night, snuggled under the soft sheets and quilt. She couldn't remember having that good a night's sleep since before her mother died.

The bedroom of the apartment was decorated like the rest of the place, in what she guessed was considered shabby chic. The small bedside table held a lamp dripping with crystal teardrops and a squat dresser fit under the one window. There was more lace here, running across the top of the dresser and framing the window. A cluster of antique perfume bottles was arranged on one corner of the dresser. She lifted one to her nose and sniffed, but no scent remained. Still, it was a sweet, feminine touch. Maybe Chloe had lived here herself once.

She checked her cell phone, plugged into its charger and resting on the bedside table. Still no service. Judging by the huge trees and jagged mountain peaks visible anywhere she looked outside, that wasn't a big surprise.

A glance at her watch showed her it was seven-thirty. Chloe had told her last night to come down any time she liked this morning, but Laurel hadn't missed the hours posted on the front door. The Cloud Café opened at seven a.m. sharp and she was late enough. She wasn't going to take further advantage of her new employer and landlady. None of this might have been in her plans, but she was going to make the most of her time in Cloud Canyon. And repaying Chloe's generosity would be a good start.

She breezed through the tiny kitchen and grabbed her purse off the chrome-trimmed table. Quick steps brought her through the living area to the door, which she locked behind her.

When she got downstairs, she saw the café was full of customers. Chloe chatted with a table full of elderly ladies, a pot of coffee in her hand. Her smile was a lot like Jack's, which Laurel had only seen briefly. The other expression on his face, though. When he'd stared at her with raw masculine appreciation.

She grabbed a white apron like Chloe was wearing from a peg near the kitchen door. "Good morning, Chloe." She looped the thin strap behind her neck and tied the strings behind her back.

Jack's sister turned and grinned. "Hey! Come and meet some of my best customers."

The old ladies tittered and turned their attention to Laurel as she approached their table.

"Ladies," Chloe began, "this is Laurel Tanner. Laurel this is Charlotte, Betty and Jane. The Bennet sisters."

The ladies looked enough alike to be triplets. They were slight of build, with heart-shaped faces topped by silvery fringes of hair. Each one nodded at Laurel, their identical pale blue eyes intent on her.

"Nice to meet you, Laurel," Charlotte said.

"She's a pretty thing," Betty added.

"No wonder Jack couldn't leave her on the side of the road," Jane said.

Laurel looked over at Chloe, who shrugged. "I told them how you ended up here. I hope you don't mind."

"Not really," Laurel said. "I'm so happy you're

letting me work and stay here, you can tell them anything."

"All of your secrets?"

Laurel's cheeks flamed and she gave a quick shake of her head. "No. Where do you want me to start?"

"Why don't you bring out the orders when they're ready. At least through the morning rush." Chloe refilled Jane's cup. "So is that 'no secrets,' Laurel? Or 'no telling?"

Chloe's eyes sparkled as she teased her and Laurel smiled. "Never mind."

The café was hopping until nine o'clock. Laurel met the other employees in passing, the stocky cook whose thick black hair spoke of Native American heritage and the skinny red-headed boy who washed dishes, as she delivered the customers' breakfasts and poured the coffee. By the time nine-fifteen rolled around, the place had emptied out.

While the redhead, Ricky, washed the dishes to the low thrum of heavy metal, the cook, Tom, prepped for the lunch crowd. The place might be small, but it did a brisk business with high turnover if this morning was any indication.

Laurel took a few minutes to acquaint herself with the limited menu. She was confident she would be able to truly help Chloe with the lunch crowd. They had talked over coffee and sticky cinnamon rolls after cleaning off the tables, and Jack's sister seemed to be as nice as she appeared. As long as Chloe didn't ask any more questions about yesterday, Laurel would make it through the day.

Laurel hummed along with the faint rock music coming from the kitchen as she put napkins and silverware on the tables. The utensils were as mismatched as the furniture, but heavy and well-made. Everything here was serviceable and pleasing to the eye, and it was little wonder that the Cloud Café was so popular with the locals.

"It's getting on toward eleven," Chloe said from the back.

Laurel nodded, her nerves tingling. It wasn't the work she was nervous about, but that she would have to talk with the customers like Chloe did. Her mother had been very comfortable around strangers. It was one of the reasons the store did so well. But Laurel hadn't inherited that gift. Again, she thought about yesterday. Her encounter with Jack had certainly made up for lost time. She let out a little snort.

"What's so funny?" Chloe asked with a smile.

"Nothing." Laurel straightened her apron. "Just laughing at myself."

"You know, that top is just gorgeous."

"Thanks. My mother made it."

Chloe's brows rose. "Wow. Where did she get that fabric?"

"She made that, too. Well, dyed it anyway." Laurel walked over to the counter and stuffed some drinking straws into the front pocket of her apron. "You know, I don't really have anything I can wear for work."

"Why don't you go into the boutique next door after lunch?"

"I can't spend any money right now. Who knows what Bo's going to end up charging to fix my car."

Chloe waved one hand. "My aunt runs the shop. I'm sure she'll give you a good deal."

Laurel blinked. Were all the Butlers this accommodating? "Maybe I'll check it out." She thought for a moment. "I could use some shorts and T-shirts."

The bell above the door tinkled, announcing the first lunch customer, and Chloe stood. "Don't be so practical." She winked. "Get yourself something fun, too."

Laurel nodded, then promptly rejected the idea. She had no time for fun right now. Yesterday had filled her quota of fun for the next ten years. She would just get her car fixed and then get the heck out of Cloud Canyon.

She walked over to a table occupied by a middle-aged couple. Putting on a bright smile, she introduced herself and took their order.

* * *

It was almost two o'clock when the lunch crowd finally thinned. Chloe was in the back refilling the tea pitchers while Laurel wiped off the table closest to the kitchen. Only two tables were occupied now, and those diners were nearly finished. Laurel patted the change and folded bills in the left pocket of her apron and smiled to herself.

Tips. It was nice to make money, even this small amount, after all the bills she'd had to pay in San Francisco not to mention a couple of months' rent on their apartment. She hadn't known how long she would have to stay in Reno, and in retrospect prepaying the rent had been a good idea. Brad certainly hadn't been any help.

The door opened to let in a late-comer. She glanced

over, then stared at the big man framed in the doorway. Her belly flipped. Jack Butler, mountain man.

He was dressed in green from head to toe. A pale short-sleeved shirt spanned his broad chest and tucked into the narrow waist of the dark pants on his long legs. There was a gun holstered at his waist, too. Bo's comment about Jack's being off-duty came back to her. There was an emblem with a tree sewn onto the ball cap he swept off his head. He ran his fingers through his dark hair, which looked glossy and rich. His cheeks were smoothly shaven and his eyes were opened wide as he stared right back at her. Wow.

She silently cursed herself. She was such an airhead. Jack was supposed to be her one fling. Her one impulsive act with no repercussions. She wasn't ever supposed to see him again! Brad's words rang true now.

She couldn't do anything right.

Chapter 4

Laurel felt Jack's sex appeal straight to her toes. She'd thought mussed-and-rugged Jack was tough to take? Clean-and-pressed Jack blew her away.

He walked into the café and sat down at the closest table, his blue-gray eyes still on her.

"Hi." His voice was throaty and rough.

"Hi." Hers was soft and breathy. She licked her lips and stepped over to his table. "Hi, Jack."

His eyes crinkled at the corners as he smiled. "I thought you said no names."

Her face burned. He reached for a menu and she watched him. Ooh, how those strong hands had felt on her. He'd held her close as he'd driven her crazy with his kisses.

She swallowed. "What can I get you?"

He flicked his eyes over her then smiled again. "What have you got?"

Heat washed over her from breast to belly. Her tongue felt too fat for her mouth. Oh, she was so out of her element. "Tom has a turkey Reuben on special."

He shrugged. "Maybe. Can I have some iced tea?"

"Sure."

She hurried from the table and ducked behind the service counter to get his iced tea. She placed her hands on a full pitcher in an attempt to cool herself off. She was just dehydrated. That's all. She downed a glass of water and closed her eyes, then placed the glass against her cheek as she breathed through her mouth.

"Are you all right?" Chloe asked.

Laurel opened her eyes and slid her gaze over at Jack's sister. "Yes."

"You look flushed."

Laurel set down her empty glass. "I'm fine."

Chloe tilted her head, then nodded. She turned away to stock the napkins behind the counter and Laurel took in a calming breath. She poured Jack's iced tea and straightened her shoulders.

Feeling more centered, she brought Jack his drink. She ran her gaze over him again. On closer inspection, his well-fitting uniform declared him a Forest Ranger. Hmm. That would explain the ruggedness. And man, was he at home in the woods. *Only you can prevent forest fires.* Well, he'd certainly lit her fire very nicely.

She set down his glass of iced tea. "Here you go."

"Thanks." He held on to the drink, stroking the glass up and down.

She stared at his long fingers.

"A straw?" he asked.

She jammed her hand into her pocket to grab a straw and handed it to him. "So what would you like?"

One corner of his mouth lifted. "Just about anything you have."

Her mouth gaped open. She wasn't any good at this double entendre stuff.

"I'll have the turkey Reuben, Laurel."

She nodded and took his menu, then realized she now had to lean across the table to return it to its holder. As she did, she caught him looking down the neckline of her apron. Her skin tingled against the cotton. Deep inside the collar of his shirt, she saw the mark where she'd nipped him yesterday.

She jerked herself upright. "'Kay."

Flustered, she hurried to the back of the café to place Jack's order. Closing her eyes again, she rubbed a hand over her neck. She felt dewy sweat there.

"You don't have to take care of my brother."

Laurel opened her eyes and faced Chloe. "What?"

"Why don't you go next door? The other tables are finishing up and Jack could be here a while."

Laurel looked over at Jack, who was still staring at her. His gaze traveled up and down and she sucked in a shallow breath. Oh, those gorgeous eyes.

"Unless you want to wait on him?" Chloe asked.

"No. I'm good."

Laurel pulled off her apron and hung it up before grabbing her purse. She was halfway across the café when Chloe called her name. She turned.

"Remember, get yourself something fun," Chloe said.

She nodded and turned to find Jack still eyeing her. Fun, huh? He was the living, breathing representation of fun. The kind of fun she'd never had before.

Keeping her eyes down, she walked out the front door. Sheesh, she was a mess today.

As she stepped into the boutique, her heartbeat finally began to slow. The place appeared to sell typical resort wear along with more practical clothes. Lake Tahoe T-shirts and sweatshirts, bathing suits and flip flops dominated the front of the store but every day wear filled the racks set further in with flannel shirts and khakis, jeans and sweaters, shorts and T-shirts on display. Several shoppers were present, and they looked like a combination of tourists and locals.

"Hi!" an older woman behind the counter called. "You must be Laurel."

Laurel blinked. "Does everybody in Cloud Canyon know me?" she muttered to herself. She nodded. "Yes."

"I'm Beth Butler, Jack and Chloe's aunt." The woman, maybe in her late fifties yet trim and young-looking, stepped out from behind the register and smiled. "Jack said you were pretty."

Laurel didn't know what to say to that, but she couldn't help but return her smile. "I wondered if you could help me. I need to buy some practical clothes."

Jack's aunt gave a vigorous nod. "You're working at the café now. I'm sure you can find some things that won't break your budget."

"Thank you."

"Sure, honey. Holler if you need anything."

Laurel nodded and began to browse the nearest rack. She chose a few scoop-necked T-shirts in yummy colors like peach and teal and buttery yellow. A couple of pairs of khaki shorts would work, too. She only had the one pair she'd worn yesterday. She crossed to a round rack and grabbed two pair in her size, hooking the hangers over her fingers.

Keeping a mental tally of her purchases so far, she drifted over to the lingerie section set toward the back of the store. She thought about the way Jack had looked at her in the café. Did he remember their kisses as clearly as she did? She would certainly never forget them.

Did he want to do that again? Maybe finish what they'd started?

She ran her fingers over the silk and lace folded neatly on one table. Something fun, huh? Why not? With her tip money and a little more of her nest egg she would splurge just a teensy bit for once.

She grabbed a few panties in different colors and found lacy bras that matched. They were little nothings, scraps of satin and lace that would feel decadent under her tame shorts and shirts. The most outrageous thought came to her. Yes, the underwear would feel lovely. But she might just still like to take it off. For Jack.

By the way he'd looked at her in the café, he was still attracted to her. Well, she knew she'd never felt the kind of heat Jack gave her with just a look. So what if she knew his name and worked with his sister? So what if she knew more about him than she'd ever wanted to? She would only be here a few days. Maybe what happened in Cloud Canyon stayed in Cloud Canyon.

Smiling wider, she took her purchases to the counter.

* * *

Jack thought about Laurel as he wiped his mouth with a napkin. Man, she was still as gorgeous as he'd pictured all last night. She seemed a little nervous maybe, but so sexy. When she bent over his table and he'd glanced down her shirt—

"What's up with you and Laurel?" Chloe took his empty plate.

Jack placed his napkin on the plate and leaned back. "Nothing."

"Yeah, right. You flirted with her, Jack. You! You never flirt."

"I wasn't flirting. I was just checking on her." Jack drained his iced tea, keeping his expression even. "She was in trouble yesterday and I helped her out." He waited a beat. "Like you're doing here."

"Maybe. But I'm not looking at her like you are." She chuckled. "Of course, she's not exactly my type."

Jack just shook his head. Chloe pulled a face at him and crossed the café to bus the other tables.

He stood and grabbed a newspaper from the rack near the front door and sat back down. As he read the paper he kept checking the front door, waiting for a flash of blue green. Laurel sure was pretty today in that thin sparkly shirt. Those pants, while not as hot as her little khaki shorts, hugged her butt.

He caught Chloe watching him watching the door. Damn. She already thought he was attracted to Laurel. Hell, what man wouldn't be? She had that long blond hair tied in a thick curly ponytail that nearly reached that sweet butt. Beneath the apron he'd caught a glimpse enough of her body to imagine more than he had seen. But when she'd taken the apron off? That flimsy shirt she wore made him long to touch it. To touch her through it. To peel those thin little straps off her shoulders and kiss her smooth-looking skin.

He rustled the newspaper and glanced at his watch. He glanced at the door again.

"Isn't your break almost over, Bro?" Chloe asked.

He folded the paper and set it on the table. "I've got about fifteen minutes."

Chloe waved a hand at him and went into the kitchen.

Would Laurel come back or would she just go right upstairs to the apartment? This was so stupid. He wasn't some kid with a crush on the new girl in school. He was thirty-two years old, for God's sake. He was a Forest Ranger. He was a divorced Forest Ranger who had no interest in starting a relationship with any woman. When the bell jingled above the door, he still couldn't help looking over to see if it was her.

It was. She stopped in the doorway, holding a bag from his aunt's boutique. Her cheeks turned pink and she held the bag to her chest.

"Whatcha got in the bag, Laurel?" he asked.

"I needed a few things for work," she rushed out.

He nodded slowly. She'd been so forward yesterday yet she was certainly shy today. The contradiction was interesting. "For work, huh?"

"I thought you were going to get something fun?" Chloe called from the back.

Now Laurel's cheeks were red. "I…" She glanced at Jack and straightened her bare shoulders. "I did."

As she walked past his table he turned to face her. "Want to show me?"

She flashed him a smile, like the one he'd seen when she'd looked up at him yesterday. It was gone in an instant but it still hit him like a punch to the gut.

"Maybe, Jack," she said. "Maybe."

Oh, he liked the sound of his name on her lips. That was what he'd wanted yesterday as he'd kissed her breathless.

She continued past him toward Chloe. His sister watched their exchange, her eyes sharp.

"So what did you find at Aunt Beth's?" Chloe asked.

Laurel shoved the shopping bag and her purse under the counter and grabbed her apron. "She had some lovely things. Thanks so much for the suggestion."

"Doesn't she have the sweetest underwear?"

Laurel glanced at Jack over her shoulder, her eyes dark. So she bought new underwear, huh? And she thought that, maybe, she would show him? His body tightened. Whoa.

He clamored to his feet. "Well, I have to get back to work."

Both women stared at him, Chloe with confusion and Laurel with…what? Desire? Did she want a replay of yesterday? To finish what they'd started?

He reached up to put on his ball cap and could almost feel her gaze on his chest. Suddenly his clothes felt too tight.

"See you, Chloe." He stared into Laurel's hazel eyes for a long moment. That heat was there again. "Bye, Laurel."

By the time he got home after work that evening, he was able to put his intense attraction to Laurel into some sort of perspective. He was just horny, that was all. Fooling around with an amazingly sexy girl after a long dry spell must have busted open a dam.

Yesterday had been like something out of a fantasy. He really didn't want any sort of relationship with Laurel. Hell, it was just his memory keeping her front and center in his mind. His head knew that. But his body apparently thought differently.

Man, when she'd looked at him in the café like that, her eyes all dark. Did she know the effect she had on him? That every move, every word, made him want more of her? Probably not. She didn't seem very experienced, despite yesterday's make-out session. Maybe he brought out her inner sex kitten. He laughed at himself. Yeah, right. She'd started that fire on her own. He was just happy to burn right along with her.

He let himself into his house, located not far from the Big Bend Ranger Station. Its location gave him the solitude and privacy he craved, especially after a long day of dealing with careless and clueless tourists and his overly-involved family.

"Smokey!" he called.

His dog came running out of the back office in a blur of gray fur. He barked and jumped and made Jack feel a little guilty about leaving him alone all day.

"Hey, pal." He bent down and got a big wet slurp on his cheek. "Miss me?"

The dog almost smiled up at him. Jack had fenced in the backyard and Smokey used a doggie door, but the three-year-old Collie mix still loved to roughhouse with Jack when he got home.

"Okay, okay," Jack laughed. "Go outside and work off some of that energy, pal."

Smokey slammed through the doggie door at the back of the kitchen and ran some figure eights in the backyard. Smiling, Jack walked toward the kitchen. He dropped his keys on the counter and took off his hat.

The house suited him, both his taste and his life. Upstairs it had three bedrooms and downstairs a living room opened off of the kitchen. The small office Smokey took over during the day was plenty big enough for Jack's purposes. Actually the house was more space than he needed.

He'd bought it right after he'd married Kelly. It was rustic, but had all the modern conveniences. She'd said she loved it and then bitched about it every day after they moved in together. It was too backward. It was too secluded. Jeez, that should have been his first clue.

He scooped some dry dog food out of the bin by the back door and filled Smokey's bowl. He pushed the door open and leaned his head out. "Time to eat, boy." Smokey stopped and picked his head up, then charged back into the house. Jack patted the dog's side as he ate, and then got himself a beer from the fridge.

He went into the living room and plopped down on the leather couch. He twisted off the cap and took a long drink, then twirled the bottle in his hands. The wide windows in front of him framed the woods he loved. The woods he protected. He didn't have any close neighbors, but that suited him, too. He had Smokey and the Tuesday night dinners at his aunt's house. He was in town every day to have lunch at his sister's and to check on his mother. And now he had Laurel to look at, at least until Bo fixed her car. He took another pull on the bottle.

How long would Laurel stick around Cloud Canyon? She wanted to show him what she bought, huh? Nice. It wasn't exactly an invitation to recreate yesterday's magic and see where it led, but it was something. He never paid much attention to the underwear his aunt sold, but just the idea of Laurel in some of it certainly piqued his interest.

Smokey jumped up on the couch beside him and flopped down with a grunt.

"What do you think, buddy?" Jack stroked the dog's

head. "Should I ask her out?"

Smokey just blinked at him.

"Thanks," Jack laughed.

This could be tricky. Pursuing Laurel in secret would be almost impossible. His sister already thought there was something between the two of them. Taking Laurel out would only put brush to that forest fire. It wouldn't be long before his whole family knew about it. But he wanted to see her again. To kiss her again. To feel her delicate hands all over him.

Maybe he could take her into Truckee for dinner. There was little chance of running into any Butlers out there. Then maybe he could bring her back to his house for dessert.

The phone rang and he set his beer on the coffee table. He loosened the top button of his uniform shirt then picked up the receiver.

"Hello."

"Hello, Jack."

He took in a slow breath, then let it out. "Kelly."

"I've been waiting to hear from you," she snapped.

To hear from him? "Sure you have. It must be that

time of the month."

She forced a phony laugh through the phone. "Funny. Can't I call and check on my husband?"

"Ex-husband, and spare me. Your alimony's deducted automatically from my checking account."

"But it's still not here," she said, that tell-tale whine present under her polished accent.

"Hey, it's not my fault July was thirty-one days long."

He could almost see her practiced pout from across the miles between them. He'd seen that expression nearly every day of their marriage.

"I was only calling to ask," she said.

"You'll have your money by the tenth. Like every month."

"Good." Now her voice was bright and put him immediately on guard. "So what's new with you?"

"With me? Well, yesterday I fooled around in the woods with a woman I just met."

She laughed. "You? Funny. Like you would ever be that spontaneous or irresponsible."

Another backhanded compliment. She was truly

gifted.

"Goodbye, Kelly."

"'Bye, Jack."

Jack hung up the phone and sat back down on the couch beside Smokey. He thought for one hot minute that he should start dating again? He was seriously considering getting involved with another woman? What if she turned into someone who would be completely dependent on him for everything but the air she breathed? Kelly had. And lightning fast, too.

He'd lived through that once, and still paid dearly for it each month. His time and his space was his own now, and he liked it that way. No. He wouldn't ask Laurel out. No matter how sexy and hot and obviously interested she was.

He wouldn't take the chance and fail another woman.

"It's just not worth it."

The dog grunted and Jack toasted him with his beer bottle.

"You said it."

Chapter 5

All through the breakfast shift Laurel could barely concentrate. Thank goodness the customers were pleasant and the menu was simple. She'd still managed to mess up a couple of orders, though. Her newly-purchased outfit, a peach T-shirt and khaki shorts, fit well and made her feel more comfortable at least on the outside. On the inside she'd taken the plunge and worn what she hoped would give her the courage to ask Jack out this afternoon.

"How's it going?" Chloe asked her as they got ready for the lunch crowd.

Laurel tried not to blush but felt the tell-tale heat on her cheeks. Surely Chloe couldn't guess that she planned to try and seduce her brother. "Just fine, thanks. Now if I can manage not to screw up any lunch orders."

Chloe waved her hand. "Don't worry about it. You're doing just fine."

"Thanks."

Chloe went into the kitchen to make sure Tom was all prepped and Laurel glanced at her watch. Ten forty-five. Just three more hours and Jack would come in for his break. She caught a glimpse of her reflection in the mirror behind the counter. Could she do it? She took a breath and felt the rasp of her lacy bra against her skin. Oh, yeah. She definitely could.

At precisely one fifty the place was empty and he was there. All hot and handsome and big as life.

Tomorrow she would go to Bo's garage and find out when her car would be ready. After that, she would have an end date to her visit in Cloud Canyon. Today, though? Today she would suspend a little time just for herself.

"Hi, Jack," she called.

His dark brows arched, as if he was surprised she'd called him by name. "Hi, Laurel."

He looked at her for another long moment, then sat at the table near the door like he had yesterday and swept off the ball cap he wore.

Without giving herself a chance to change her mind, she hurried over to him. "What are you in the mood for today?"

His blue-gray eyes sparkled and she waited for his answer. He started to smile. "Um, what's the sandwich special?"

"Hot Tuna Melt."

"Hot?" he asked.

She nodded slowly and leaned closer. "Melts in your mouth."

He stared at her mouth and she almost licked her lips. His gaze ran over her, lingering on her front. The unseen touch made her skin tingle.

He cleared his throat and brought his eyes back up to hers. "Sounds good."

"I'll put your order in," she said. "Iced tea?"

Jack nodded and she went behind the counter. Chloe's gaze flickered between her and Jack, but she didn't say a word. With a small smile, she picked up a tray of dirty glasses and took them into the back. Laurel was all alone with Jack for the moment.

Another glance in the mirror confirmed her rosy cheeks. Oh, so what? She was in Cloud Canyon, darn it. And what happened in Cloud Canyon...

She brought Jack his drink and set it in front of him.

He stroked the glass like he had yesterday, with his long strong fingers. "Straw?"

She withdrew a straw and, grasping the tip, pulled most of the wrapper off. Slowly. She let the straw slip into his drink and watched as he peeled the scrap of paper off the top of it. Okay, that was it. Her heart began to pound in her chest. *Here goes.*

"Come up to the apartment tonight?" she breathed.

His lips parted and his eyes rounded. She could read the surprise in those eyes, just like she had when she'd first kissed him in the woods. Watching him, she willed her heart to slow its pounding as she waited for his answer.

He shook his head. "That's not a good idea."

In that instant her stomach dropped five thousand feet. She was tempted to dive back behind the counter, but she held her ground. If anonymity had made her bold Tuesday, this time-out-of-reality made her determined. "Um, I'm only going to be here a short time, Jack. We could get to know each other better. No strings."

He looked like he wanted to say yes. Actually, he looked like he wanted to grab her and throw her down on the table. Hunger flared in his eyes as he gripped his glass. Laurel lifted her chin and summoned all the courage she'd ever possessed.

"I." Jack fisted his hands on the table. "Maybe."

She stood still, her sneakers rooted to the floor as she

wondered if she'd heard him wrong. It wasn't a yes, but?

"Great." Brushing a curl behind her ear, she managed a smile. "Maybe I'll see you tonight, then."

She forced herself to walk slowly toward the back of the café. Maybe? She placed Jack's sandwich order and turned. Maybe??

Chloe was on the phone when Laurel stepped in the back. She cupped a hand over the mouthpiece. "All cleared?"

"Yes. I'll wipe down the tables and get them set for tomorrow morning."

"Thanks, Laurel. They have a new kid at the bakery and I've been on the phone for— Yes, the Cloud Café." She turned back to her conversation about bread and pastries.

Laurel didn't want to get her hopes up about Jack's visit. This was the first time she'd ever propositioned a man and she got such a lukewarm answer?

Maybe. Maybe he hadn't been all that tempted the other day. Brad had told her very clearly that she had never made him happy. Maybe Jack hadn't enjoyed their kisses as much as she had.

True, Jack's eyes had been intense on her. And his nostrils flared. Every muscle had tensed beneath that crisp uniform shirt. He wanted to see what was between them, too. She nibbled her lip. Didn't he?

No! She wouldn't turn back into meek Laurel Tanner, so unsure and keeping her wants and desires to herself. There was time enough for that after Bo Butler fixed her car.

She went over to the service counter and poured herself a glass of water. As she drank it she couldn't help wishing it was something much stronger. She kept her back to Jack. Maybe?!?

She set down her glass and picked up the wiping cloth and cleaner. Bending over the first table, she sprayed and wiped. She wouldn't turn around. Nope. She would just wait for Tom to ding the little bell announcing Jack's food was up and ready. She would ignore the gorgeous man who sat so silently at his table.

Blowing a curl out of her face with a puff of air, she moved on to the next table. By the time she'd cleaned the sixth table she could almost imagine she was alone in the café. How could such a big man keep so quiet?

She snuck a peek at him and saw he was still watching her. He was perfectly motionless in his green uniform, pressed and precise except for his wavy hair. His chiseled features were grim, his full mouth set in a line.

The bell dinged in the back. Jack's melt-in-your-mouth sandwich was up. Good. He could eat and get the heck out of here for all she cared.

Leaving the cleaner and cloth on the table, she walked toward the kitchen. She carried the plate to Jack's table and placed it in front of him. Before she could withdraw, he grabbed her wrist. His touch was soft yet firm, his fingers rough against the inside of her wrist.

She stared at his hand, unable to bring her gaze to his face. "Jack," she whispered.

"Laurel," he responded, his voice low.

She swallowed again and slowly met his gaze. His eyes were hot. Dark. Deep. So that's what they meant by "bedroom eyes." *Whoa.*

He stroked her pulse with his thumb. "Is seven okay?"

Her heart skipped. "Seven is great."

Then he smiled, that crooked expression she'd briefly

glimpsed before. He released her but she could still feel his touch, like he'd branded her.

Good Lord, what would she feel like after tonight?

* * *

Jack got into his fifteen-year-old Cherokee. The door closed with a ear-splitting creak and he winced. "Time to have Bo take another look at you, girl."

The aging SUV was the other thing Kelly hadn't wanted in the divorce. That and his house.

He reached into the backseat and grabbed his wide-brimmed Ranger hat. Setting his ball cap on the seat beside him, he put the Ranger hat on and rolled down the window. He was parked several spaces back from the café, right in front of his mother's shop.

The wide café windows drew his eyes, and he easily imagined Laurel bustling around in there. He'd tried to stay strong. He'd tried to stick to his guns and keep their brief encounter in the past. The recent past, but still.

He'd watched her gather her courage to ask him up to the apartment. And he'd watched as she'd started to think herself out of it. There was no way he'd been able to let her take back that invitation, no matter what it might lead to.

He turned the key in the ignition. "So much for willpower."

Pulling back onto the road, he headed toward the Soda Springs Recreation Area. He tried to focus on the rest of his day and not on the rest of his night. Thinking about Laurel and her pretty new underwear would only drive him nuts. Besides, the summer help was starting to get lazy. More than one of the college kids had called in sick in the past few days. The day he'd met Laurel out on Old Mill Road had been the first day off he'd had in over two weeks.

Gravel crunched beneath the Cherokee's tires as he made his way down to the Springs. The skinny kid at the guardhouse waved as Jack pulled to a stop beside it.

"Good afternoon, Director."

"Hey, Randy." Jack leaned an arm on the car door. "Anything going on I should know about?"

"No, sir. Just the usual."

Jack looked at the people wading and fishing in the water or lounging on the rugged bank. He could pick out a green-clad staff member on the far bank, and another farther up near the covered picnic area. "At least everybody showed up today. I expect we'll be busy through the end of this month."

Randy let out a breath and Jack smiled at him. "Buck up. You're off the next two days, right?"

"Yep." Randy grinned. "Then I get to play tourist."

"Just remember to read that list of safety rules you hand out to every carload of visitors."

"Yes, sir."

Jack shifted his car into drive. "Keep up the good work."

He drove down a curving road toward the crowded parking lot. The kid wanted to play tourist? Jack remembered that feeling well. Growing up in Cloud Canyon, watching the ebb and flow of tourists through the town, he'd wanted to kick back and enjoy himself too. Something bigger had beckoned, however.

His father had been a Forest Ranger, and Jack had never wanted to be anything else. After college he'd gone into the training program, focusing on Recreation Management. It had sounded fun, but it was a lot more work than it appeared. Safety checks, guest mediation, constant vigilance, law enforcement, EMT training. It had been a lot of schooling and a lot of training, but it had been more than worth it. His dedication and hard work paid off about a year ago when he'd risen to the rank of Director of Recreational Management for the district.

Taking a break between sessions of Ranger School at Lake Tahoe one summer had brought him into contact with the elite, those tourists who didn't want to take their time to explore the Forest but preferred to play and party on the south shore of the lake. His ex-wife Kelly had been one of those partiers.

When she'd overturned the canoe she'd had no business using Jack had come to her rescue. She'd appeared sweet and helpless and Jack had fallen for it. The helpless part wasn't an act, though. She'd grown needy and clingy soon after their wedding vows were exchanged. Ultimately, Jack hadn't been able to give her what she'd needed.

At first, soon after their wedding, he'd felt like a big man. But as time passed, it became clear that she depended on him for even her own contentment. When she'd come to him and told him she wasn't happy, he'd had no clue how to fix it. She'd refused to consider any counseling. In the end, he'd had no choice but to agree to the divorce. Guilt had mixed liberally with his sense of failure. He hadn't been happy with her in a very long time.

A shout of laughter brought him to attention. A few twenty-somethings were playing and making the most of their time in the Springs. Jack suddenly felt like an old man.

"Tourists," he grumbled.

Was Laurel one of them? Someone just passing through? Jack didn't know what she was doing in Cloud Canyon or where she'd been headed when he'd found her by the side of the road. She seemed like she was in no hurry to get out of town right now. Nope. She seemed like she had nothing but time.

Hey, if she wanted Jack to help fill it? To see what could be between them? He was more than happy to oblige.

Chapter 6

Laurel stepped out of the claw-foot tub and grabbed a thick towel off the brass rack set beside it. The tile floor was pleasantly cool beneath her feet as she dried herself. She wrapped the towel around her body and stepped in front of the small vanity. Using the heel of her hand, she wiped away the fog on the mirror. Her hair was pinned up on her head, and some loose strands curled around her flushed face. She suspected more than steam put those particular roses in her cheeks.

She was still amazed she'd had the nerve to ask Jack to come here. Heck, she'd ask him to come up to the apartment, like she was Mae West!

She stepped over to the narrow closet where she'd hung some of her things. The top she'd worn for her first day of work in the café was one of her favorites. Her mother had always looked to her for ideas about color combinations, and she could indulge some of her own artistic energy in that way. Brad had managed her mother's store in San Francisco, but it apparently hadn't been the stellar retail venue he'd hoped. He had nickel-and-dimed everything, making sure that if they added a simple row of beads it was reflected in the price. Jackass.

Laurel withdrew her sketchpad from her suitcase and sat down on the bed. Thumbing through the pages, she considered the designs she planned to pitch to the gallery owners. They seemed pale, somehow. Maybe it was a trick of the lighting. She shut the book and placed it beside her suitcase in the closet and closed the door.

Jackass or no, maybe Brad had been right about the business after all. Laurel hadn't been able to make the rent on the store after that first month on her own.

She unwrapped her towel and draped it over a small chair. "I'm not going to think about it."

She slathered on some lotion and thought about the coming evening instead. A glance at the ornate little clock on the nightstand showed her it was six fifteen. *Is seven okay?* Jack had asked. How the heck was she going to last until seven?

She stepped over to the bag from the boutique. She'd put the T-shirts and shorts away yesterday, but now she dumped the remaining contents on the bed. Cherry, rose, grape, midnight and orange. She'd treated herself to several sets of the prettiest underwear in the store. Today for work she'd worn the pink. "Which color would you like, Ranger Jack?"

The purple, maybe. She lifted the bra and rubbed the lace between her fingers. It was soft with just a hint of friction. Mmm. The "nothing" panties were a wisp of lace, but they were soft, too.

She put on the bra, took a breath, and stepped in front of the mirror. The color complimented her fair skin, and the bra made her B-cup breasts appear larger.

"Not too shabby."

She wriggled into the panties. It was like wearing nothing. She took her short terry robe from the closet and slipped it on, tying the belt around her waist. Grabbing her makeup bag, she went back into the bathroom. Some mascara, a touch of lip gloss. A sweep of purple eye shadow to go with the underwear, though Jack wouldn't see the connection right away.

She zipped the bag shut and studied her rosy cheeks again. "Well, I don't need any blush."

She returned to the bedroom. Running her fingers over the few shirts hanging in the closet, she murmured, "Which top should I wear, Mom?"

How she missed her mother. Astrid Tanner had been funny and sweet, and always a little off center. Her tie-dyed clothes weren't cheap, which made losing the shop so much more of a mystery. Brad had managed the place, leaving her mother and Laurel to create the designs. That wasn't a bad thing, since he didn't have an artistic bone in his body. Her hand fisted. Anger was preferable to the hurt and regret she'd first felt when he'd broken their engagement. Brad was such a waste of air.

A knock came at the door, startling her. It couldn't be Jack. Not so early. Maybe Chloe needed something.

She padded into the kitchen on bare feet and stood in front of the door. "Who is it?"

A beat of silence met her ears. "Jack."

Her heart did that girly skip thing again. She reached for the knob, gave it a twist and pulled the door open.

Ooh. He'd changed out of his uniform and now wore jeans and a flannel shirt. He was the rugged mountain man she'd kissed in the woods again and she clutched the doorknob to hold herself steady. The next second she realized she wasn't even dressed yet.

"This isn't how I wanted to greet you on our first... Is

this a date?"

"Maybe." He held up a brown shopping bag. "I brought dinner."

She took the bag from him, breathing in the familiar scent of oil and spices. "I love Chinese." She set the bag on the counter and turned. "I didn't expect you so early."

He closed the door and stared at her for a long moment, those blue-gray eyes dark. "I couldn't wait."

The next instant she was in his arms, holding tight to him as he kissed her cheek, her ear, her neck. He loosened her hair and tilted her head back before plunging his tongue deep into her mouth. Oh, he tasted so good!

She tugged his shirt out of his jeans and ran her hands over his back. He was so smooth. So warm. Impossibly, he held her closer still. She ran her hands over his shoulders. He was tense and strong and so firm beneath her fingers. "Jack."

He eased her robe off one shoulder, kissing every bit of skin as he revealed it. "Mmm, you smell good," he rasped. He stroked a finger along her bra strap and lifted his head. "Is this one of the things you were going to show me?"

Laurel stepped back from his arms. Emboldened, she shrugged and let her robe slip a little off both shoulders. "What do you think? Is purple my color?"

He growled low in his throat. "Laurel, you're killing me."

Any thoughts of Brad and his constant derogatory comments fled as she saw the masculine appreciation in Jack's eyes. This man wanted her, and that realization was as heady tonight as it had been that afternoon in the woods.

He grabbed her again and urged her over to the table. He sat, drawing her between his outstretched legs. Running his hands beneath her robe, he tugged on one thin strap of her panties. "I thought you said 'no strings.'"

She stifled a giggle. He leaned closer until his tongue brushed the lace covering one breast.

She let her head fall back. "Oh, and I thought you could kiss!"

He murmured something she couldn't catch then teased her other breast with his fingers as he worked his tongue and lips over her.

The lace of her bra grew wet, and the friction was almost unbearable. Then with one flick of his wrist he unfastened her bra and drew hard and deep on her breast. Shivering, she nearly climaxed.

"Mmm. And I thought your kisses tasted good," he murmured. His talented fingers moved to her belly, tickling her navel as she gasped. He hooked his thumbs in the straps at her hips and stilled.

She met his gaze, and saw the question there. She had never been very adventurous, but she could grasp what he was silently asking her. He was waiting for something, like permission, from her. Nibbling her lip, she gave a shaky nod.

Heat flared in his gaze. One finger brushed her through the lace and then he touched her. There.

Oh my God, this was amazing! Closing her eyes again, she gave herself over to him. She couldn't focus on anything but his mouth and hands and what he was doing to her. Her blood pounded in her ears as she rose to passion she had never before experienced. She peaked, and her climax seemed to go on forever, her cries echoing in the small kitchen.

He stroked her belly, her breasts, and then tugged her into his arms. She sank against him. His heart hammered against her cheek as he held her close, his lips moving over her hair as her heartbeat began to slow.

She kissed his neck, tempted to put another hickey on his rough and delicious skin. "Wow."

His laugh was low and rumbled against her cheek. Looking him in the eye, she could see the banked heat there.

"Jack, you're amazing."

"It was my pleasure, Laurel." He took in a shuddering breath. "It's been a while for me."

"And it still is, isn't it?"

He shrugged. "I'm good." His big hands cupped her butt and he gave a quick squeeze. "Leaves us something for next time."

"Next time?"

His brows rose as if to challenger her.

"Yeah." She couldn't help but grin. "There will definitely be a next time."

Laurel finally disengaged herself from him and turned away from the temptation that was this remarkable man. While Jack went into the bathroom, she donned her bra and robe with fumbling hands. She stood on shaking legs and stared at the chair he'd just vacated. She knew she would never be able to forget it.

She would just try to focus on the food instead of him. She wouldn't think about what had happened at this table minutes earlier. What he'd done to her! And now they would sit and talk as if she hadn't let herself go. As if he hadn't held her close as if she mattered.

Oh, she was in so much trouble.

* * *

Jack returned from the bathroom. Laurel got down some plates from the cabinet and spooned out the lukewarm Chinese food for them. Egg rolls, noodles and sweet and sour chicken. It smelled delicious but not nearly as good as Laurel herself.

"This isn't the café, Jack." She brought the full dishes to the table. "Don't get used to my serving you all the time."

He grabbed a lo mein noodle off his plate and drew it into his mouth. He chewed slowly, replaying every motion, every sound, of their recent encounter in his mind. He was a little uncomfortable after making her come apart in his arms, but he would just power through. If this, whatever this was, would go to its obvious conclusion there would be time for him to have his share too.

He swallowed, then looked at her evenly. "I can think of at least a couple of other things I can get used to instead."

Her cheeks turned a pretty shade of pink. She kept her eyes down as she picked up an egg roll and brought it to her mouth. He couldn't imagine what she was thinking.

"This is all new to me," she said after a while.

He didn't know what to say to that. He wanted to ask about the other guys, but who was he to pry?

He took a bite of chicken and chewed. She was the most sensual woman he'd ever met and yet she seemed…naïve wasn't quite the word. As she ate, her robe dipped off of her left shoulder again. Her skin was red from the scratch of his beard stubble when he'd buried his face against her sweet neck. The skinny purple bra strap held his attention.

"Now that should be a crime."

She looked over at him, her brows drawn together. "What?"

He reached out and stroked her bare shoulder, then

toyed with the strap. "With a body like yours, you should never wear clothes."

She snorted, then covered her mouth. "Sorry."

"Was that a laugh?" When she nodded he smiled. "I'm dead serious."

"I think that's called 'afterglow.'"

He laughed now. "Maybe. But I still say you should never wear anything but that underwear."

"Are you going to arrest me?"

"I could. Don't have my sidearm, though."

"Do you make arrests and stuff?"

"And stuff," he answered with a grin. "Life in the Forest is pretty tame most of the time, though."

"You're certainly intimidating in your uniform." She glanced down at the table. "Among other things."

Jack blinked. Was she thinking about him in his uniform? She'd certainly stared holes in his chest this afternoon in the café. His ex-wife Kelly had never liked it.

"I've been told my uniform makes me look like Smokey the Bear."

She snorted again.

"Now what?"

She tried to hide her grin behind a napkin. "Nothing."

There was something sexy and comfortable about sitting with her, sharing dinner after fooling around. It took a lot of effort to stay rooted in the chair. He wouldn't get up and hold her again. He wouldn't keep her on his lap as he cuddled with her. He wouldn't stroke her soft skin or smell her incredible hair. He frowned at his plate and went back to eating.

Yeah, he would put up with a little domesticity with Laurel. If it meant they could have a repeat of tonight sometime? And more? Sure he would. But they'd agreed to "no strings."

And for once in his life he was going to keep a promise.

Chapter 7

The next afternoon Laurel walked down the slanting street toward Bo Butler's garage. The day was bright but there was definitely a nip in the air even though sunset was hours away. Her day in the café had been what she was coming to view as usual. Hopping busy, capped with Jack's late visit marking the end of her day. He hadn't said much today, not that she'd exactly been a Chatty Kathy herself.

Those eyes of his, dark blue when he wore that green uniform, told her he remembered everything from last night. After their—she guessed it would be considered a romp?—in the kitchen, talk between them had dwindled. But it hadn't been an uncomfortable silence, surprisingly. Maybe he was the strong, silent type. He certainly wasn't as outgoing as his sister.

Neither she nor Jack had made a date to see each other again. Not last night and not today. But the expectation hung thick in the air. Their evening together hadn't really seemed like a date though, since they hadn't left the apartment. It was more like a booty call followed by a light dinner. Well, she didn't need anyone in Cloud Canyon labeling her as the stopover mistress or something equally gross.

Dating had never been her strong suit, really. Brad had all but taken over her life when she was still in college. She'd been so meek and mild then, letting him tell her what to do and how to dress. She hadn't changed much during their time together, either.

Her mother had never told her not to date Brad, but then again she'd let Laurel make her own decisions since she'd hit high school. Her mom had never been one for rules. It was by sheer luck and the grace of God that Laurel had never got into any real trouble.

On her walk she found herself drawn to a store displaying dream catchers. Some were as small as a fifty-cent piece and some as large as a dinner plate. Done in suede in different colors, their feathers danced in the breeze like silent wind chimes. She stepped close to one rack, then reached out to finger a pretty dream catcher wrapped in rose-colored suede. The ring was about the size of a jar lid. Super-soft narrow laces hung from the dream catcher, weighted at the bottoms with wide smooth beads of pink, red and white. White feathers also hung from the wrapped ring, touched with beige on their tips. She knew the dream catcher would look lovely hanging in the bedroom window of the apartment.

"Ah. That's made by a Navajo." The storekeeper, a stout woman with dark lined skin and thick black hair, stepped over to stand beside Laurel. "Not traditional Ojibwa but authentic."

"It's pretty." Laurel touched the crystal bead suspended in the web of twine strung through the center of the dream catcher. "Very pretty."

She checked the price tag. Surely her dreams were worth seven dollars. "I'll take it."

The woman gave a curt nod. "Come. I'll wrap it for you."

Laurel followed her inside the store. More dream catchers were on display here, along with Navajo rugs and ceramic and wooden statues of wolves and eagles. She spied a little golden sticker on the underside of a wing on one wall-mounted eagle. Made in China, it read. She hid her smile. Not exactly authentic.

There was no store like this in San Francisco, at least not in Haight-Ashbury. No, that place had been built by people who found their dreams in different ways, usually involving a bong. Many of the residents still liked to wear tie-dyed "authentic" clothes, which had helped her mother's business while she was alive. In this region, in this store, the colors were muted. To Laurel they reflected the mountains and woods just outside the door. Yes, Cloud Canyon was a far cry from San Francisco. But very pretty in its own way.

The woman totaled her purchase. Laurel paid out of her tips from today, and took her carefully-wrapped parcel.

"You dream new dreams," the storekeeper said.

Laurel began to smile when saw that the woman was serious. Her mouth was set in a thin line. The little hairs on the back of Laurel's neck tingled. "Thank you."

The woman stared at her and Laurel thanked her again and left the store.

"New dreams, huh?" She tucked the parcel into her purse. "I'm having enough trouble trying to realize my old ones."

She continued down the street, musing over the life she'd had so recently in San Francisco. She'd helped her mother in her shop in Haight-Ashbury, creating color combinations and embellishments to compliment her mother's designs. Her own art had taken a back seat out of necessity. There hadn't been any extra money for her to have more than a small work area in the apartment they'd shared. She'd had to keep her designs small too, stained-glass sun catchers mostly, but they were well received by tourists in her mother's shop. Brad never had any use for them, and hadn't spared her his opinion either.

Laurel had never shared her dreams with Brad, though. Not more than the one time. That should have told her head what her heart had already known. He'd laughed when she'd told him that she wanted to open her own gallery. A gallery with a big enough studio to create the art she knew was inside of her. Art as big as the dream that had urged her toward Reno with the hope to get a commission of enough money to finance it.

The road began to grow steep, and she leaned back as she continued down to Bo's garage. Dreams. Hers were still waiting, delayed by the deer and the rock wall.

"Maybe Bo will have good news," she mused aloud.

Or not. She could definitely think of worse things than having to spend a few more days with Jack. She thought of him last night, so forceful and passionate as he'd driven her crazy. So gentle and tender as he'd held her close afterward her release.

"Yep. Worse things could definitely happen."

She spied the garage to her left as the ground leveled out. The sound of banging and grinding came from the three open bays on the right side of the building. She didn't see her Beetle on any of the lifts, though.

"Hey, Laurel!"

She turned and waved as Bo stepped out of the bay closest to her. He wore a gray T-shirt tucked into blue work pants, with "Butler Service and Body" stitched over his left pec.

"Hello, Bo."

He wiped his hands on a rag and stuck it in his back pocket. "What brings you by?"

"Not my car," she quipped. "Have you made any progress?"

He shook his head. "I started on the fender and hood, but it's going to be a few days 'til I get the parts in to fix the engine."

"Oh." She toed the gravel with her sneaker. "A few days?"

"Yeah. Maybe a week, even. I'm sorry, but there isn't a lot of call for German parts up here. Folks need their four-by-fours and they like them to be American."

"SUVs." Laurel sighed. "I never needed one in San Francisco."

"That's where you're from?" Bo's brows rose. "Jack never said anything about Frisco."

"I never told Jack."

Bo studied her for a moment. "But Chloe said…" He just trailed off.

"What did Chloe say?"

Bo rubbed the back of his neck and smiled that almost-Jack-like smile. "Not much. Just that you and Jack have been talking when he comes in for lunch."

She lifted her chin. "That's right."

Bo didn't say anything more, but his eyes twinkled. He couldn't really know anything. Jack wasn't one to kiss and tell, was he? Sneaking around wasn't something she was used to, but she didn't want Jack's family to think that she'd lured him into an affair.

"Please let me know when the parts come in?"

Bo's expression sobered and he nodded. "Sure.

Shouldn't be more than a week or so. Do you need a ride back to the café?"

She started to shake her head then eyed the street she'd just descended. It angled sharply up in front of her and suddenly it was like every muscle was tired just considering the walk. She'd had no problem climbing up and down some of the most crooked streets in the country in San Francisco, but that was when she was at sea level.

She turned back to him. "You know, a ride would be great."

She followed Bo to his pickup, her mind working on the possibilities Bo's little slip presented. So Chloe had told Bo that she and Jack talked at the café, huh? There had to more to it than that for Bo to presume some sort of personal communication between her and Jack. Her stomach clenched.

Just what did Chloe say?

* * *

"Just what did Chloe say?" Jack asked.

His mother shrugged as she continued to run a duster over the hutch near the front of the antique store. "Nothing really, Jack. She just said that you seem to be taking an interest in this Laurel girl."

Sure, she did.

"Laurel's not a girl, Mom. She's a woman."

His mother glanced at him over her shoulder. "I assumed as much. I didn't think you were interested in one of the young things training at the Station."

"Hardly."

"Chloe said you were flirting."

He blew out a breath. He removed his ball cap and dragged his fingers through his hair. "I don't flirt."

She looked at him, her brow furrowed. "I know."

"I helped her out, Mom. Just like I said at dinner Tuesday."

She nodded and began to lift a heavy washstand set over near the window. Jack put on his cap and lifted it for her. Following her direction, he set it off to the side. "I don't know why everyone is so interested in my love life all of a sudden."

She shifted the washbasin and pitcher to the center of the stand and brushed her hands over the smudged apron covering her jeans. She wore her long hair, still dark and thick, twisted into a braid. To him, she didn't seem liked she'd changed at all over the years. He didn't miss the gleam in her dark eyes today, either.

"You have a love life now, do you?" she asked.

Jack kept his mouth shut. There was no way he would tell her what was going on with Laurel.

His mother continued to peer at him, her eyes narrowed. Man, he knew that look. She'd always been able to make him or Bo confess any little transgression in a minute's time with that expression. Well, she wouldn't have any luck with him today.

"I just came by to say hello," he said.

She ceased her silent interrogation and stepped close to him. "I know." Her eyes grew shiny. "You take good care of me."

He felt his throat tighten. He cleared it with a cough. "Where's Josh?"

"Chloe picked him up already."

He walked toward the back of the store and noted there were some new additions to her crowded inventory. Two primitive, roughhewn tables and a stout bookcase sat against one wall, fighting for space with a finely-carved curio cabinet.

"How's business been, Mom?"

She beamed. "Very good. You might not like tourists but they sure like to spend money. Just ask your aunt."

"I don't dislike tourists. I work with them. Every day."

"You keep them from drowning. Or getting lost. Or setting our woods on fire."

"And?"

"I'm just saying that one tourist mistake doesn't have to color the rest of your life."

He knew just what mistake she was referring to. "Don't bring Kelly into this. It's bad enough she called me the other night."

"She called you?" Her brows drew together. "Why? What does she want?"

Jack hid his smile. His mother barely reached his shoulder yet he knew that she would defend him in a heartbeat against anything, especially his ex-wife.

"She just wanted to make sure her alimony payment was on its way."

She crossed her arms. "I don't trust her, Jack. I never did."

"Maybe I should have listened to you."

She waved a hand in the air. "If you had told me how much of a... Well, I would have said something sooner."

Jack just looked at her.

"Oh you never say much, Jack. You're quiet like your father." Her eyes grew misty again and she blinked. "But..."

God, *but*. Did he even want to know? "But?"

"But you shouldn't let a bad marriage keep you from enjoying the rest of your life."

A bad marriage? Maybe she had a point there. But how about a bitter divorce? He wouldn't waste another minute thinking about Kelly. Not today.

He ran his fingers over the scarred surface of the bookcase beside him. "Is this new?"

"That just came in. I knew you would like it. Why don't you take it up to the house?"

He bent down and kissed her cheek. "Maybe I will. My office has been looking a little ragged lately."

Her eyes lit up. "Maybe I can come by and organize the place for you? I have some very nice pieces to spruce things up. Just in case."

"In case of what?"

"In case you want to entertain."

"Mom, please."

"All right." She blew a strand of hair out of her face and put her hands on her hips. "Just promise me you won't let Kelly ruin you for any other woman."

"Laying on the melodrama a little thick today, aren't you?"

Her gaze softened. "She left you wrung dry. And it's killing me that you're still paying her after three years. After all she took from you in the divorce."

"I had to give her half for the house. At least I get to live in it without her."

"That's a comfort." She put her hands on his shoulders and stared up at him for a long moment. What she was searching for, he wouldn't guess. Finally, she urged him to turn toward the front door. "Go. Finish your shift. Then relax. Promise me."

"Okay. I'll stop by tomorrow and pick up the bookcase."

"Good."

He left the store and climbed back behind the wheel

of the Jeep. He looked toward Chloe's café. Laurel had left before he'd finished eating. He'd heard her tell Chloe that she had to go see Bo, no doubt to check on her car. She hadn't stopped by his table before she left, not that he really blamed her. He hadn't been able to do more than grunt in answer to her questions, ever aware of his sister's sharp gaze on the two of them.

Laurel seemed to take her cue from him, though. She hadn't seemed hurt that he didn't suddenly play the boyfriend this afternoon. Well, he wasn't going to become this smooth-talking guy all of a sudden. That had never been him.

Yeah, things changed after last night. They weren't strangers any longer. They were lovers now, or just about. It was what she expected. What she'd asked for. He vowed to deliver.

If his heart sped up when he saw her, it was just a response to the memories of last night. It had nothing to do with how sweet she looked today. Or the sound of her voice even when she wasn't talking to him in particular.

He would stop by the apartment tonight, though. He didn't know any other way to get a hold of her. He wanted to know what Bo told her about her car, that was all. He'd found her by the side of the road, right? It was his responsibility to make sure she was taken care of. That her car was fixed to her satisfaction.

Satisfaction. Again he thought about last night. He'd pleased her in the kitchen, even though he'd been left wanting. Still, she was amazing. And she seemed to find him pretty amazing, too. Maybe tonight he could show her just how much he wanted her. When would Bo finish with her car? He was tempted to ask his cousin to take his damn time.

Biting out a curse, he jammed the key in the ignition and started the Jeep. He pulled out into traffic and headed back to the rec area.

"She insisted on 'no strings,'" he muttered. "Okay, then."

He would just focus on removing the tiny little strings on whatever pretty underwear she had on tonight.

Chapter 8

Bo dropped Laurel off in front of the café, and let the engine run as she grabbed her purse off the seat.

"Thanks." She opened the door and climbed out. "I'll hear from you, right?"

"Yep. Just give me a call."

She shook her head. "I haven't had cell service since I climbed up past five thousand feet."

"Yeah, that's how it is. I use the radio."

"Huh. I hadn't even thought about how Jack called for your tow truck the other day."

Bo looked at her expectantly, as if she would give more away in this conversation. Well, he could just forget it. She thanked him again and shut the door.

The café was closed and Chloe was long gone. She was probably with her Josh, whoever he was. Laurel wasn't going to ask. If she didn't pry into Chloe's personal life, maybe Chloe wouldn't watch her so closely whenever Jack was around.

She glanced at her watch. Four-fifteen. She crossed the street to the little market she'd discovered yesterday. Maybe she would buy something to make for dinner, not that one of Tom's sandwiches wouldn't make a great grab and go dinner. The apartment had a small stove that she guessed worked. Everything else in the place was old but clean and functional. There was even a stacked washer and dryer tucked into a small hall closet.

She'd explored this morning and found pots and pans in the painted cabinets. Maybe pasta for dinner tonight. There was no shortage of healthy foods here in the mountains, so she thought she'd pick up some of that chicken sausage she'd seen in the market yesterday. Some grated cheese, some spices. She didn't know if Jack would stop by tonight. He'd been so quiet in the café.

"But a girl has to eat, right?" she asked herself. "And if someone stops by, it would only be polite to offer him dinner."

Humming, she entered the store and picked up a basket.

* * *

"I don't know, Mom." Chloe leaned against the bathroom doorjamb and kept one eye on Josh in the tub. "Maybe twenty-five or twenty-six."

"But what is she like?" Her mother ran the water in

the kitchen and Chloe knew she was washing the dishes.

"Is she nice?"

"Very nice." Chloe picked up the bottle of shampoo and squirted some on her son's head. "Scrub, boy."

Josh began to rub his hands in his hair, singing a song about pirates.

"Where is she from?"

"I don't know. Someplace to the west."

"Oh, no. Sacramento?"

Chloe laughed. "She's nothing like Kelly."

She watched Josh pour his rinse cup over his head and she absently toed the towel on the floor closer to the bathtub's bottom edge to catch the spillover.

"Thank God."

Chloe jumped to find her mother standing in the doorway. "It's been three years."

"She called him the other day."

"So?"

Her mother shook her head. "I don't like it. Maybe she's tired of her latest man and wants Jack back."

"Jack would never take her back."

Her mother knelt beside the tub and finished rinsing

Josh's hair. "She's the one who wanted the divorce."

Josh looked at them, his eyes round. "The Force?"

"Never mind," they both answered at once.

"Kelly couldn't make him happy, Mom."

Her mother held up the towel. "Come here, hon." The little boy stepped out of the tub and into the waiting towel. She rubbed him until he giggled. "I still don't like it."

Chloe pulled the drain plug and ran the shower to rinse the tub. "Maybe he's finally moving past it."

She took the towel from her mother and rubbed Josh's head until his golden hair stood straight up. "Go get your PJ's on."

Her son streaked down the hallway, whooping as he ran to his room.

"He's all boy," her mother said.

She turned to find her mother tidying the bathroom now. "Don't I know it."

Her mother faced her. "Do you ever hear from him?"

Him. Josh's father. Chloe hadn't seen nor heard from him in almost five years. She so wasn't going to talk about him. Period. "Nope."

Her mother's eyes clouded. "Honey, don't you think

he deserves to know our little guy?"

"He doesn't deserve anything, Mom." Chloe blew out a breath. "Don't worry about me." She circled a hand in front of her mother. "Focus all of that energy on Jack."

Her mother opened her mouth, then shut it with a snap. "Okay, okay. I didn't press you when you came back from Reno with that hang-dog expression five years ago."

"I know."

"I didn't judge you when you told me you were pregnant."

"Mom, please?" Her mother, her entire family really, had been nothing but supportive at that critical time in Chloe's life. She was grateful but she wouldn't take her mother's prying now.

Her mother's hands flew up. "Fine." Her mouth turned down in a frown. "She's pretty, huh? Let's hope your cousin doesn't get any ideas."

"I wouldn't worry about that. Bo might be a charmer but he would never poach on Jack's territory."

"Jack's territory?" Her eyes widened. "Really? What do you know?"

Whoops. "Nothing," she rushed out. "I think Bo just

got the idea that Jack's attracted to her, that's all."

"Bo thinks Jack's staked a claim, huh?"

Chloe rolled her eyes. It had to be due to living here in the Sierra Nevada. Everyone talked like they were still in the middle of the gold rush.

"I don't know about a claim. I do know that Bo wants Jack to be happy."

"We all do, sweetie." Her mother sighed. "I could have strangled that Kelly myself, the way she'd torn him up."

"And Laurel seems like the farthest thing from Kelly, Mom. She's sweet and nice and...I like her."

Her mother smiled slyly. "And Jack does, too. Hey, if that loveable lunkhead Bo sees something there it must be clear as crystal."

Chloe thought for a second, then shrugged. She wouldn't tell her mother about the hickey or the sparks flying between Jack and Laurel over the past few days. Nuh uh. The woman would take it and run with it.

She touched her mother's arm and urged her out of the bathroom. "Let's go check on that boy of mine and make sure he didn't take his Star Wars PJ's out of the hamper."

Her mother laughed and they headed down the hallway toward Josh's bedroom.

* * *

Laurel pulled the pot of water off the stove and drained the penne pasta into a colander in the sink. It felt good to be doing for herself again. She barely remembered eating in the weeks following her mother's death, let alone cooking. Brad liked to go out for almost every meal, to trendy spots and places to be seen. Most nights she would have been happy with a crab cake down on one of the piers, but not Brad.

She lifted the strainer and shook it gently. "Pompous ass."

The sausages sizzled in the pan on the stove. She breathed in the delicious smells filling the small kitchen. Garlic and sun-dried tomato and basil drifted past her on fragrant steam. Chloe kept the place furnished down to the last utensil, and Laurel picked up a wooden spatula to flip the slices of sausage into the pot next to the frying pan.

"You're swimming in jarred sauce, fellas. Sorry." She stirred the sauce and meat. Everything looked and smelled great and her stomach growled.

"If Jack doesn't show up tonight, I'll just have leftovers for tomorrow," she told herself. "No big."

She would miss seeing him, though. Today she hadn't passed more than a few minutes at a time without thinking about last night. But tonight was Friday night, and she had no idea how he spent his weekends. The café was closed on Sundays, so if she didn't see him tonight she would probably have to wait until Monday. And by Monday Bo might have a better idea of when her car would be ready.

After tossing the sauce and pasta in a big bowl, she sprinkled cheese on top and set the bowl on the table. She took off the apron she'd found tucked in one drawer and ran her hands over her top. At least tonight she was dressed, if only for herself. She wore one of her mother's creations again, a camisole done in shades of peach and orange to match the new underwear she'd chosen. A pair of tan Capris and sandals completed her outfit.

"All dressed up and no place to go." Glancing at the door, she sighed. "I guess I dine solo."

As if on cue, a knock sounded. Her heart did that silly leap again and she crossed to the door.

"Who is it?"

"It's me."

It's me? That was a little familiar, but she couldn't ignore the things Jack's voice did to her. She pulled the door open. Jack filled the doorway, holding a bottle of red wine in his hand. His face was expressionless, and she couldn't guess what he was thinking.

She arched a brow at him. "You assumed I would cook?"

"No." He gave her a small smile and stepped in. "I assumed we would drink."

She stared into his eyes for a long minute. His eyes turned that dreamy blue-gray when he flirted with her. She'd missed that this afternoon.

"Thanks." She took the bottle from him and set it on the counter. Turning it, she glanced at the label. "Nice vintage."

"I have no clue." He still stood there, his mouth set. "I uh, stopped by to find out what was up with your car."

She blinked up at him. Okay. If he chose to ignore the way his eyes ran over her body, she'd play along.

"Bo said the parts for the engine could take a few

more days. Maybe a week."

There was a subtle softening of his jaw line. "Ah."

She didn't know what to make of that, but she knew what Bo's words meant to her.

"A few more days to fix the car. A few more days in Cloud Canyon for me."

When his eyes darkened, she knew he grasped her meaning. He glanced over at the table. "I guess you're about to eat dinner."

"Yes." She brushed a hand over her hair. "With you. If you'll stay."

Jack stood there as if unable to make his feet move either toward the table or out the door. "I just wondered about the car."

She braced herself for his exit but he only rubbed his hands on his thighs.

"And the wine?" she asked.

He shrugged. "My mother drummed it into my head that you never go anyplace empty-handed."

She waited a beat, saying nothing as he mentally talked himself either into or out of staying for dinner. She wasn't going to beg. She'd been the submissive one with

Brad all those years. Taking any scrap of attention he gave her and acting ever so grateful for his company. Thinking about the girl she'd been then turned her stomach now. So, she merely arched a brow as she waited for his decision.

"Um. Thanks," he finally said. "Sounds good."

She couldn't help but smile. "Grab two bowls out of the cabinet, will you?"

That seemed to finally get him moving. He closed the door and opened a couple of cabinets before finding the dishes. He handed the bowls to her and stood while she spooned out the food. "Looks good, too."

"Thank you, but I can only take some of the credit. The market made the sausage. Someone in Illinois made the sauce." She grinned. "I boiled the pasta, though."

She settled in one chair and he sat across from her. The steam from the pasta had made her cheeks heat and her hair curl around her face. She looked up to find him staring at her hair. She'd left it loose, tumbling down her back, and she tucked a few strands behind one ear.

"Thanks for inviting me," he said.

She nodded, then jumped up out of her chair and pulled open a cluttered drawer. "Corkscrew, corkscrew…

Ouch!"

He was up and beside her in an instant. He grabbed her hand and must have seen that she'd jabbed her finger on the darn thing. It was just a little prick. "It's not bleeding."

He still brought her finger to his mouth and kissed it.

"It's all right." She pulled back, her cheeks hotter. "Really."

He released her hand. "Let me open the bottle?"

She handed him the corkscrew and stepped back from him. "This is hard to believe."

He wrenched the cork out of the bottle and set it on the counter. "What?"

She waved a hand toward the table. "I'm standing here, flustered and uncomfortable, when last night we… Well, you know what we did last night in this kitchen."

He grinned and carried the bottle to the table. "You'll be here for a few more days. Maybe we'll get to spend some time in another room."

She chuckled, and then brought two glasses over to the table and sat across from him. He poured the wine and then drank half a glass in one gulp, watching her over the rim.

"That shirt is pretty. Did you get it at my aunt's shop?"

She shook her head as she picked up her fork. "No. At my mother's."

Jack followed her lead and began to eat. "Your mother has a shop?"

"She used to. In San Francisco. But she…"

"She what?"

She shook her head. "No. We're supposed to keep this light, Jack. We're not supposed to know anything about each other."

"Yeah." He drank some more wine. "But I remember how long 'no names' lasted. Besides, I'm sure my sister has told you everything about me."

"No, she hasn't. And I would never pry into your life that way."

Setting down his glass, he leaned forward. "I only meant that Chloe has a mouth as big as my cousin Bo."

"Oh." She relaxed a bit, and brought her glass to her lips. "Well, my mother had a shop in San Francisco." She took a small sip of her wine. "She died two months ago."

"Man, I'm sorry. My dad died when I was in high school. I still miss him."

She blinked at him, her eyes stinging. "She was all I had."

He cursed softly. "I'm such a clod."

She glanced over at him. "No, you're not."

"Yes, I am. I just complained about my sister and my cousin. I sometimes feel like I have too much family and you don't have any."

"Never mind." Brushing her hand over her cheek, she sniffed and straightened her shoulders. "I'm sorry."

To her relief, Jack began to eat again. Laurel didn't say anything more about her mother, so they ate in that comfortable quiet they'd shared last night.

After dinner, he helped her clear the table. She arched her brow as he turned on the water to rinse the dishes in the sink.

He shrugged. "Habit."

She brought the glasses over to the sink, and when she leaned close he took a sniff of her hair. "You smell nice. Soft and powdery." Catching her by the waist, he turned her toward him.

She braced her hands on his chest. "Jack, I have garlic breath."

"The thing about garlic breath?" He brought his mouth close to hers. "It doesn't matter if you both have it."

She smiled under his lips and he took her mouth. He tasted like garlic and wine, and that flavor she now knew was just him. When she reached up to wrap her arms around his neck, he lifted her. She clung to him as he carried her to the bedroom. Her pulse raced as he stopped beside the bed and set her down.

Emboldened by the attraction she saw in his eyes, she gave a push at his shoulders. "Sit."

Jack sank down on the edge of the bed and removed his shirt. She took a moment to take a good look at him. His chest was sprinkled with swirls of brown hair, thinning to a line over his ridged stomach that disappeared into the low waistband of his jeans. It was clear he wore no underwear. She kicked off her sandals, slipped off her pants and touched the hem of her shirt. She lifted it up and off and he stared at her, his hands in fists on the comforter beneath him. Her bra and panties matched, both in a light shade of orange.

She stepped over to him, her head tilted to one side when she caught his smile. "What?"

He put his hands on her waist and pulled her closer. "You look like a creamsicle, baby."

She laughed and he grabbed her, rolling on the bed until she was under him. He stroked his tongue against her cleavage. "You taste even better than you look."

Her skin was prickly hot as he began to taste all of her. Like last night, he brought her to delicious pleasure that caused her to moan his name. But unlike last night, he came over her and rolled again to pin her above him. Her body still trembled but she couldn't wait to see what he would do next. He didn't disappoint.

Between kisses, he shucked his jeans and managed to grab a condom out of his pocket. Almost before she knew what he was doing he pulled her down on him. "Oh!"

He was hot and hard and high up inside of her. He held her hips and she began to move.

He growled in his throat. "You're so tight."

She rode him, her hands braced on his chest and moving until she could feel him begin to lose control. He gripped her hips, his hands rough, and she had to grab on to his wrists to steady herself. He lifted her, up and down, as he threw his head back. His throat worked, his jaw clenched, as he obviously fought to hold on to his control.

"Let go, Jack," she whispered.

"No." He gave a shake of his head then leaned forward to kiss her throat. "Not yet. It's been too damn long. I want this to last."

What he did, what he said, made her climb toward ecstasy once more. "Oh, oh…" She climaxed as he thrust into her one last time. He shuddered beneath her as his own release took him.

Minutes or hours later, her mind was mush at the moment, Laurel stretched on the bed while she waited for Jack to get back from the bathroom. After she'd blubbered about her mother at dinner, he hadn't said another thing about it. Of course, he was a very quiet man.

He got back into bed beside her, and the springs creaked to echo the sounds they'd made earlier. She shouldn't feel this comfortable around him, not after being naked with him and as close as she could get. She shouldn't cuddle up against his side as he closed his eyes with a look of contentment on his face. He was sexually satisfied. That was all.

But she rubbed her cheek against his shoulder anyway, breathing in his scent as she gently moved her fingers through the crisp hairs on his chest. He smelled like pine and musk, fresh and hot at the same time.

His arm came up to wrap around her and he buried his face in her hair. "Mmm." He stroked her back, slowly, and it was as arousing as the way he'd touched her before. "I should get going."

So much for cuddling, then. She nodded and sat up, resting her back against the scrolled headboard. "Right."

He got up and pulled on his jeans and shirt, his back to her. Had she expected him to stay the night? She wasn't going to play the clinging vine, like she had with Brad. Nope. She was happy with the way things were, right at this moment. And wasn't Jack nice to look at as he bent down to put on his work boots?

He faced her then, running his fingers through his hair. "What are you doing this weekend?"

She brushed her hands over the sheet covering her, tracing her finger along one seam. "I have to work tomorrow, but the café's closed on Sunday." She glanced at him. "But you already know that. What about you?"

"I'm going fishing with Josh tomorrow morning."

"Chloe's boyfriend?"

He smiled. "Josh isn't her boyfriend. He's her son."

Her son? "Oh."

"How about dinner tomorrow night?"

She began to shake her head. "I don't know. Dinner here is one thing—"

"I thought we could go into Truckee. It's about a half hour from here."

She smiled at him, she couldn't help it. "Sneaking me off to a secret rendezvous?"

"Hey, I'm only thinking of your reputation."

"Oh, yeah?"

"Yeah." He sat beside her on the bed. "That's why I'm leaving now. I don't want anyone in my family spotting my Jeep out front."

"You're sweet to be concerned."

"Sweet?" He raised his brows. "Never been called that before." He kissed her and stood. "This was, well it was amazing, Laurel."

She couldn't keep the grin off of her face if she tried.

"Amazing."

His lips quirked in a smile. "Good night."

"Good night."

She listened to his firm tread on the wood floors as he walked down the hallway and through the kitchen. He sounded as solid as he looked, yet still he moved with the grace of a guy comfortable with himself. She had never been that way, though a few more days of Jack's praise and attention was sure to leave her self-confidence seriously boosted.

Oh, the things he'd done to her in this bed. Snuggling beneath the sheets, she brought them to her nose and breathed in. The linen still carried his scent, and with it sharp memories of what they'd shared tonight. It was so far from anything she'd experienced before.

And now they were going to dinner tomorrow night. This would more than likely be her one and only weekend in Cloud Canyon. By the end of next week Bo would probably have her car ready to go. Reno waited, and hopefully she would have enough nerve to push herself and get a commission or two.

Her eyes settled on the dream catcher she'd hung in

the window that afternoon, the crystal bead near the center winking at her.

"New dreams, huh?" She fell back on the pillows and smiled. "Maybe for a little while."

* * *

"What a mess." Brad Covington rifled through the file drawers he'd taken from the back of Astrid Tanner's old store. "No wonder the business failed. I couldn't be expected to do everything. I'd told her time and again to keep things in order. Stupid hippie."

That had made it easier for him to keep more than his share of the profits over the years, though. As he thumbed through the hanging green folders, he spotted the corner of a piece of paper down at the bottom of the drawer. He spread the folders wider apart and saw there were two computer-printed sheets. "Tell me that flake didn't miss another supplier's bill." He yanked the pages out of the drawer and quickly scanned the contents. "A bank statement? What the hell?"

They were apparently only two pages from a statement, so he had no idea what bank issued it. He read the dates on the deposit entries, from back in May. The statement must have come in right before her heart attack in June.

The deposits weren't large, ranging from about seventy to nearly two hundred dollars each, but there had to be over thirty listed just on these two pages. The backs of the pages didn't tell him any more about the account. Did Astrid have this kind of money stashed somewhere? Did Laurel know about it? No. Otherwise she would've used it to try to keep him.

"Clingy witch," he muttered.

"Where did you put the money, Astrid?" He sat down in his leather desk chair and leaned back. "And how much of it belongs to me?"

Chapter 9

When Jack stepped into the café, his eyes immediately settled on Laurel. She stood in front of a table of three guys who were probably off to the Forest today like he was. They were dressed in camp shirts, chinos and new hiking boots. Out-of-towners, probably.

She wrote down their orders and turned away. Jack saw the three guys at the table watch her butt as she walked back toward the kitchen. One guy leaned close to the one next to him, and must have said something dirty because all three of them laughed low.

He took a breath and started to walk over to them when he caught his sister's eyes on him.

"Good morning, Jack!" she called.

Out of the corner of his eye, he saw Laurel still. It was only a brief moment, then she turned a smile in his direction that sent a spark through him.

"Oof!" Josh barreled into his midsection, and Jack held out his hands to stop him from hitting him in the groin instead of his belly that second time. "How's it going, buddy?"

His nephew grinned up at him. "Great. Let's go!"

Jack picked him up and walked over to Chloe. "Did this guy eat?"

When Josh lowered his head, Jack had his answer. "We men have to fuel up before we hit the trails. How about we order something?"

Josh sighed and Jack lowered him to the floor.

"Okay." Josh climbed up on a chair.

"Your mom will have Tom make you something, pal." Jack sat down. "I'd like an omelet, please."

"Sure you don't want Laurel to wait on you?"

"You're standing right here, Sis."

She glanced toward the back and Jack followed her gaze. Laurel was setting clean glasses behind the counter, apparently oblivious to their conversation.

Chloe's eyes met his again. "I know there's something going on. I've never seen you act like this."

"Like what?"

"Don't be obtuse, Jack. It doesn't suit you."

"Is that a kind of bird?" Josh asked.

"No," Jack answered. "Let it go, Chloe."

She shrugged. "For now. I'll go get Tom started on those breakfasts."

Jack turned his coffee cup upright and waited for Chloe's return. He hadn't counted on Laurel being the one with the coffee pot.

She filled his cup and stood back. "Good morning."

He looked into his coffee cup and blew at the steam. "'Morning."

"Uncle Jack said we have to fuel up, Laurel."

"I'd think that would be true, Josh," she said. "Your mom told Tom to fix you something special."

"Uncle Jack is having an om-o-let."

Jack chuckled. "Omelet, pal."

Josh lifted his cup of chocolate milk and shrugged. "Whatever." He took a big sip and wore a mustache as a result. "I just want to go fishing already."

"Doesn't fishing take a lot of patience?" Laurel asked.

Jack caught her eye and nodded. "Yep. Patience is everything."

She bit her lip and he wondered if she was also thinking about tonight. "It's hard to be patient sometimes."

Oh, yeah. She was thinking about it.

Josh rolled his eyes. "Mommy says I have to have a

lot of patience for everything."

"I heard the bell ding, Josh. Maybe that means your breakfast is ready now." She turned to Jack and leaned a fraction closer. "Jack, what time—" She straightened as Chloe approached with their plates. "Enjoy your breakfast."

Chloe put their plates down and stared at him. "Yeah, tell me there's nothing between you two."

"Me and Uncle Jack?"

"No, honey."

Josh's eyes got big. "I didn't see anything between Uncle Jack and Laurel."

"I did." Chloe laughed as she cut up his pancakes. "I sure did."

"Go bother somebody else," Jack grumbled.

Josh picked up his fork and dug into his pancakes. Chloe finally left their table and Jack started to eat.

"We'll catch lots of fish today, Uncle Jack?"

"Hope to. You have to remember what I told you."

"Sit still and be quiet?"

"That's right."

Josh sighed. "I always have to sit still and be quiet."

Jack glanced over to where Laurel was refilling the

coffee maker. She rose up on her toes, and the backs of her legs flexed nicely. Those legs were strong, and fit just right high up on his hips while he buried himself inside her.

He took a sip of black coffee. "Good things come to those who wait."

The little boy shrugged again and kept eating while Jack thought about what would come to him tonight.

After they finished eating, Chloe took Josh to the bathroom. The out-of-town guys had left a few minutes earlier, and the place was pretty quiet. Jack grabbed Josh's jacket and stepped up to the counter where Laurel was stacking clean glasses by the soda machine.

"Hey, Laurel."

She turned, her eyes falling on the jacket in his hands. "Where's your sidekick?"

He angled his head toward the restrooms. "Pit stop. How about I pick you up around six?"

"Okay," she said without hesitation.

He saw her eyes darken though, and felt that punch of desire again. Taking a step back from the counter, he nodded. "See you then."

"Come on!" Josh called as he ran out of the bathroom

and headed for the front door.

Jack grabbed his hand. "Easy, pal. Here. Put on your jacket."

Josh wriggled but Jack got it done.

"You listen to your uncle," Chloe said.

"Yep," Josh said, tugging on Jack's hand again. "Come on, come on!"

"Thanks, Jack," Chloe said.

Laurel was watching the little boy, a soft smile on her lips. She hadn't known about him before last night, but this morning it seemed like she was already fond of him. He looked down at his nephew. Who wouldn't be? The kid might have gotten his blond hair from his father, but everything else showed he was all Butler boy.

They left the café and Jack buckled Josh into his booster in the backseat of the Jeep. Josh immediately put on Jack's Ranger hat. Jack got in, closed the door and rolled down the window.

"Laurel's pretty," Josh said.

"Yep."

The traffic was still light this morning and he drove out of town and headed toward a quieter section of the

District, away from the Soda Springs rec area.

"Laurel's nice, too."

"She is."

Jack glanced in the rearview mirror and saw Josh staring out the window, his brow furrowed.

"But I didn't see anything between you," Josh said.

Jack chuckled. Thank God for small miracles.

Jack parked at what was now their favorite fishing spot, and Josh reluctantly removed the hat. They left the car and made their way down to the still pond. Jack wore his pack and carried the poles, leaving Josh's hands free to grab onto his belt loop. Birds sang their song high in the trees, and a breeze carried a hint of the warm day to come. There were no tourists around, but this wasn't their favorite time of day or their favorite spot. He guessed it was too tame for them.

Jack sat down on the bank and Josh plopped down next to him. Jack rifled through the pack and took out the tackle box. Flipping the box open, he let Josh choose his fly.

"The purple one, Uncle Jack," he said, careful not to touch any of them as he pointed to his choice. "The fat one."

"You got it." Jack tied the big fly on the end of Josh's line and cast it out to float on the surface of the pond. He handed Josh the slender rod. "Hold this and stand here."

They didn't bother with hip waders, but just stood on the bank of the pond. Fly fishing was definitely a man's sport, but the boy had taken to the fuzzy lures the first time Jack had brought them out. And this was about the only time Josh ever stood still.

As Jack tied a fly to his own line, he caught Josh watching him.

"They don't really look like flies," Josh said.

Jack cast his line. "I know."

"Then why are they called 'flies?'"

"To keep things simple. They look enough like bugs, right?"

"I guess." Josh fingered his line like he'd seen Jack do. "Do the fish think they're real flies?"

"Mostly."

"That's why they try to eat 'em, right?"

"Yes."

But probably not today, as the little boy's chatter

would keep all but the deaf fish away from their edge of the pond. Jack breathed in the scent of the woods around them and let out a breath. He heard Josh breathe in deep and let it out in a whoosh, and hid his smile. He would have to be careful around the kid, especially as he got older. Jack was pretty much his only male role model.

Josh never knew his father. In fact, Jack had never met him either. He was just some smooth-talking out-of-towner Chloe had met in Reno. She never talked about him, not to her big brother anyway. And Jack wasn't going to pry. He didn't think the jerk even knew about Josh.

"Look at that big bird!" Josh shouted.

Jack looked at the owl soaring overhead. Josh watched it until it disappeared into the trees across from them, his eyes bright. Jack saw the pride on Josh's face.

"Way to spot him. Maybe you'll be a tracker like Bo."

"Nope. I'm gonna be a Ranger like you."

Jack's mouth dropped open, but he couldn't say a thing. Chloe might have made a tourist mistake like Jack had, but while his had left him with guilt and alimony payments hers had left her with Josh. And Josh's father had missed out on one great kid.

After about a half hour, Jack pulled in their lines.

They sat on the bank and Jack opened his pack. As he reached in for a couple of bottles of water, memories of that first day with Laurel in the woods struck him hard. Had that only been Tuesday? He took out the water and opened one for Josh.

"Why don't you take Laurel fishing?"

Jack shrugged as he grabbed two soft granola bars from the pack. "Girls don't really like fishing."

Josh laughed. "You don't have to really go fishing."

He froze, then zipped the pack closed. "What?"

"Have a picnic. Tom could make sandwiches."

Letting out a breath, Jack tore open one bar and handed it to Josh. "Maybe. Why Laurel?"

Josh blinked at him. "Who else?"

Jack had to agree with that. "Yep. Who else?"

* * *

Laurel didn't know where they were going to eat in Truckee, but from what little she knew about Jack she assumed the place wouldn't be too fancy. Another of her mother's tops would do, then. She chose the green and blue one she'd worn for her first day in the café. Holding it up in front of her, she glanced in the mirror. The top made her eyes look more green than hazel, but she knew the fabric wasn't what put the sparkle in them.

"Nope." She grinned at herself. "That's all Jack."

She laid the top on the bed and picked the blue underwear out of the top drawer of the dresser. He hadn't seen these on her yet. After she slipped on the underthings, she stepped over to her suitcase. She'd packed a couple of skirts, but not the pretty broomstick ones her mother had made. Those hadn't seemed right for Reno. These skirts were kind of short, one in denim and the other in khaki. "Denim," she decided.

She zipped it on and stepped over to the bed to put on her sandals. There was something naughty about wearing just tiny panties under the skirt, the fabric brushing against her butt with every step. It was like she was going commando!

After putting on her sandals, she took out her make-up bag. "A bit more makeup tonight." She brushed on some mascara and a sweep of green shadow. Some blush on her cheekbones and gloss for her lips.

It was nearly six o'clock, and Jack would be here soon. She hurried out to the kitchen. She still couldn't look at the retro chrome table without picturing what had happened there. True, they'd also eaten two meals together there, like civilized people. Her stomach gave a flutter. Oh no. When she got nervous her mouth didn't stop. And he was so quiet! Dinner conversation should be fun, not to mention the drive out to Truckee.

The knock came right at six. "Hey, it's me."

She didn't know why, but she liked that he was an "it's me" to her. It didn't mean anything really, just that no other man visited her in the little apartment. Something about the familiarity felt good tonight, though.

She pulled the door open and smiled up at him. He was dressed in khakis and a navy golf shirt. His hair looked like it was still damp, and he smelled like heaven.

"You look nice," she said.

His gaze ran over her. Slowly. "You too."

Two words, but they made her feel like he'd gone on and on about her clothes and her hair. A poet he wasn't, but those eyes…

"Ready?" he asked.

Oh, yeah. "Yes."

She locked up behind them and he followed her down the stairs. A rugged tan Cherokee sat at the curb, and she didn't have to guess that it was his. When he opened the passenger door for her, she smiled. "This feels like a date."

He leaned on the open door. "It is a date."

Then he kissed her and she felt it to her toes. He closed the door and crossed over to get in. The Jeep was pretty old, but it was very clean inside and when he started the engine it sounded more than capable.

"I like your car."

He shrugged and pulled out onto the street. "Bo keeps her running."

"That's convenient. Is that your Mountie hat on the backseat?"

"It's my Ranger hat, yes."

She pictured him in it, all tall and broad, and grinned. "Would you wear it for me?"

He glanced at her, then grinned. "Are you asking me to make love to you in my uniform?"

Make love? Ooh. "Nope." She laughed. "Just in the hat."

Jack shook his head but his eyes sparkled. "I don't think so."

They drove out of Cloud Canyon toward Truckee. They didn't talk much on the way, but she didn't feel uncomfortable with him. Of course, that could be because she'd slept with him already.

"I don't get into Truckee much," he said as they slowed on the exit ramp.

It looked untamed, with a river running right along the highway. Rocks jutted out of the river in places, and there were rafters making their way through the churning water. They seemed to work as a team, riding the water and leaning toward each side as one.

"I've never been rafting," she said.

"You should try it."

"I'm not much of an outdoor girl."

He laughed and winked at her. "Could have fooled me."

She flushed. "Do you go rafting?"

"Not much. I prefer kayaking."

"Why?"

"When I kayak I don't have to rely on anyone else's

skill with the paddle."

That told her a lot about his independence. "I bet kayaking helped give you those big shoulders."

He slid her a look. "Maybe."

They pulled into the parking lot of the restaurant. It was a huge thing, with thick timber peaks and rough rock walls. Nestled right beside the river, it was framed by towering trees. Jack parked and walked around to her door again.

She stepped out and gazed up at the restaurant. "This place is lovely."

"I don't come here often, but they have the best meat around." His brows shot up. "You do eat meat, don't you?"

"We had sausage last night."

He pulled a face. "Chicken sausage."

She laughed. "I eat meat."

He waved her in front of him and they went inside. Linens dressed the tables, balancing the rustic beamed ceilings and massive chandeliers made out of antlers. Jack had apparently called ahead, because they didn't have to wait with the dozen or so people in the flagstone entry. They were led to a table tucked right against one of the wide windows which showed a spectacular view of the river.

The meal was as good as Jack had promised. Her steak was prepared like she'd asked, and the crisp rosemary potatoes were delicious. They didn't talk much during the meal, but every time she caught his eye she could see the promise of the passion to come later. Was it like this because they both knew they only had a short time together? Or was he always this passionate? She certainly had never felt this burning hunger for anyone before.

At last they were finished and Jack paid the check.

"Did you enjoy it?" he asked as they walked out into the parking lot.

"Very much, thank you."

As they neared the Jeep, she shivered.

"Are you cold?" he asked.

She rubbed her arms. "I keep forgetting how chilly it gets up here at night."

He opened the back door of the Jeep and pulled out a worn brown leather jacket. "Here." He draped it over her shoulders. "Better?"

She rubbed her cheek against the collar. The leather

warmed and as it took her heat it released that fresh, hot scent of Jack. "Much."

He turned then and pinned her against the car. He kissed her, his tongue plunging deep into her mouth. He'd caught her by surprise, but she welcomed it as she wound her arms up around those big shoulders she'd admired earlier. The jacket slipped off of her but he was making her even warmer.

His lips trailed down to her throat, her shoulder, and he nipped her. "I've wanted to kiss you all night."

"Me, too," she breathed.

His hands went to her bottom and lifted up the hem of her skirt. "This is a short skirt."

"Not so short."

He reached beneath, his hands warm on the bare skin just below her little lacy panties, and froze. "Tell me you're not just wearing panties under here."

She giggled. "Sorry."

"I'm glad I didn't know that in the restaurant." He opened his eyes and kissed her mouth. "Come on."

He grabbed his jacket from the ground and helped her into the car. Gravel spun as he peeled out of the parking space. She watched as he visibly calmed himself and slowed the car down.

"Where are we going?" she asked.

He glanced at her, his gaze hot. "My place."

Chapter 10

Jack gripped the wheel as they headed down US 80.
He kept thinking about Laurel's sweet ass all but bare
under that skirt while they'd sat at the restaurant. It was all
he could do to keep to the speed limit.

The house was dark as he drove toward it, except for
the hall light he'd left on for Smokey. He managed to park
the Jeep without hitting the trees near the drive, then
yanked the key out of the ignition. He came around to her
side and opened the door, watching her legs as she swung
off the seat. They were smooth and sleek and her skirt
hitched up high on her thighs as she stepped down. Man.

The porch light came on automatically as they
stepped up onto the steps, and he opened the door for her.
She walked in as he flicked on the overhead light, her eyes
wide as she looked around. It was stupid, since she was
only in Cloud Canyon for a few more days, but her opinion
mattered.

"Wow." She walked over to the fireplace, which he'd
framed himself and built up with rock taken from the creek
behind his property. Her fingers traced the rough beam he'd
installed as a mantle. "This is something."

"It's a little rough, I know."

"It's rustic." She smiled. "And very pretty."

He shook his head. "First you call me sweet and now my fireplace is pretty?"

She walked over to him. "Questioning your manhood?"

He reached for her just as Smokey barreled back into the house through the dog door. He tried to catch the dog's squirming body. "Down, boy."

Laurel laughed and crouched down, letting Smokey lick her face. The dog went crazy, obviously starved for company of any kind in the house. Finally Smokey calmed and sat in front of her, his tail thumping on the wood floor as he stared up at her in blatant adoration.

"What's his name?"

"Smokey."

She laughed again and stood. "Does he get to wear your hat?"

He smiled and grabbed the dog's collar, leading him through to the kitchen. He heard her follow, her heels clicking lightly on the floor.

"Outside again, boy," he said, urging Smokey through

the dog door. He slid the latch on top and the dog sat there, staring through the window in confusion.

"Aw, Jack."

He turned. "He'll be fine outside."

As if to prove him right, the dog scampered off the porch out into the yard. Jack took a moment to stare at her, to watch that pretty flush move up her neck to her cheeks. "We're finally home."

He swallowed. *Home?* Where had that come from?

She didn't seem to take much notice of what he'd said, but just leaned back against the counter of the center island. "I like your kitchen, too." Her hands smoothed over the granite counter he'd installed. "This is nice and smooth."

He saw the glint in her eye and swallowed. "Laurel."

"You said you were glad you didn't know about my panties while we were in the restaurant."

Had he said that aloud? "Mmm."

Her head tilted to one side. "Why is that?"

He stepped closer to her. "Because I wouldn't have been able to stop myself."

She breathed in, her lips parted. "To stop yourself?"

He took her in his arms. "But I don't have to stop myself now."

"Stop yourself from what?" she whispered.

"From licking you until you scream."

She gasped and he caught it in his mouth. He lifted her skirt, the denim folding up and gathering at her waist as he revealed everything. She wore a blue lacy panties. "Ah, Laurel."

He removed the panties and put her up on the counter. In an instant he was where he wanted to be, between her legs and tasting her.

She clutched at his head, arching back as she began to move against his tongue. "Jack!"

He kept up the pressure, hungry to feel her release, hungry to taste her until he couldn't taste anything else. He wanted to taste her climax, to feel her pleasure. Then she cried out, and he reached up to hold on to her waist as she came apart against his tongue.

His breath rasping, he kissed her belly and stood.

She opened her eyes and sighed. "Oh, my."

Her gaze was soft, her lips parted in a smile.

"Come on, baby," he said, gathering her in his arms.

"Where are we going?"

"If I don't get you upstairs I'm going to do you right here on the kitchen floor."

She seemed to consider it for a moment, her gaze on the wide-plank floor, and he kissed her. He carried her up the stairs to his bedroom and set her on her feet. When she leaned against the footboard to steady herself, a beat of masculine pride struck him.

"You feel all right?" he asked.

"Oh, yeah," she said softly. "I feel fine."

He began to take off his clothes as she did the same. Grabbing a condom from the nightstand, he turned. He was naked now and she'd only taken off her shirt.

"You better hurry," he said.

She stopped, then began to slowly unzip her skirt. "And why is that?"

"I need you now, Laurel." He stepped closer to her. "Right now."

Her eyes grew wide. "Jack—"

"Now." He stepped closer to her. "And you better not take more time to get those clothes off than it takes me to put this condom on."

She grinned and wriggled out of her skirt in the next instant and unfastened her bra. He could look at her all night, but there was a more pressing need right now. Everything in him seemed focused on getting inside her.

He tumbled her onto the bed, staring into her eyes as she welcomed him.

He growled low in his throat and tumbled her onto the bed, staring into her eyes. "This is going to be fast."

"Y-yes."

He brought his lips to her ear. "And hard."

"Oh, yes."

He stroked her with his fingers. "You're so wet," he growled. He couldn't wait any longer, his body screaming for release. He spread her legs and drove inside.

"Jack…" She began to move, lifting her hips to meet every thrust.

"That's it, baby."

It only took a few hard thrusts before she came again, her body pulsing around him. He kissed her neck as he finally gave in himself.

He held her close afterwards, like he had in the apartment last night, and he could feel her heart beating against his chest. He should get up. He should give her space. But she felt so damn good curled up against him. A thought niggled at the back of his mind.

He might never get the chance to feel this closeness again.

* * *

Laurel stretched and buried her face in the pillow beneath her. The sheets felt like a comfy T-shirt. Reaching her arms out, she found the bed was much larger than her little iron bed in the apartment. She popped one eye open. Wood paneling and simple decorations reminded her of exactly where she was. She turned and sat up.

Jack was gone. Her clothes were draped over a chair in one corner. They must have been placed there by him since she didn't remember doing that. At the moment, she couldn't remember anything but what they'd shared on these comfy sheets.

She rolled over and looked around the room. It was very masculine, with a buffalo plaid comforter and furniture that looked handmade with bark showing in places. It was definitely Jack's space, and she felt privileged that he'd shared it with her.

She rose and went into the bathroom off the bedroom. It was also simple in decoration, with a huge tub set in one corner. The rug in front of the tub was damp, as was the towel hung on the rack on the wall beside it. Jack must have showered already. She must have slept like the dead.

She took care of herself and washed her face at the stout pedestal sink. The mirror hung above showed there was really nothing she could do with her hair at this point.

She saw he'd left a robe out for her, one of green flannel. The man certainly liked his plaid. She put on the robe and walked out into the hall. A short hallway showed three other doors, probably a couple of bedrooms and another bathroom. The smell of coffee reached her and she breathed deeply.

Padding down the stairs, she smiled to find Smokey waiting below for her. He seemed to smile up at her, his long bushy tail sweeping back and forth.

"Good morning, Smokey." She scratched behind his ears and he rolled his eyes. "There's a good boy."

The dog trotted over to the wide windows at the back of the house. The door was wide open and she could see Jack sitting in one of two Adirondack chairs, his damp hair sort of sticking up in the back. After pouring herself a mug of coffee, she stepped out onto the cedar decking. The wood was cool beneath her feet, the mug warm in her hands.

"Good morning," she said.

He turned and smiled. "'Morning."

He was dressed in jeans and a T-shirt, his feet bare. She reached out to smooth down his hair then sat in the chair beside his, tucking her legs underneath her. Smokey curled up on the deck in front of her, letting out a grunt of canine comfort.

She blew on her coffee and drank. "Mmm. Nice and strong."

His eyes flicked over her. "How did you sleep?"

"Like a rock. I didn't hear you get up."

"I had to feed Smokey." His eyes lingered on hers. "Believe me, I wanted to stay wrapped up with you all morning."

She stared down into her coffee. "Me, too."

He looked back out at the trees and she followed his gaze, her heart dipping. "This view is incredible. The colors! I'd never imagined there were so many shades of green. I wish I could…" She shook her head.

"Could what?"

"Recreate it."

"Are you a painter?" He held up a hand. "Don't tell me. We're not supposed to know anything about each other."

She shrugged. "No, I'm not a painter. Just a frustrated artist."

She could tell he wanted to ask more, but he sipped his coffee instead. After a few minutes spent enjoying the view and the quiet, he stood.

"Let me get breakfast today," he said.

"You'll wait on me?" she teased.

"Your wish is my command." He winked. "Or have you forgotten last night already?"

Maybe he didn't see her blush as he went back inside. She'd been very demanding last night after that first time, and he'd been only too happy to oblige her.

Smokey looked up at her, obviously torn between staying with his new friend and following his master to where there could possibly be scraps of food.

"Go on," she said with a tilt of her head.

The dog ran through the open door toward the kitchen. She finished her coffee, listening to the waking forest around her. Unseen birds sang in the trees, but otherwise it was utterly still. She could almost hear her heart beating, it was so quiet. Sounds of dishes and pans reached her from the kitchen. The smell of bacon came next, and she couldn't sit still any longer.

Leaning against the kitchen wall, she watched Jack as he flipped pancakes on the stove. There was something sexy about a man being so domestic, but from the lack of feminine touches in the house she guessed he'd been alone for a while. She thought about his off-hand statement about preferring kayaking, and knew his independent streak ran deep.

"Looks good," she said.

He glanced over his shoulder. "I admit I like my own pancakes better than Tom's."

She walked over to the cabinets and found dishes to set the table. They worked smoothly together, like they had done this before. Maybe because there was no emotion dangling between them, they could be comfortable with each other. She just knew she'd never felt like this with

Brad, even after years of knowing each other.

Smokey sat at her feet as she settled at the table. Jack set out a platter of pancakes and bacon and grabbed a carton of juice. She poured for both of them and they started to eat. Her first bite was…interesting. She took a big swallow of juice and he chuckled.

"Buckwheat," he said. "Not as fluffy as Tom's but they last me 'til lunch."

"I'll bet." She wiped her mouth. "They're good, though."

"Thanks."

He ate his plateful and most of the platter while she managed to eat one of the heavy cakes.

She picked up her glass of juice and toasted him. "That will keep me for days."

Leaning back in his chair, he eyed her. What was he thinking? About what a mess she looked? No, there was heat in those eyes. And there was no denying that crooked smile she was seeing more of each day.

"Now I know how to keep you happy," he said.

She sipped her juice and shot him an even look. "I think we established that last night, too."

His brows rose and his smile widened. "What do you want to do today?"

"I hadn't thought about it."

"I thought we could spend the day here. I could buy some ribs to throw on the grill."

"That sounds great. This could be my last Sunday here."

Something flickered in his eyes. Regret? Well, maybe he would miss her a little bit. Her stomach gave an odd flutter. Maybe she would miss him, too.

"Good." He stood and began to clear the table. "Why don't you go shower and I'll go into Big Bend."

She brought the glasses to the sink. "Clearing the table and hunting-and-gathering?"

He just shrugged. "Makes sense."

So simple and straightforward. "Thanks."

She stood on tiptoes and kissed him, lightly, like it was the most natural thing in the world.

He kissed her back, sweetly. Leaving him to the dishes, she went back upstairs to shower. She didn't have her toiletry bag, so she just used his soap and shampoo. There was no conditioner to be found. He was such a man.

When she was finished, she realized she had nothing to put on but last night's clothes. She got dressed and ran Jack's comb through her hair. Again, the intimacy struck her. How odd that such domestic familiarity felt more intimate than what they'd done to each other last night? It was like these few days really were time suspended.

She took the opportunity to peek into his closet. Whoa. He must have a dozen flannel shirts hanging in there. She ran her fingers over one of the shirts. "Mountain man."

Several Ranger uniforms hung there too, with a Mountie hat and a few baseball caps on the shelf above. His boots and shoes stood in rows. He really seemed very self-sufficient.

There was no sign that any woman had ever shared the house with him. She'd opened his vanity drawer to find his comb, and hadn't seen any lady's disposable razors, a tube of lipstick or even a bobby pin. If there had ever been a woman here, Jack had gotten rid of any sign of her. Was that a good thing? Or would he just as easily set her aside as well? That was what she wanted, so that shouldn't bother her. Why it did, just a little bit, she wouldn't consider.

Slipping on her sandals, she left the room and went downstairs. It struck her how he trusted her to be in his home alone. Smokey came through the dog door as she walked into the kitchen, a doggie smile on his face.

"Hi, boy." She gave him a scratch. "It's just you and me."

The dog tilted his head.

"For now. Jack will be back in a little while."

Smokey just went back outside to lay on the porch decking. She poured herself another mug of Jack's coffee and joined him. As she settled into the chair, the phone rang. The dog stood and looked at her expectantly.

"I'm not getting that," she told him.

The phone rang again, followed by a click that signaled its switch to voicemail.

"Hello, Jack."

Laurel straightened and turned at the sound of a woman's voice.

"It's me." The unseen woman sighed dramatically. "I guess you're not home. Probably out in those damn woods of yours. Call me when you get in."

The phone clicked off. Laurel looked over at Smokey. "It's me?"

The dog seemed to shrug in answer.

Was that a girlfriend? No. Her voice was cold near the end. And what was with the crack about the woods? She sounded very familiar, though. An ex, then?

Laurel stared back out at the "damn woods." Who would ever willingly give up Jack? Well, she would. When her car was fixed. But this was different. This wasn't a relationship.

"Then why am I sitting here, waiting for him to bring food back to the cave?"

Again, the dog had no answer.

Well, she would enjoy it while she had the chance. What would happen later this week was inevitable. Bo would fix her car, she would hand over most of her money, and end up heading back to San Francisco. That thought depressed her. Back to what? Her lonely apartment? Maybe she could get a job in a gallery that would let her display some small pieces of her art. But would that be enough to satisfy the artist in her?

She only had a few more days in Cloud Canyon with

Jack. Looking at the way he lived his life, there wasn't any room in it for more than a casual relationship. There really was no other choice for her to make.

A few days with Jack would have to be enough.

Chapter 11

As Jack drove home, the shopping bags on the seat beside him rustled in the breeze coming through the open window. It was still chilly but there was a promise of warmth in the air, too. The market had been open early as usual, a nod to the locals who didn't sleep their free time away. Let the tourists hide under the covers and miss the beautiful morning. Jack wasn't going to waste a minute of this one.

He thought about Laurel then, moving around his house as she showered and dressed. Over three years had passed since Jack had anyone to come home to other than Smokey. He usually spent his Sundays alone, going over paperwork in his office or just sitting outside on the porch with the dog. His mother hadn't pressed him to come over for Sunday dinner in months. She had Chloe and Josh for that duty. Tuesday night would be soon enough for the family to get together. His hands tightened on the wheel. Tuesday. His "week or so" with Laurel would be half over by then.

Ignoring the odd feeling in his stomach, he turned down the road toward his house. After parking the Jeep, he rolled up the window and grabbed the bags.

He climbed the stairs and unlocked the front door. "I'm back."

She peeked in from the back door, a smile on her face. Smokey shouldered past her legs as he barreled toward him. He pet the dog, holding the bags up over his head. "Not for you, pal."

Laurel came up and kissed him. "Hi."

Her lips were soft against his. He could get used to that kind of a greeting every day. "Let me put this away."

"I've got it." She took the bags and walked into the kitchen. "Anything in here not go in the fridge?"

"The bread, I guess."

He watched her moving around his kitchen, looking very right there. That clench in his belly came again. It was just lust, right? She looked pretty hot standing there, too. He loved it when her hair was loose down her back.

"What's this?" She turned and held up the shirt he'd bought her.

He tilted his head toward her green shirt. "I thought you might be chilly in that, not that it doesn't look as good on you this morning as it had last night."

She blinked at him, then unfolded the shirt. It was a thin sweatshirt, off-white, with a painting of a pink dream catcher on the front.

"Jack, this is lovely." Spreading the shirt out on the counter, she traced the hand-painted design with her fingers. "These colors, rose and pink and russet." She lifted her head. "It's so pretty."

He set his keys on the counter. "It reminded me of the dream catcher you hung in the apartment."

"The dream catcher." She looked at it again. "It does look like it. How did you know that was mine?"

"Chloe wouldn't have left something like that behind."

"The Butlers are superstitious?"

He shrugged. "Why tempt fate?"

"Fate." She blinked at him again. "Well, I'm going to wear this now." She stripped off her shirt and let the new one settled down over her body. She smoothed the fabric down and flipped her hair out of the neckline. He hadn't realized the neckline was notched low in the front, but the smooth skin between her breasts peeked out at him.

"Thank you, Jack."

He lifted his gaze to her eyes. "You're welcome."

He took the empty grocery bags and began to fold them. After stuffing them into the drawer near the fridge, he turned to find her watching him.

"There was a call for you," she said.

"Yeah?"

"I let the machine pick up."

He glanced over to see the message light blinking on the answering machine. Without thinking, he crossed to it and punched the button. Kelly's voice filled the kitchen. He glanced at Laurel, but her face didn't show anything other than mild curiosity. He wasn't going to call Kelly back, not with Laurel here. He didn't want Laurel to see him lose his patience, and Kelly could press his buttons.

He stopped Kelly in mid-whine and turned back to Laurel. "My ex-wife."

Laurel nodded. "Oh."

He didn't want to talk about Kelly. Hell, he didn't want to think about Kelly. Laurel was a different thing entirely, and he wouldn't let his ex-wife spoil his Sunday even if she had no idea she was doing it.

Taking Laurel's hand he drew her closer, kissing her

mouth again. "Mmm. Come on."

He led her out onto the porch and sat down, welcoming that comfort he'd felt earlier. He'd bought a newspaper in town and they shared it, the paper rustling softly as they turned the pages. Kelly's voice faded from his mind as he focused all his senses on the woman seated beside him. She'd showered, and from the scent of her he guessed she'd used his soap. There was something satisfying about that, like she was marked with his scent. *Don't be a fool, Jack.* Laurel wanted the same thing out of their time together that he did. No strings.

After a while, Laurel clicked her tongue.

Jack turned to her. "What?"

"You're a quiet man, Jack Butler."

He didn't know what to say to that. Kelly had always given him a hard time for keeping his thoughts to himself. Toward the end, that quietness was the only thing that kept him from telling her just what he thought of her. But Laurel didn't looked annoyed at his silence. No. A smile played around her mouth.

"Yep."

She shook her head and grinned. "I swear, the only

time you like to talk is when you're naked."

"That's not true. I also like to talk when you're naked."

Her eyes widened, and he wanted to tell her everything he wanted to do to her. And everything he wanted her to do to him. He'd had to restrain himself in bed with Kelly, in his words and his actions. She'd never looked at him like Laurel was looking at him now. Laurel was a world apart from his ex-wife, though. Hell, Laurel was a world apart from any woman he'd known.

* * *

Jack stretched with a loud groan, his arms wide on the bed. He opened one eye and peered at blurry numbers on the clock on the nightstand. Six-thirty. Leaning up on one elbow, he ground the heel of his other hand against his eye. He glanced at the other side of the bed, empty now. He'd taken Laurel home after midnight last night, after trying to make their weekend last as long as possible. He should have taken her home after they'd eaten out on the deck, but she hadn't seemed to be in any more of a hurry to get home than he had been for her to leave.

He swung his legs over the side of the bed and went

into the bathroom. Something caught his eye, dark blue and crumpled like string to the left of the bathroom door. He picked it up, lust hitting him as he recognized Laurel's tiny lace panties.

"Going commando under that little skirt, Laurel?" he asked aloud. The image that provoked made his grin widened. He went back to the bed and tucked it into the nightstand drawer. At least he'd have something to remember her by when she left Cloud Canyon.

He turned on the water and stepped into the shower, letting the cold water pound his back until it turned warmer. He began to wash his hair, closing his eyes and breathing in the crisp scent of the shampoo. Laurel had taken a shower here yesterday, her hot little body soaped up and glistening in the same space he occupied now. His body tingled as his belly tightened. He soaped up, then turned the water back to cold.

Toweling off as he went, he walked into the closet and pulled out a fresh uniform. The hat on the shelf above caught his eye. Laurel wanted him to wear that when they made love? Ridiculous. But he could see it perched on her head. And her wearing nothing else. Shaking his head, he got dressed and tied his boots.

He went downstairs, brushing his damp hair out of his eyes. "Smokey."

Crossing to the kitchen, he opened the dog's food bin. The dog came running, then skidded to a stop on his hindquarters. He peeked behind Jack, his doggy brows raised.

"She's not here, boy." Jack would swear the dog looked disappointed. He poured a scoop of food into the dog's bowl. "Maybe she'll come another day."

Smokey was apparently satisfied by his vague promise, and began to eat. Jack closed the bin and straightened. Would Laurel come to his house again? She'd asked him to visit her tonight, an invitation he hadn't turned down. Tuesday he had the family dinner at his aunt's. Laurel could be gone by Wednesday, if Bo performed his magic on her little Beetle.

Measuring coffee into the machine, he focused on getting through his work day. On looking forward to flirting with Laurel at the café without Chloe noticing. On later joining Laurel, upstairs in that creaky iron bed in the apartment.

The dog finished eating and dashed out into the backyard. Jack's gaze followed, settling on the two chairs side by side on the porch. They'd done it out there too, he and Laurel. While the ribs slow-cooked, he'd draped her legs over each arm of the chair and loved her until she'd lost control. And when she'd screamed his name? He'd never heard a sweeter sound.

He turned from the view and the memory and made his breakfast. The routine settled him, and he made a big bowl of oatmeal with honey. He ate and straightened the kitchen. He'd made too much coffee. Way too much for just one person. He poured the extra down the drain.

Putting on his sidearm and ball cap, he left the house. He drove through Big Bend to the Visitor's Center to check today's assignments. Thoughts of Laurel kept intruding, though. Images of her on his bed, all rosy and naked. Lust struck him low in the belly. He prayed all the kids showed up today.

If he had to do more than supervise, the tourists were in trouble.

Chapter 12

Laurel poured coffee into the Bennet sisters' mugs, making herself focus to keep from spilling.

"What are you thinking about, Laurel?" Charlotte asked.

"Yes, dear," Betty put in. "You're wearing that smile again."

Laurel shook her head. "I don't know what you're talking about."

"And you're flushed from head to toe," Jane added.

That did it. Laurel knew she was grinning like a fool even as she tried to fix her expression. "Let me go check on your breakfasts, ladies."

The three of them stared at her, their eyes narrowed. She guessed they never missed a trick. She was really glad they were always gone by the time Jack came in.

She took the coffee pot back to the counter and headed toward the kitchen. The truth was, she'd felt so darn good ever since she woke up this morning. Her muscles were pleasantly sore, from hours of hot sex with her hot mountain man. Yesterday had been a day like none other she'd ever spent. Or would ever spend again, probably. She couldn't imagine feeling so free with some faceless guy she'd meet in San Francisco sometime in the future.

She leaned on the pickup counter. "Do you have those poached egg orders, Tom?"

"Almost ready," Tom said in his rumbling voice. "Tell the ladies to keep their garters on."

She laughed. "I'm afraid they'd show me their garters if I said that."

"They probably would," Chloe said from behind her.

Laurel turned with a smile. "They're too cute, though."

"Cute?" Chloe rolled her eyes. "Those biddies are the Three Fates of Cloud Canyon. And the self-appointed keepers-of-the-knowledge."

"What?"

"Gossips. They put my cousin Bo to shame."

Sure enough, the ladies' gray heads were close together as their eyes darted around the room. "Oh."

Chloe tore a slip of paper off her order pad and stuck it in the rack above the pickup counter. "If you have any secrets, guard them close."

Laurel paused a beat. "I have no secrets." She poured

herself a glass of water, in the habit of keeping hydrated now. "I've told you that."

"And you don't flirt with my brother every time he comes in, either."

Laurel set down the glass and faced her. "I'm not a flirt."

Chloe shook her head. "That's not what I said."

She traced the rim of the water glass with her finger. "Would you have a problem if I—if someone flirted with him?"

"Not at all. Jack could use some loosening up. He's been pulled tighter than a crossbow since his divorce."

She thought about that cold voice on the answering machine. "How long—?"

The bell dinged and Laurel picked up the ladies' orders. She brought the plates to their table and they thanked her, their eyes sharp, as Laurel managed to keep her composure. She picked up the empty plates on a nearby table and dropped them off in the kitchen.

When she returned to the dining area Chloe was wiping the counter. "Three years."

"What?"

"It's been three years since his divorce."

Laurel just nodded, focusing on stacking the clean glasses and mugs Ricky had left in the rack beside the counter. Three years since his ex-wife had walked away from Jack? Or since he'd left her?

"And not a date in all that time," Chloe went on. "At least, I don't think so."

Laurel found her watching her closely. Could she tell Laurel had done more than date her brother over the past few days?

"No dates." Laurel turned the mugs so all their handles were to the right. "Hunh."

Chloe laughed softly. "Nice try."

Laurel wiped her hands on her apron. "I don't know what you're talking about."

Chloe placed her hand on Laurel's arm, the touch gentle. "Hey, it's okay if you're attracted to Jack." She grinned. "It's only natural. We Butlers are a good-looking bunch."

Laurel took the escape Chloe's light-hearted teasing gave her. "Never mind. I'm only going to be here a few more days. In fact, I'm going to good-looking Bo Butler's garage today to find out just how soon I'll be putting Cloud Canyon in my rearview mirror."

"I'll miss your help." Chloe removed her hand from Laurel's arm. "And your company."

The warmth in Chloe's eyes touched Laurel even more than her words. The bell dinged again and Chloe turned to pick up her orders.

Laurel watched her chat with her customers as she delivered their breakfasts. Her smile was a lot like Jack's. And she was so generous toward her, a stranger thrust on her a week ago. Laurel didn't have any close friends in San Francisco. Heck, with her mother gone and Brad out of the picture, she had no one there except for some of her mother's old friends. Funny, but she never realized how lonely and dependent she'd been. Chloe's job and apartment had given her more than a little money and a place to stay.

She blinked back tears. "I'll miss you, too," she whispered.

* * *

Jack turned the Jeep toward Cloud Canyon, tapping his fingers on the steering wheel as he stopped for a traffic light. "Come on, come on." The light turned green and he pulled forward.

Yeah, Tom's lunch special was always worth the trip. And he had to check on his mother. But Laurel was there, too. He couldn't remember when he'd ever had the urge to see a particular woman. He hadn't had a real date since Kelly left, just a dinner here or there with women from the department. He was always careful not to push any of those acquaintances into something physical. He could count on one hand the times he'd had sex this past year. Before running into Laurel, it had been four months since he'd gone into Truckee. Singles bars were a necessary evil in his mind, and the women who came on adventure vacations were very physical and open for the most part. And as long as the lady knew where he stood, he'd had no real problem scratching an itch now and then. It was nothing compared to the wildfires he and Laurel lit together, though.

She was going to see Bo today. That would put an end date to their…whatever this was, and he would miss it. Yeah, the sex was incredible. But he liked talking with her, too. Sitting together, sharing a meal. And holding her. She fit just right against his side in his big bed, and he'd missed her this morning.

"Jeez, Jack," he grumbled as he parked in front of the café. "You're turning all sentimental."

He tugged on his ball cap and got out of the Jeep. One step into the café and he immediately spotted her. She stood by the back counter, filling two glasses with iced tea. She hadn't seen him yet, so he took the opportunity to watch her for a minute. She blew a loose curl out of her eyes and lifted the tray. After she placed the glasses in front of an old man and woman, she straightened and smiled. He felt a punch to his gut in response. Her expression was so bright and open, and the way she stood with the tray propped on her hip did nice things to her curves.

"Take a picture, it'll last longer."

Jack turned to find Chloe grinning at him. "What?"

His sister waved her hand. "You can't deny it."

"Deny what?" He sat at a nearby table and took off his cap. "I'm just here for lunch."

She turned to watch Laurel head back toward the kitchen before sitting across from him. "I like Laurel."

"Oh, yeah? She seems nice."

"You're attracted to her, Jack. Do something about

it."

"Look, I don't need anyone messing in my love life."

His scowl apparently did nothing to deter her. He shouldn't be surprised by that. Even when they were kids, his little sister had her own mind. She did what she wanted no matter what her big brother had to say about it.

"It's been three years, Jack. Three long years since Kelly. You deserve to have some fun."

"Laurel's not like that."

"Oh? Not up for some fun, then?" Chloe's eyes lit and she leaned forward. "You've discussed more than the lunch special, I guess."

"What I mean is, she's just here for a few days. I'm not going to take advantage."

"Take advantage?" Chloe laughed. "I'm thinking she wouldn't mind a bit."

Jack looked up to find Laurel watching them, her brows raised. When her gaze met his, that punch to his gut moved lower. He grabbed a menu and pretended to consider his lunch choices.

"I'm no hound dog like Bo, Sis."

"I know that. You're one of the good ones. That's

why you need to let go a little bit."

Jack just kept his eyes on the menu.

"I can take a hint." Chloe stood. "Apparently *you* have to be hit over the head," she added.

Jack ignored her until she stepped up to Laurel. Then he watched their exchange. Just what was his sister up to?

As he watched, Laurel's eyes flicked toward him again and she nodded. As she walked over, he admired the front of her as he had her back. Her apron couldn't stop his memory of what he knew was beneath it.

He felt a smile curve his mouth as she stopped in front of his table. "Hey."

"Hi."

She glanced at Chloe over her shoulder, but his sister was busy talking with Tom at the pick-up counter. For a second, he thought Laurel was going to kiss him. Disappointment mixed with relief when she straightened. This wasn't the place for that kind of stuff. Especially with his sister watching his every move.

"How's your day so far?" she asked.

Better now. "Same old. How about you?"

She fingered her apron. "I'm going to see Bo this

afternoon."

"Yeah." He folded and unfolded the edge of the menu. "Let me know what he says?"

"Sure." Her brows raised a fraction. "Of course."

Jack searched her face. Maybe she would miss him when she left. He sure would miss her. At least he could admit that to himself.

"Are you going back to San Francisco?"

She shrugged, leaning a hand on the table. "I guess so." Her brows knit as she clicked her tongue. "After Bo takes all my money, that's pretty much all I can do."

He opened his mouth to ask what that meant, but he remembered her rules. Damn. "Oh."

The bell dinged and she turned toward the back. "That's Mr. and Mrs. Olsen's lunch." She turned back to him, her pretty eyes wide. "Do you know what you want?"

He felt that punch again. *I have no clue.*

"One of Tom's big burgers will do me," he said. "With some thick-cut fries." He kept his expression flat as he looked her in the eye. "Worked up an appetite this weekend."

That pink blush spread from the neck of her T-shirt

and up her face until her eyes sparkled. "Me, too."

He watched as she walked away from him, rubbing one hand over his face to hide his smile. How long did they have left? Who knew? Well, they had tonight. That much he did know. And maybe a couple more days after that until she went back to her real life, whatever that was.

He would just have to make sure she remembered him when she left. He damn sure knew he would remember her.

* * *

Laurel paused in front of Bo's garage, her stomach twitching. She pressed one hand to her belly and took in a breath. Why was she nervous? She was just checking on her car. Nothing major.

Her talk with Jack had been too brief this afternoon. One look at him and she couldn't help remembering everything he'd done to her over the past two days. She hadn't thought much about their dinner date since Saturday night, though. He was his strong-and-silent self when they were out there in Truckee, and fell into that stillness again throughout the day on Sunday. It wasn't an uncomfortable silence. Even in their short time together, she'd come to recognize that as his natural state. He didn't waste words, that was for sure.

"Can I help you?"

She looked toward the open bays of the garage at a big man in the coveralls. He had a shock of red hair and a matching handlebar moustache.

"Hi." She smiled. "I'm looking for Bo?"

Bushy red brows shot up as his eyes ran over her.

"Lucky bastard," he grumbled.

Her mouth gaped open. "Um…"

"He's in his office."

Big Red, as she quickly named him in her mind, went back into the bay behind him. She stepped toward the front of the building into a tiny waiting area. As she pulled the door open, she heard a faint buzz come from the back of the place. There was no one at the desk set near the windows, so she just let the door close behind her. She could see down the hall behind the desk toward the service waiting room. "Hello?"

"I'm back here," she heard Bo call from an open doorway midway down the hallway.

Walking around the desk, she headed for his office.

"I get what you're saying," Bo said into the phone. He waved her into the chair in front of the desk and swiveled his own slightly away from her. "That's what I thought. Too long."

Laurel sat and tried not to eavesdrop on his conversation.

"Well, what do you want me to do?" His voice was a low rumble, but carried a bright note. He laughed, the sound light. "Easy for you." He laughed again, his eyes sliding toward Laurel. "I gotta go. Yep. I'll see you tomorrow."

He cradled the phone and folded his hands on the desk, wearing a smile as bright as his Butler-blue eyes. "Hi, Laurel."

"Hi." She took her purse off her shoulder and traced her finger over the beaded clasp. "Are you busy?"

"Not too. What's up?"

She took a breath and forged ahead. "I'm here for an update."

His gaze slid to the phone and he rubbed his chin. "The part still isn't in. I've got the fender done, if you want to see it."

The part wasn't in? She gripped the arms of the chair to keep from jumping up and hugging him. "No, that's all right. Will it be here in a few days?"

Bo shrugged his big shoulders. "Hard to say. I called down to Sacramento, but they don't have the part in stock right now. I have a couple more places I can call. We'll get her fixed up, though. You can count on it."

Count on it. Her mind spun with the possibilities. Count on a few more days in Cloud Canyon, definitely. A few more days to delay going back to her dull life in San Francisco. A few more days to spend with delicious Jack Butler.

"I'm real sorry, Laurel."

She focused on Bo's earnest expression, struggling to keep a smile from breaking out all over her face. "That's okay," she rushed out. "If it's not ready, it's not ready."

One corner of Bo's mouth lifted as he dropped his gaze to the desk top. "Yeah."

His cheeks were ruddy now. Maybe he was embarrassed that he couldn't make good on his initial promise.

"It's really all right." She came to her feet. "It's not

so bad here in Cloud Canyon." She thought about Jack. "I'll survive."

She caught a glimpse of a smile before he faced her again.

"Good," he said. "Can I give you a ride back to the café?"

"No, thanks. I have to pick up a few things on the way ho— on the way back to the apartment."

Bo's eyes narrowed and she guessed he hadn't missed what she'd almost said.

"I'll let you know when I get the part."

"Thanks." She headed back out onto the street and started to climb up toward the café. Passing the Native American shop, she paused to look at the dream catchers on display. How sweet was Jack, buying her that shirt? He'd noticed the thing hanging in her window. What else had he noticed? Did he see how flushed she got whenever he looked at her? Did he see how much she'd wanted to kiss him this afternoon?

Well, she wouldn't hide what she was feeling. She would enjoy the pleasure she got from just looking at him, let alone touching him. And if that made her a fool? She would be one happy fool.

Chapter 13

"A few more days, huh?" Jack asked.

Laurel nodded, the motion bringing her face into direct contact with the sensitive spot between Jack's neck and shoulder. "Mmm hmm."

He held her closer on the bed and ran his hands over her bare shoulders. For once he preferred the narrow bed in the apartment. And he liked it when she nuzzled his neck. It reminded him of that first day when she'd nipped his skin and left a mark Bo hadn't missed. *Bo.* He never thought he would be grateful that his cousin couldn't get that damn part for her car.

"That's a shame," he said.

She lifted her head to look at him in question and he grinned at her.

Her lips curved in a smile. "Mountain man."

He kissed her open mouth. "Mountain Laurel."

She snorted. "So I'm a flower?"

He could only shrug. Flattery wasn't his strong suit. "Fits."

Shaking her head at him, she settled back down on his chest. "A few more days." She sighed. "At least that buys me some time."

"Time for what?"

She didn't look at him, just ran her fingers over his chest. It was one of a growing list of questions she visibly hesitated to answer in her attempt to keep their relationship baggage free. Well, his mother raised a curious son. Baggage or not, he was interested in her.

"Stop that." Grabbing her fingers, he brought them to his mouth. "I can't concentrate when you do that. Time for what?"

She nibbled her bottom lip but still kept her eyes from his. "Time to figure out what the heck I'm going to do with my life."

That sounded ominous. *Nice going, Jack.* He didn't think she was in trouble. Not the legal kind anyway. She didn't seem secretive when she evaded his questions, just very private. He wanted to ask her to let him help her through whatever it was. It was what he did. Helping Bo through a rough patch now and then. Giving Chloe a hand with Josh. Checking on his mom every day.

But had no right to mess in Laurel's business. He wasn't her boyfriend. Just her lover. For now.

"Hmm."

She dropped a kiss on his chest and turned her head to face him. "I can think of worse places to do my thinking, though."

As he brushed a curl out of her eyes, he paused to feel its silkiness in his fingers. "I guess Cloud Canyon has its assets."

"Uh huh." She rested her chin on her hand and gave him a wink. "Quite a few I can think of. I think my favorite perk is the supply of big mountain men eager to help out a damsel in distress."

He chuckled. "I meant its scenery, Laurel. Nature."

"Like the view behind your house?"

"For starters. You haven't gotten out of this apartment much, have you?"

"I'm in the café during the day. And in your arms at night." She nuzzled his ear. "Works for me."

He thought back to a few minutes earlier, to her sweet cries as she'd clutched the iron headboard so tightly her knuckles had shown white. Yeah, it worked for her. And him, too.

"Let me take you on a hike."

One fair brow arched as she pulled back. "Where?"

"In my woods, Laurel. Where I like to go when I'm not working."

"Like last Tuesday?"

He stilled. Had it really been less than a week since he'd found her by the side of the road? "Yep. Maybe Saturday?"

"If I'm still here."

"Sure." He pushed aside his own worries that she'd be long gone and simply nodded. "If you're still here."

Her brow furrowed, then cleared. "I'd like that." She settled down again, then jerked upright. "Wait! I don't have any boots."

"I can find you a pair."

She slanted him a look. "Not your ex-wife's."

"No. She never hiked with me. Chloe should have a pair you can borrow."

"Okay." She shook her head. "I don't kayak, you know. Or raft. Or any of that stuff."

"I'll go easy on you. Just hiking."

Her gaze grew soft. "I'd like to see your woods," she said, her voice low. "Again."

Desire struck him and he rolled, pinning her beneath him. "I'd like to see you in my woods again." He kissed her throat and she arched toward him. "Like last Tuesday," he said, echoing her words.

His mind whispered that he was living on borrowed time. Tomorrow was the weekly dinner at his aunt's, but he could probably see Laurel afterward. Hell, he couldn't stay away from her if he wanted to. He just wouldn't think past Saturday. But he would show her his woods.

The memory of their first kiss was still burned on his mind, even after all the times he'd kissed her since. He wanted to make love to her in the woods this time. With nothing but the trees and mountains he loved to witness it. The scent of the trees mingling with the scent of Laurel as he got as close as a man could get to a woman.

He closed his eyes. They were something else together, and he was going to take advantage of the cosmic glitch that brought her to him in the first place. For as long as she was here.

Even if Bo fixed the damn car this week, Jack would make sure Laurel didn't leave Cloud Canyon until he took her on that hike. Memories were all he would have left after she was gone.

He was going to make sure they were damn good ones.

* * *

Laurel felt wonderfully tired as she stretched and cuddled against Jack. Mmm, he smelled so good. She pushed aside her uncertainty about the future, at least for tonight. He was breathing evenly now, obviously recovered from the passion that had shaken his big body as he'd come apart. He'd probably leave in a little while. His work day started as early as hers. That, and she knew he didn't want his family seeing his Jeep parked out front. Jack Butler, mountain man and gentleman.

They hadn't made a date for tomorrow, but she wouldn't worry about that either. There were no strings tying him to her, and that was just how she wanted it. She would focus on Saturday's hike. She would stay around for the weekend, if only to be polite.

Yeah, right. As if having Jack in his natural habitat wasn't enough of an incentive. Hadn't she jumped him that first day? He'd been so big and strong, smelling as fresh as the woods and tasting just as good. She'd never felt an attraction like that before.

But, hiking? At least she didn't have to use his ex-wife's boots. That would have been beyond icky. Like some sort of metaphor for filling her shoes. No thanks. That cold voice on his answering machine was worlds away from what Laurel knew about Jack's personality. Sure, he was quiet. But he was warm and alive and so…there. Real.

"I should go," Jack said.

Her breath caught and she swallowed. "Okay." She'd known this was coming, right? Then why was she disappointed?

He got up and went into the bathroom, and when he came out he was dressed. Leaning down, he kissed her. "Good night."

"Good night."

She listened to his even tread as he left the apartment, then cuddled back down under the sheets. She'd only spent one entire night with him, but it had felt so right. It was a bummer they couldn't do that again. Maybe Saturday? She smiled to herself. That gave her another incentive for staying through the weekend.

Closing her eyes, she breathed in that fresh yummy

Jack smell as sleep tickled at the edge of her mind. Mmm.
Don't get used to this, Laurel.

She wouldn't listen to that voice. Not tonight.

* * *

Laurel hummed to herself as she wiped down the last
table. Jack had come in for a late lunch, as usual. He'd told
her he was busy for dinner tonight, but that he would come
by afterwards if that was okay. If that was okay? He'd
looked incredible in his uniform and she'd barely managed
to keep from kissing him right there in the café. She could
still taste his good night kiss from last night, the sweetness
of it making her stomach do that now-familiar flip thing.
She straightened, the cleaning rag clutched in her hand.

Whoa. If she wasn't careful, she would fall in love
with him. Her body tingled with awareness every time she
saw him. It wouldn't take much for her foolish heart to
want the impossible.

Well, she wasn't that simpering girl she'd left in San
Francisco. She didn't need a man to realize her dream. Just
a sympathetic gallery owner who wouldn't mind sharing a
tiny bit of space for an aspiring stained glass artist. If she
didn't have the chance to raise enough cash to open her

own gallery she would use her mother's old contacts to find a sliver of a place she could call her own.

She walked into the kitchen and put the rag in the dirty linen bin. Yes, Bo had unwittingly given her a temporary reprieve from making any decisions regarding her future. But she was no fool. She had to decide what she was going to do, and soon.

She would be at least fifteen-hundred dollars in the hole after her car was fixed, leaving her with precious little stake for Reno. She snorted and hung her apron on its hook. Not to gamble, like she knew anything about gambling in the first place. That was why she'd planned to book a reasonably-priced room and start her search for a gallery to take her work on consignment. It had been a pipe dream, really. Apparently her dream of having her own gallery was the same thing.

Her heart sank at the possibility. "I'm a fool."

"What did you say?" Chloe asked as she came out of the kitchen.

Laurel shook her head. "Nothing. Just facing some hard truths."

"Hard truths, huh?" Chloe tilted her head to one side,

her gaze searching. "You never told me where you were headed last Tuesday."

A self-conscious smile curved her lips. "Reno."

Something flickered in Chloe's eyes, a dimness that seemed out of character. "Oh. Do you go there often?"

"No." Laurel shook her head. "I've only been there a couple of times, actually. It just seemed like a good place to start. To look for opportunities that I couldn't find in San Francisco."

Chloe opened her mouth, then shook her head. "Nope. I'm not one of the Bennet sisters. Your business is your business."

As Chloe locked the front door and flipped the "open" sign to "closed," Laurel leaned on the edge of the counter. "I need to make some money, Chloe. There's no big mystery, believe me."

"Money for what?"

Laurel grabbed her purse from behind the counter and straightened. "It's just a foolish dream."

"A dream?" Chloe came closer, her eyes bright. "Dreams aren't foolish. Sometimes, they're all we have."

Laurel folded her arms and sighed. "You have your

café, your family. You have that adorable son of yours."

"Yes. But that's not all I want."

"What do you dream about?"

A half-smile twisted Chloe's mouth. "I gave up my dream and found a new one when I had Josh."

"He is amazing." Laurel shrugged. "I just want…"

"What?" Chloe touched her hand. "What do you want?"

She took a breath. "I just want something of my own. Maybe find some validation."

Chloe was obviously waiting for her to elaborate, but Laurel was just getting used to the idea that the dream of her own gallery would probably never come true. Brad's hurtful words coming so soon after her mother's death, closing the store when she couldn't make the rent. He'd called her a mess. Well, no one deserved to be dragged into her mess. She couldn't pour out her problems to Chloe, no matter how kind she'd been.

Forcing a smile, she held her arms at her sides. "Never mind. I'll let you get out of here."

For a moment Chloe's face was as still as Jack's. Then she smiled. "Hey, what are you doing tonight?"

Your brother. Laurel dipped her head to hide her blush and her smile. "Um, nothing."

"Come to dinner with me."

"Dinner?" She faced Chloe again. "Where?"

"Every Tuesday we have a family dinner at my aunt's house." Chloe waved her hand. "You know my aunt."

"Yes. She's very nice."

"Well, the whole Butler bunch will be there as usual. I know she wouldn't mind if you came, too."

Jack's whole family? Oh, man. No one knew about their involvement, and she knew Jack liked it that way. She wasn't looking to be the topic of Butler gossip herself.

"I don't want to intrude."

"Not possible. The real trick will be trying to get a word in edgewise. Though you're almost as quiet as my brother."

Jack at dinner. With his family. Would he think she was intruding? "Let me think about it?"

"Nope. Dinner's at seven, so I'll pick you up at quarter 'til."

"I…" What the heck? "Thanks. That sounds great."

"Good. My aunt's a terrific cook."

That was one consolation. Laurel thanked her again and went upstairs to her apartment to figure out what to wear. Gee, it wasn't like Jack was bringing her home to meet his mother. He had no idea she was even coming to dinner. She would just think of herself as Chloe's waitress and boarder. A single woman with nothing else to do, stranded in a town where she didn't know a soul. What would his family think if they knew she did know someone close to them? And very intimately?

Laurel turned the faucets on the tub and pinned up her hair. A good soak would relax her. Then maybe she could manage to sit at the table across from Jack and not give any signs that she knew him as more than the guy who'd come to her rescue last week and ate lunch in the café every afternoon. That she didn't know what his hands felt like on her skin or that he liked to talk dirty as he drove her crazy.

She groaned and sank down into the tub.

⁕ ⁕ ⁕

Jack pulled on a pair of chinos. He'd gotten through the day somehow, managing to keep from wrapping Laurel in a hug when he'd first walked into the café. He'd read the warmth in her eyes, too. Her lips had parted and he'd nearly kissed her hello. Jeez. You'd think he was sixteen and experiencing his first crush.

He chose a blue golf shirt and finished dressing for dinner at his aunt's. "Just make it through dinner, Jacko." He put on his shoes. "Then you can go over to Laurel's."

He went downstairs and fed Smokey. As the dog began to eat, the phone rang. Caller I.D. flashed and he cursed softly. Kelly.

Picking up the phone, he took a breath. "Hello?"

"Jack, it's me."

"Kelly. What do you want?"

"Pooh. How do you know I want something? Can't I just call and ask how you're doing?"

He sank onto the couch and rubbed a hand over his brow. "Okay, I'll play. How are you?"

"Fine. Why didn't you call me back?"

"I've been busy." He leaned his head back. "And we've been divorced."

"I just wondered what you've been doing."

Laurel flashed in his mind. He wiped the smile off his face even though Kelly couldn't see it. "Why?"

"I'm going to the lake next week and I thought we

could get together."

He lifted his head. "Are you kidding me?"

She clicked her tongue. "Jack."

"Excuse me. I don't believe I'm free, Kelly. Now what do you really want?"

"Well, I'm not seeing anyone right now."

"So?"

"I thought if I could drag you away from your woods, maybe we-"

"There is no 'we.'"

"Oh, never mind."

He could almost see her pout. Needy Kelly. Well, he couldn't give her what she'd needed when they were together. He sure as hell wouldn't worry about what she needed now. "I'm not your entertainment anymore."

"You know, some of my friends are on the very best of terms with their ex-husbands."

He pinched the bridge of his nose. "Imagine that."

"I guess I'll see you on my next trip through Crap Canyon, then."

Jack said nothing to that.

"What's with you, Jack?"

"I don't know what you're talking about."

"You used to be civil."

"I am being civil. I answered the call even when I saw your name on the caller ID." He stood. "Look, I have to go."

"Yes." Her voice was flat. "Dinner at your aunt's."

"It's Tuesday."

Again, she sighed. "Fine. But I'll figure out what's up. I know you too well."

You never knew me at all. "Good bye."

He punched the "off" button as she said good bye. That was weird. Was she crazy? Did she actually think he'd want to see her? If she did, she really didn't know him at all.

He walked to the front door. "See you later, Smokey."

The dog turned from his post at the back window and tilted his head in question.

He smiled. If he had his way, he'd be at Laurel's before the table was cleared. "Okay. See you much later."

When Jack arrived at his aunt's house, the evening air was taking on that familiar chill as a breeze kicked up.

Bo got out of his pickup as Jack stepped out of the

Jeep. "Hey, Cuz."

"Hey, Bo."

Bo's eyes searched Jack's face. "Bummer about Laurel's car, huh?"

"What? Oh. The part." He held the screen door for Bo and knocked on the door. "Yeah. Bummer."

Bo barked out a laugh behind him, which Jack ignored. The door swung open slowly, Josh practically hanging off the handle on the other side.

"Hi, Uncle Jack! Me and Mommy been waiting."

"For what, pal?"

Josh ran into the dining room. "For you to meet our guest, silly," he called over one shoulder.

Jack stilled. What had Chloe done?

Bo walked past him toward the dining room. He paused and threw a grin in Jack's direction before walking through the doorway. "Well, hi there, Laurel!"

Chapter 14

Jack couldn't breathe for what felt like a whole minute. Laurel was here? Deflecting Chloe's suspicions was hard enough at the café. How could he act indifferent around Laurel with his whole family crammed into the room?

He heard Laurel's answering greeting to Bo, the soft husky sound of her voice causing sparks to prick his skin. He'd never felt that with another woman.

Making himself move toward the dining room, he kept his expression flat. "Hello, everyone."

"Hi, Jack." His mother came to her feet and walked over to him. "We've just been getting to know Chloe's friend Laurel."

Jack kissed her cheek and nodded to his aunt and sister. He couldn't put it off any longer.

Letting his gaze settle on Laurel, he cleared his throat. "Hi, Laurel."

Laurel looked as uncomfortable as he felt, seated on the far side of the table with her hands folded in front of her. Her hair was down and loose, the way he liked it. She wore one of those pretty shirts, too. This one was pink. But

he didn't miss the resignation in the set of her bare
shoulders. Of course, she'd known he would be here. What
had Chloe told her to pull this one off?

"Hi," she said, her tone perfectly friendly yet neutral.

"Sit next to me, Uncle Jack."

Chloe shook her head. "Let Uncle Jack sit next to
Laurel."

"Why?"

"Because she's the guest," his aunt said.

Jack held back a snort. Like that made sense.

Josh shrugged. "Okay."

Jack walked behind the table and ignored the brush of
Laurel's hair against his arm as he took his seat to her left.
Were the chairs always placed this close?

"How was your day, Jack?" his mother asked.

"The usual, Mom."

"No rescues this week?" his aunt quipped.

A glance at Laurel showed him she was studying the
tabletop.

"Yeah, Cuz?" Bo asked. "Nothing major today?"

Jack reached for a roll as he'd done last week,
keeping his hands busy. He was used to keeping his mouth

shut during these dinners, and his family's blatant prying wouldn't change that.

"Bo, check the grill?" his aunt asked.

Bo stood. "Sure, Mom."

Laurel was quiet at Jack's right, picking apart her roll and eating it one tiny piece at a time. He could kill Chloe for putting her through this.

Bo brought in a platter of chicken grilled with rosemary and balsamic vinegar. It was one of Jack's favorite meals, but he doubted he'd taste any of it tonight. Like last week's dinner, talk went on around him.

"Did you grow up in San Francisco, Laurel?" his mother asked.

"How did you…?" She looked at Bo, who shrugged. She smiled at his mother. "Yes, I did."

"Do you still have family there?" Chloe asked.

Jack froze, finally taking a drink of his iced tea.

"No." Laurel fiddled with the napkin on her lap. "My mother passed away in May."

"Oh, how terrible," Jack's mother said. "You poor thing."

"I miss her." Laurel put on that bright smile Jack had

often seen when she was nervous. "She was a wonderful mother."

"She made Laurel's top," Chloe said. "Isn't it beautiful?"

"I was going to ask you where you got that," his aunt said. "You only bought shorts and T-shirts in my store. Well," she added with a wink, "that wasn't all you bought."

Jack swallowed hard. Man, the underwear. He peeked at Laurel, who was flushed as pink as her shirt.

"You have some lovely things," she said to his aunt, her gaze sliding over to him.

Jack's mouth went dry as he wondered which panties she had on under her tan skirt. He drank more tea.

"Thirsty?" Bo teased.

Jack looked at Bo, who barked out another laugh.

"How long will you be in Cloud Canyon?" his mother asked.

Laurel shrugged and shot Bo a pointed look. "A few more days, according to my mechanic."

"Is he taking his sweet time?" his aunt asked. "Bo, you shouldn't do that to the girl."

"Hey, I'm doing the best I can." He glanced at Chloe.

"It's not my fault the part isn't in yet."

Laurel sipped her tea and smiled. "Cloud Canyon is lovely. I don't mind having to stay here for a few more days."

"Why are you smiling, Mommy?" Josh asked. "What's so funny?"

"What?" Chloe stood and grabbed up her plate. "I'm not smiling, honey."

Jack watched his sister go into the kitchen and turned to find Bo studying the tabletop now. Laurel rose to help clear the table and Jack joined her.

"Let me get that," he said, taking the dishes from her hand.

"That's a gentleman," his aunt said. "Poor girl waits on folks all day."

Chloe came back into the dining room, sliding past Jack as he followed Laurel into the kitchen. For the moment, he and Laurel were alone. She placed the forks in the sink and glanced over her shoulder at him. Her eyes were large. Sparkling. "Thank you."

"You're welcome." He stepped close to her. He placed his mouth against her ear. "Soon, baby."

She moved slightly toward him, tilting her head to the side. He could smell her, the scents of soft perfume and warm skin filling his head as he breathed in deeply. His body reacted in a heartbeat and he stepped back.

"Bring in dessert, Jack," he heard his aunt say. "It's on the counter."

"Dessert," he groaned.

Laurel took in a breath and waved her hand toward the tray of lemon squares. "Well?"

He rolled his eyes and picked up the tray, following her back into the dining room. Bo arched a brow at him, but Jack just returned to his seat.

"Dinner was wonderful, Mrs. Butler," Laurel said.

"Beth, honey," his aunt said.

"Beth. The lemon squares look delicious, but I should get home."

Jack began to stand.

"I'll drive you," Bo said.

Jack glared at Bo. *Like hell.* "I can take her home."

They stared at him, all except Josh. He was busy licking the icing from between his fingers. Chloe and his mother wore looks of satisfaction. They were definitely matchmaking.

"I have to go through town to get to Big Bend anyway," Jack said.

They said their good nights and he waved her ahead of him out the front door.

"You don't have to drive me home," she said, her voice low.

Jack kept himself an arm's distance away, in case the family was watching. "Like I want to hang around on the street until Bo leaves?"

She faced him as he opened the car door for her. "Why do you think he would follow me upstairs?"

"Bo's a hound dog." He watched her swing her legs into the car and gripped the door's frame. "And you're gorgeous."

"Flatterer."

That made him still for a second. Him? He closed her door. Getting into the Jeep, he jammed the key into the ignition and took a breath. He'd managed to block his thoughts, his senses, from her during dinner. But in the closeness of the Jeep it all came back full force. The touch of Laurel's hand across his knuckles made him realize he was clutching the steering wheel.

Risking a look at her, he let his hunger for her wrap around his belly as he sucked in a breath. He loosened his grip and reached for her, but she pulled back against the door.

"Someone might be watching," she whispered.

He held himself still, willing his blood to slow its pounding. Finally, he took a breath and started the Jeep.

Pulling away from his aunt's drive, he headed for the apartment. Laurel was quiet beside him on the bench seat, busily fingering the beads at the bottom of her shirt. Her skirt rode high on her thighs and her skin looked as smooth as he knew it felt.

Keeping to the posted speed limit, he silently counted backwards from five hundred to keep the blood in his brain for a little while longer. When he saw the turnoff for the service road that ran parallel to Route 80, he turned the Jeep with a squeal of tire rubber.

"Jack?"

He pulled over to the side of the deserted road and shut off the engine. In an instant he was holding her, kissing her, as she wrapped her arms around his neck. She felt so damn good against him, her body rubbing his in all the right places.

"Ah, baby," he said, bringing his mouth to her throat, unable to do more than feel as she reached up under his shirt and over his back to clutch his shoulders.

"Jack…"

He began to unfasten his pants when a thought pierced his sex-fogged brain. "Shit." He pulled away from her with a jerk.

She held on to his arms, her fingers clutching his biceps. "What?" she breathed. "What is it?"

Pulling himself away from her to sit back behind the wheel, he closed his eyes. "I don't have a condom."

He heard the fabric of her shirt rustle as she moved closer to him. "Oh."

He opened his eyes and chanced a look at her. Big mistake. Her lips were rosy and parted, her hair all over the place. "Ah, Laurel. I'm sorry." When she touched his arm, he flinched. "Give me a minute."

She smiled. God help him, she smiled. "Let me take care of you."

He couldn't speak. She unzipped him and reached

into his boxer briefs. "Not going commando?"

He could hardly breathe let alone laugh. Her fingers wrapped around his shaft, tugging and stroking until he was so close he thought he'd die. Then she lowered her head and took him in her mouth and he let his head fall back against the seat. "Oh, baby…"

She licked him, sucked him, until he began to arch toward her. "God, I'm so close."

She lifted her head and he groaned at the loss of contact. His flesh was blister hot, damp and cooling off now without her soft lips on him.

"Let me, Jack."

He stared at her, at the sensual curve of her lips as she began to stroke him again. Her pupils were dilated and he could see she was almost as turned on as he was.

He managed a shaky nod and she lowered her head again. She made the sexiest little sounds in the back of her throat as she drove him closer to climax, and he could feel every vibration of her lips as she moved up and down. It was too much. Gripping his hands on the wheel again, he arched toward her and gave himself up to the pleasure as his orgasm roared through him. And she was there, holding him, stroking him, as he slammed back down to earth.

"Laurel." It was all he could manage to say, his pulse still pounding in his ears.

"Let's go." She sat up and kissed him. "I have condoms at the apartment."

He took in a deep breath, attempting to make his brain process what she'd just said. His limbs felt like lead weights and he didn't think he could do more than just breathe.

"Jack?"

He opened his eyes and turned toward her. She looked beautiful. A smile played on her rosy mouth and her hazel eyes sparkled.

"Are you okay?" she teased.

"Better than okay," he managed to say.

"Then let's go."

Her earlier words penetrated his brain. The apartment. Condoms. Laurel spread and ready for him on the bed. He sat up straighter. Amazing. She'd just given him the best blowjob he'd ever had and he felt himself getting hard again.

"Let's go," he echoed.

* * *

Laurel's body tingled on the seat beside Jack. She glanced out the window at the darkened woods at the side of the road, and realized she had no idea where they were. Hopefully the ride to the apartment wouldn't take too long.

Glancing over at Jack, she saw determination on his face. A muscle ticked in his jaw and she knew he wanted her. Her mountain man wanted her.

He pulled the Jeep in front of the café and cut the engine. They hurried upstairs and almost before she realized it she was on her back on the bed. The quilt was soft beneath her as Jack peeled off her shirt, her skirt, her panties. And then his mouth, that incredibly talented mouth of his, was on her. She bucked against him, running her fingers through his hair as he drove her quickly to climax with his tongue and his fingers.

He came up and kissed her, his hands on either side of her head as he rested his forehead on hers. "Where?"

She blinked up at him. "W-what?"

"The condoms, baby." He stroked his hands over her bare breasts and she arched toward him. "I can't wait to get inside you."

She stared up at him, at his dark eyes, and shivered in anticipation. "N-nightstand."

And when he was deep inside her, giving her so much pleasure she nearly screamed, it seemed like the most natural thing in the world. Only afterward, when he was still beside her, did she realize the thought that had struck her that afternoon might have a touch of truth to it. Their affair was sexually satisfying, yes. And she genuinely liked to be around him, even with their clothes on. Squeezing her eyes shut, she turned away so he wouldn't see the truth.

She was falling in love with him.

* * *

"There must be more than fifty thousand in this account." Brad shuffled the pages from several bank statements on his desk. "When did she set this up?"

The brown-haired girl seated across from him didn't answer, but he hadn't expected her to. He glared over at where she worked on a laptop perched on the corner of the desk. Sometimes she was so quiet he forgot she was there. And if he didn't need her to do his filing and correspondence she wouldn't be. Even Laurel was more animated than this girl. But she was gifted on the computer, and hopefully she would figure out Astrid's bank account password soon.

Brad sat back in his chair, his mind on Laurel. She had to know about this account. Her name was on it, for Christ's sake! "Chasing Dreams" was the business name on the account, not that it rang any bells in his mind.

"Damn Astrid," he grumbled. "Flake."

He'd managed to locate more bank statements by using the key to Astrid's apartment. Why shouldn't he? He'd been engaged to Laurel, right? She lived there too.

Where was Laurel? It was a pity he hadn't known about this account two weeks ago. He'd have put up with plenty to get his hands on this money, even Laurel's insipidness. As it stood now, he only had a few pages from a couple of bank statements. Either Astrid was patently stupid or deviously clever. He'd give his right ball it was the former.

"Anything?" he asked.

The girl, Mary, looked up. "On the password?"

Brad stared into her brown owl eyes. "Yes. On the password."

Mary shook her head. "No. Even using the latest

encryption software, I can't seem to find the right combination."

"You tried birthdays, right? Anniversaries?"

"Those you gave me, yes. In different combinations, and reversing the coding so that the—"

"Spare me the details."

Brad swiveled his chair toward the window behind his desk. Even after spending years with Astrid and her daughter, he knew very little about their extended family and milestones. Who would have thought that crap would be important now? He looked at his cell phone out of the corner of his eye. He'd tried to reach Laurel several times over the past week, with no luck. He let out a breath. If at first you don't succeed.

He grabbed up the phone and tried her number again. Damn thing didn't even ring, just went right to voicemail. He forced himself to leave a calm and friendly message, asking her to call him back when she got the chance. Where the hell was she?

He punched end call and let the phone clatter to the desk. Mary jerked in response and he bit back a snide comment. She was just another timid mouse.

"Keep looking, Mary." He stood and turned his back on her. "I need to know everything you can find out about that account."

"Damn it, Laurel," he muttered, staring at the Bay stretched out below him. "Where are you?"

Chapter 15

As she tidied the counter before the lunch rush on Wednesday, Laurel felt a tug on the hem of her shorts. She looked down to find Josh Butler staring up at her.

"Where's Mommy?"

She took a clean napkin from the counter and wiped the jelly off of his chin. "I think she's in the back."

"Nope. Tom was watching me back there."

"Well, maybe she—"

The bell above the door drew her attention.

Chloe walked in and Josh ran up to her. "Where were you?"

Chloe bent down to kiss his cheek and straightened. "I had to talk to Grandma."

"About what?"

Chloe's eyes slid toward her. Laurel could guess what the Butler women had discussed. Her and Jack. They'd clearly been matchmaking Tuesday night.

"Yes, Chloe." Laurel propped an elbow on the counter. "About what?"

Jack's sister actually blushed. "Never mind." She ruffled Josh's hair. "Did you finish your pb and j?

"Yep."

"Then why don't you head down to Grandma's?" She turned to Laurel. "Can you take him for me?"

Sensing a setup, Laurel hesitated. "Where?"

"Mom's shop is on the end of the strip."

"Sure." She untied her apron. "Ready?"

Josh ran to the table where he'd left his backpack hanging. "Yep."

He took Laurel's hand and she swallowed. The kid barely knew her, but because of his mother's obvious trust in her he gave her his own. She could see how easy it must have been for Chloe to give up her dreams for this sweet little boy.

"I'll be back in a few," Laurel said.

"Don't hurry," Chloe answered. "Mom has some pretty things that would look great in the apartment."

Laurel stilled. "You know I'm leaving in a few days."

Chloe smiled. "Maybe."

Rolling her eyes, Laurel let Josh tug her out the door. "Show me where your Grandma's store is."

"Right down here." He tugged her to the left of the café. "She has furniture and some ugly pictures, but she has old toys too."

"And I bet she lets you play with them?"

"Yep," he said again.

Jack's aunt waved to them as they passed the boutique.

Laurel seemed to be on friendly terms with more people in the short time she'd been in Cloud Canyon than in six months' time in San Francisco. Everyone there was always in a hurry or preoccupied with their careers.

Like Brad. With every passing day in Cloud Canyon she realizes how foolish she'd been to take everything that jackass said as gospel.

"You're in Mommy's old 'partment?"

"Yes, sweetie. For now."

"I lived there when I was in Mommy's tummy."

"Then you don't remember it?" she asked with a smile.

"Nope. We lived with Grandma when I was little. Now we live in our house."

Laurel knew Chloe was a strong woman, but her esteem grew at Josh's simple statement. A single mother who found a place for herself and her son, with only some help from her family. What Chloe had managed to do on her own humbled Laurel. Surely she could find the wherewithal to open her own gallery someday. She was on her own, true. But she didn't have a child to provide for.

"Here's Grandma's."

The word "Antiques" was painted in big letters across the wide window on the storefront, a window that was crammed full of eye catching furniture, lamps and knickknacks. Everything was displayed with care, speaking to the artist in her. But if the Victorian beaded lamp was placed closer to the whitewashed dresser, the pinks and reds of the shade would pick up the tone of the wood grain...

"Come on, Laurel!"

She realized she'd been gaping at the window. "Sorry."

The door opened, its bell's jingling echoing the ones at the café and Beth Butler's boutique. The store was filled with lots of finds as well, leaving pathways for customers to meander through various displays.

"Grandma, we're back!"

"Hi, honey." Jack's mother stepped out of back room,

a dust cloth in her hands. "Laurel! How nice to see you."

Laurel could see that familiar glint in the woman's eyes, but smiled in spite of herself. "Hi, Mrs. Butler. Chloe asked me to bring Josh down."

Josh let go of Laurel's hand and made his winding way toward the back of the store. She saw that he had a small table and chairs set up in one corner. An old coffee can full of crayons sat on top of the table and a wicker basket of books sat beneath. The Star Wars action figures scattered across the tabletop weren't really antiques, but as Josh began to arrange them she knew he thought they were pretty valuable. His brow was furrowed with concentration.

"Was the café busy this morning?" Jack's mother asked.

"Yes. And Chloe's so great with the customers."

"That's my girl."

Laurel was struck with a flicker of melancholy. Her mother used to say the same thing when a customer admired one of Laurel's sun catchers. Turning, she looked at an impressive breakfront set not far from Josh's play area. "Wow, you have a lot of china here."

"Mostly mismatched, unfortunately."

"That's the charm of it. You can rearrange the patterns to coordinate the displays and people would buy a whole 'set,' so to speak."

"Do you think so?"

"Well, I don't want to tell you your business."

"Did you help out in your mother's store?"

Another pang struck her. "Yes, but she made her designs from scratch. Not a lot to display, really." Except for her own sun catchers.

"Well, you have an eye. Why don't you have a hand at that display?"

"Oh, I don't know."

"You'd be doing me a favor."

She glanced at the china and her mind began shifting the patterns and colors. "All right."

The bell above the door jingled again.

"Excuse me." Jack's mother walked toward the door to greet the two ladies who entered.

Laurel stepped closer to the breakfront. There had to be enough dishes to make three complete settings for four, including a few serving pieces. At first she picked out one or two predominant colors in a pattern and searched for the same in another piece. Then she opened one of the glass doors and withdrew a few of the larger plates. She began to see the complimentary patterns. Arranging a large plate with delicate forget-me-nots beside a salad plate with cabbage roses on the surface below the glass doors, she saw the greens in the leaves nearly matched.

Reaching for a tea cup, she spied a saucer that was broken. It was wedged between two salad plates, which explained how it had broken. Carefully removing the plate it had sat on, she slid the pieces in front of her. There were about three dozen jagged pieces, so there was no hope of repairing it. The plate had been pretty once, glazed with an abstract design in rich greens and blues. Tilting her head to one side, she fiddled with the crockery.

The greens could look like the towering trees visible from anywhere in Cloud Canyon, and she moved them around to replicate that shape. The blues could be the mountains in the distance or maybe the Truckee River she'd seen with Jack when they went to dinner last week. A swirling path of blue passed in front of the "trees" in the design, and she moved and shifted the pieces until they more closely resembled the river.

The way the pieces fit together looked a lot like one of her stained glass pieces. Her sun catchers had been Art Deco in design though, appealing to San Francisco natives and visitors. But this design, taken from nature, really came alive for her. Maybe she would do some sketching tonight.

"That's lovely."

Laurel turned. "I was just playing around."

She clicked her tongue. "I'm not surprised that broke, the way I had those dishes stacked in there. "I tend to put off arranging them. Jack helps me with the furniture and heavy pieces, but he's not going to notice if the dishes or knickknacks are jumbled."

At the mention of Jack's name, Laurel forced herself to keep her expression neutral. "Does he come into the store often?"

"Every day."

"He's a good son, then."

Jack's mother smiled. "The best. Ever since his dad died, he's looked out for me and Chloe."

"When he was in high school."

"Jack told you."

"He's been in for lunch every day."

She leaned against the breakfront. "He doesn't usually talk about his father."

"I guess it's easy to talk to me, since I'm not going to be around very much longer."

"Would you like to stay?"

Had Jack's mother heard something in her voice? A longing, maybe?

"I have to get back to my life, Mrs. Butler."

"Do you have a boyfriend back in San Francisco? Is that why you're eager to get back?"

Laurel blinked in response and the woman laughed.

"Listen to me," she said. "I'm as bad as Chloe."

Laurel shrugged. "It's all right. I'm getting used to the Butlers, I think. No, I don't have a boyfriend."

She gave Laurel's hand a pat and looked at the broken pieces of the plate. "But the design there, Laurel. It's lovely. It looks like a mosaic."

"Sort of. I do stained glass. Well, I used to."

"In San Francisco?"

"A little. I made sun catchers and sold them in my mother's shop."

Jack's mother traced her finger over the branches of

the tree Laurel had created out of the broken china. "This would be beautiful in a larger design, though. Have you thought about doing big pieces of art?"

"Only every day."

She gave a firm nod. "You should do it. Maybe that's what you're meant to do."

Laurel tamped down the excitement the woman awakened. "No. I have to get back to San Francisco and try to find another place to sell the sun catchers. That's pretty much the only chance I have now. Maybe someday."

"Well if you do make some more designs, I'd love to sell them here in the store."

Laurel couldn't dim the hope that flared at the suggestion. But she had nowhere to create any designs. She just nodded at the offer, her throat tight.

"I should get back to the café. I'm sure Chloe's swamped."

Jack's mother watched her for a long moment, her gaze searching. "Okay. It was nice talking to you."

"You, too." She touched Josh on the shoulder. "See you, Josh."

"See you, Laurel," he answered, his head now bent

over his coloring book.

Her design drew her eye again, and Laurel pulled her attention from the jagged pieces and what they represented. Her shattered dreams, really. She nodded at Jack's mother and left the antique store.

Jack's aunt waved from the open door of the boutique as she passed, and Laurel raised her hand in response. The Butlers were a friendly bunch, if a little nosy. She really didn't mind, though. It was fine, as long as they didn't get her to admit anything that would embarrass Jack. She didn't want to leave him with anything more than memories of their time together. If she took more than memories back with her to San Francisco, that shouldn't be his concern.

Chloe greeted her with a smile as she stepped into the café, and Laurel knew that she'd take more than memories of Jack with her when she finally left Cloud Canyon.

Funny how people she'd known for so short a time could come to mean so much to her. It must be the thin air or something in the water.

* * *

Jack stepped over the fallen log as he approached the

abandoned campsite. Lucky for the campers, and Cloud Canyon, the fire they'd left smoldering had been surrounded by sandy soil with little brush. Stomping on the embers, he bit back a curse. What was it about vacation that made people take leave of their senses? Or maybe they'd always been fools and just recently decided to spread their idiocy to his part of the Sierra Nevada?

"Lucky me." He saw that at least they'd carried out whatever they'd brought in. There was no trash lying around. Randy had called Jack about fifteen minutes ago, having caught a whiff of smoke. Kid had a good nose. Jack would probably lose him to the Fire and Aviation Management part of the Forest Service.

Jack headed back to the Jeep, parked down near Soda Springs. A quick glance at his watch showed it was nearly two o'clock. Time for lunch at the café. Time to see Laurel. It was Thursday. Bo would probably have her car fixed today or tomorrow.

As the gravel crunched beneath his tires, he looked up at the trees. He'd asked her to hike with him on Saturday, and she'd accepted. He would just have to hold her to that even if her car was fixed. He knew she was just passing through.

There had to be a man waiting somewhere for her, either on the other side of the Sierra Nevada or back in San Francisco. The guy had to be an idiot. If Laurel was his, he would never let her out of his sight. He shook his head. Here he was, going all caveman.

He pulled the Jeep into a space in front of his mother's shop and cut the engine. As he stepped from the car, his mother peeked out the door.

"Jack," she called.

"Hi, Mom." He slammed the door shut and stepped toward her. "What's up?"

"I thought I'd talk to you before you had lunch."

He followed her into the shop. "Why?"

"Hi, Uncle Jack."

He nodded at Josh. "Hey, buddy. Why, Mom?"

"Laurel was here," she said.

"Look, I already told Chloe. No matchmaking."

"I'm not." He arched a brow at her and she smiled. "Well, not really."

As he stepped toward where Josh was sitting, he saw the broken dish on the breakfront. "What's this?"

"Laurel did that." She laughed lightly. "She didn't break the dish, just arranged the pieces."

"Really?" He ran his fingers over the wood, tracing around what even he could see were trees. "She's an artist too, then."

"Too?"

"Like her mother."

Jack's mother leaned against the breakfront. "How well do you know Laurel?"

He kept his expression neutral. "Not very."

"But you like her."

"She's nice." He looked back down on the china pieces. "We've talked a little."

"I saw how nervous you were at Aunt Beth's last night. You like her."

"She's a beautiful woman, Mom. And I haven't been around one in a very long time."

"She is beautiful. And very sweet."

"Yep." He turned and headed toward the front of the store. "I'm gonna go get lunch."

His mother was quiet behind him, never a good sign in his experience. He chanced a look at her and saw the thoughtful crease of her brow. *Uh oh.*

"She's leaving in a few days," she said.

"I know."

His mother didn't say anything when Jack turned away again. He didn't need anyone to tell him Laurel was leaving. He also didn't need them telling him what Laurel's leaving would mean. His family thought they would be losing their shot at matchmaking, that was all. To him it meant a hell of a lot more.

He put that out of his mind and left the antique store. He would have lunch. He would see Laurel. He would go hiking with her on Saturday. He would just worry about the rest later.

When he stepped into the café, his eyes found her immediately. She stood near the back counter, her head tilted down as she worked. A curl had escaped her low ponytail and brushed the side of her neck. Her skin looked so fresh, even from here. Fresh and smooth, and he knew it tasted as good as it looked. He sat down at the nearest table.

Chloe came over and placed a glass of iced tea in front of him. "How are you?"

"Fine."

She looked over to where Laurel was and Jack followed her gaze. Laurel was looking straight at him, a smile teasing her lips, and Jack sucked in a breath. Wow. There was no way Chloe could miss the expression on Laurel's face. Or on his, probably. Their connection was as clear as if she'd greeted him with a big wet kiss.

When was the last time a woman had looked at him like that? Like she wanted to wrap her arms around him and never let go? Not once in his recent memory, that was for sure. They might not have a "relationship," but the connection was there. Funny, but it didn't scare him like he might have expected. It felt right somehow.

Chloe's soft laughter drew his attention away from Laurel. There it was, stamped on her face. His sister was pretty shrewd, and he had never been able to hide much from her growing up. He sure as hell couldn't hide this.

"How much do you know?" he asked in a low voice.

"Only what I've seen." She leaned closer. "And what I can guess. I won't say anything."

"Man." He rubbed a hand over his face. "Does Mom know?"

Chloe straightened. "No. She thinks you're attracted

to her, though."

That knowing look on his mother's face had shown that clearly enough. "Well, yeah."

She punched his shoulder. "You're a master of understatement."

He wanted to ask her what she thought about Laurel, if she thought she would stay around longer if he asked her. But he couldn't. Hell, he didn't know what he wanted and he expected Chloe to guess what Laurel did?

"Bring me a burger, will you?" he asked instead.

Chloe nodded. "Yep. I'll have Laurel bring it over."

There was no use pretending. His sister knew. Jack just nodded and drank his iced tea. The bell above the door jingled but he barely noticed as Laurel began to walk toward him. She still wore that half smile, and he thought of everything they'd shared just last night at the family dinner. With none of the intensity of Tuesday night after dinner at his aunt's house, it was sweet and hot and still amazing.

He smiled as she drew closer, until he saw her eyes flick toward something over his shoulder. The scent of a familiar perfume struck him before a pair of slender arms wrapped around his neck from behind.

Shit.

Chapter 16

"Jack, you're here!"

He turned and got out of the chair to step out of Kelly's grasp. "Kelly, what are you doing here?"

"I thought you'd be here." She stood on tiptoe and kissed him on the mouth.

He stepped back, his hands in fists to keep from swiping at his mouth like Josh would have. "What do you want?"

Kelly tilted her head to one side, a practiced pout on her smoothly made-up face. "Is that anyway to greet your wife?"

"Ex-wife. What are you doing here?"

Kelly smirked in Laurel's direction. "Bring me a mineral water." She sat down at Jack's table and folded her arms. "We need to talk."

Jack looked over at Laurel, who'd turned away to get Kelly's drink. He sat down and leveled a glare at Kelly. "What do you want?" he asked again, each word bit out clearly, deliberately.

"I wondered if you would think about selling the house."

"I bought you out of the house. *My* house."

"I know." She waved a hand above the table. "But maybe I was too hasty. You know, the land values are up all around Pig Pen."

"Big Bend," he corrected automatically. "And what do you know about the land values in Yuma County?"

"Well…" She pulled at the napkin in front of him. "I have this friend."

"Let me guess. A new boyfriend?"

"Not yet." She grinned, a predatory expression he recognized, and his balls seized up tight.

"He's a realtor," she went on. "He said that if you sold the house, you might give me a share of the profit. If you sold for more than the appraised value three years ago, of course."

Nothing showed in Kelly's eyes but greed. This was so much easier to deal with than her vague request for his company on the phone the other night.

"It's a done deal, Kelly. And I wouldn't think of selling the house anyway."

That crease appeared in her smooth forehead, a sure sign she was pissed. "Pooh."

Chloe brought his burger and coolly ran her gaze over Kelly. "Kelly."

"Chloe!" Kelly jumped up and wrapped his sister in an insincere hug. "How are you?"

"Fine."

Chloe looked at Jack as Kelly sat back down. *What does she want?* It was unspoken, but he knew his sister's mind. He shrugged in answer, somehow managing to keep his temper.

* * *

Chloe stepped away from the table as Laurel brought Jack's ex-wife the bottled water she'd demanded. Kelly took it without a word of thanks and almost dismissed her without another glance. Suddenly her eyes narrowed. "You're new."

Laurel stiffened, finally nodding. "Yes. I'm Laurel."

She raked her eyes over her, obviously finding her lacking in her simple work clothes. Kelly Butler was dressed like she was going to a country club, in a pale pink skirt and cream silk blouse. Her auburn hair fell in a shoulder-length bob, shiny and straight. Her eyes were light blue, her complexion pale. Not the outdoorsy type, then.

Well, that explained why she'd never gone hiking with Jack.

"I'm Jack's wife."

"Ex-wife," Jack quickly corrected.

Laurel had known as much, but she couldn't imagine him married to her. Couldn't see him doing the wonderfully naughty things to her that he'd done to Laurel this past week. But they'd been married. He must have loved her once.

She ignored the little lurch her belly gave in reaction to that realization. And this woman had let him go? It was little wonder she looked like she wanted him back. Any man would pale after you've been loved by Jack.

"Nice to meet you." Laurel walked back to the counter to find Chloe scowling in Kelly's direction.

"Bitch."

Laurel busied herself with folding napkins. "She seems…cold."

Chloe's mouth thinned and she turned to Laurel. "She took Jack for almost everything. What he ever saw in her, I'll never know."

As she glanced at Kelly Butler through her lashes,

Laurel could guess. Jack's ex-wife looked like the type of woman to play on a man's sympathies. A real lost little girl type, despite the polish. Well, hadn't Jack come to Laurel's rescue last week? She twisted the napkin she held. Oh, God. Was she just another girl to be rescued?

She couldn't keep from watching Jack and Kelly. He was ramrod stiff as she ran her fingers over his arm. When she leaned close to him, he pulled back. A flip of that shiny hair, a tilt of her head, and Jack didn't respond. Whatever she'd used to catch him apparently didn't work now. Laurel didn't know if that meant he was over Kelly or if his passion was given easily and burned out fast.

Finally, Kelly stood. "Oh, never mind. You're still as stubborn as ever."

Jack didn't get up, didn't offer her a farewell kiss, and she all but stomped out of the café. Chloe was right. Kelly Butler was a bitch.

A glance at Jack's face told Laurel that he wasn't as unaffected as he'd acted in front of his ex-wife. No. He looked angry as he stared at his untouched burger, his eyes hard. She wouldn't pry. Nope. Jack's business was just that. *His* business. Besides, she was leaving Cloud Canyon in a few days. What did it matter to her if he was still entangled with his ex-wife?

She put Kelly Butler out of her mind and walked over to his table. "How's the burger?"

"What?" He glanced up at her, and his gaze softened. She could get lost in those Butler-blue eyes.

"Hey," he said. "Sorry about that."

She feigned indifference and shrugged, playing with the ties of her apron. "So that's your ex-wife."

His mouth thinned for a moment before he shook his head. He picked up his burger. "She's a piece of work."

She waited until he took a bite and finished chewing, but he didn't say more. He was a gentleman, but she was seized with the urge to ask about Kelly. How did they meet? How long were they married? Did he miss her? She pressed a hand against her belly. That last question was one she wouldn't ask on a dare.

He put down the burger and wiped his mouth, finally smiling. "How about dinner tonight?"

"On a Thursday?" she teased, placing her hand on the table.

He tapped the back of her hand with his fingers.

"Tick tock."

She straightened, but didn't remove her hand. So he felt it too, the rushing of time until she drove away from Cloud Canyon. "Come to the apartment."

"You'll cook?"

Now she smiled. "Nope. Pizza?"

He nodded, his eyes holding that sparkle she hadn't seen since Kelly had arrived in the café. "I'll pick it up and be over around seven."

He was stroking her hand now, probably in full view of Chloe's watchful eye. She didn't care. His fingers knew her skin, completely.

She nodded, drawing her hand away to hold it at her side. "Seven."

He picked up his burger again as she stepped away from the table. Yes, Chloe had definitely seen their exchange. Jack's sister was watching, her eyes sharp.

Laurel blew out a breath as she stepped over to her friend. "Okay. I give."

Chloe grinned. "About time you admitted it."

* * *

At six-thirty she was once more in the tub, trying to

send all thoughts of Kelly Butler out of her mind. Falling into her art had worked, for a little while at least. Her latest sketch replicated the design she'd fiddled with back at the antique store.

Kelly. Jack must have loved her. He didn't seem like the kind of guy to ask a woman to share his life if he didn't. And he must have wanted her at one time, too. He was a very passionate man, with a big appetite.

It had been obvious to Laurel that Kelly still wanted him in spite of her pouts and chilly words. For the life of her, Laurel couldn't imagine how Kelly could have let him go. To have Jack to herself, in that wonderful house in the woods he loved? To let him make love to her on the porch, on the sofa, in his big bed? Each and every night of the year? Laurel could admit to herself that she would love that.

True, Laurel didn't have a hold on Jack except for his desire for her right now. But what would it be like to have the love and devotion of a man like him?

And now Jack's sister knew about their involvement. Chloe hadn't seemed anything but vindicated when she'd grinned at Laurel's admission. But what would the rest of

Jack's family think if they found out? That she was just a tramp passing through Cloud Canyon, grabbing a good time with the town hottie?

She stepped out of the tub and wrapped herself in her short robe. None of that should matter. *Jack is just for here and now.*

She'd managed to swipe on some mascara before she heard a knocking on the apartment door. "Jack, are you impatient?" she said to herself. She hadn't even had time to put on underwear yet!

She padded through the kitchen and stopped before the door. "Who is it?"

"It's me."

That deep Jack voice coming through the door, just those two words that spoke of some sort of relationship, caused her skin to tingle. She'd never had an "It's me." Not even Brad had used those words.

Running a hand over her hair, still pinned up on top of her head for her bath, she sighed. She pulled the door open and Jack stepped inside. The pungent smell of pizza and the fresh scent of him filled her senses. He put the pizza box and the bottle of wine he'd brought on the counter and wrapped her in his arms. Mmm, he smelled even better up close. She buried her face in the crook of his neck and breathed in deeply.

"I love it when you do that," he murmured, cupping the back of her neck. He closed the door with his shoulder and shifted her upward until they were eye-to-eye.

"Jack, the pizza."

He kissed her then, plunging his tongue into her mouth, and in a flash she was only hungry for him. She pressed against him, feeling every glorious inch of him through her robe. He pulsed toward her for one hot moment, his entire body rigid, then released her.

"Pizza." He leaned against the counter as if he had to catch his breath. "Mmm, right."

She tightened the belt of her robe and bit her lip to hide her grin. A girl had to feel good when she affected a man like that. She heard the slide of cardboard as he put the pizza box on the table. Reaching into the cabinet, she got down dishes as he found the corkscrew and opened the wine. Again, the feeling of domestic comfort teased at her. She pulled open a drawer and grabbed two forks, then closed it deliberately.

Jack is just for now.

She sat down at the table and watched as Jack poured wine into two glasses, telling her stupid heart to cease its pounding and let her body take over. She surrendered her senses over to the pull of him, to her attraction to him, and nothing else. And that was as it should be.

* * *

Jack took a minute to collect himself before he joined Laurel at the table, his hands braced on the edge of the counter. When she'd opened the door he'd felt like he was home. Home? What the hell was wrong with him? Hadn't seeing Kelly today reminded him how foolish it was to give yourself up to another person?

He wasn't an idiot. He knew Laurel didn't want a relationship any more than he did. But one look from her, one touch of her skin, and he wanted to hold her for as long as she would let him. When he'd kissed her, it had seemed the most natural thing in the world. And when she'd kissed him back, mirroring his hunger, it had shaken him to the soles of his boots.

He picked up the two glasses of wine and carried them to the table. She watched him, her hazel eyes round,

and he wondered what she was thinking. He wouldn't ask
her. Jack Butler didn't engage in those kinds of penny-for-
your-thoughts conversations.

"Pizza smells good," he said as she handed him a
plate.

She nodded and picked up a fork. "I love
mushrooms."

She speared a mushroom and began to eat as he
quickly devoured his slice.

He took a sip of wine and served himself another
piece of pizza. "That was awkward today."

Her brows arched slightly. She took a sip of her wine.
"Your ex-wife." A smile teased her lips. "Nice girl."

He barked out a laugh. "Yeah. I don't know what I...
Never mind."

"That's kind of what Chloe said."

Jack stilled. What else had his sister said about his
marriage? About his failure? It wasn't a subject they'd
discussed, but despite his silence on the matter his whole
family had to know how he'd taken Kelly's defection.
"Chloe isn't Kelly's biggest fan."

"Chloe loves you," Laurel said. "She's very

protective."

"That's my sister in a nutshell."

"You're lucky."

He knew now that she had no one. When she didn't say more, he felt the need to fill the silence. It was a first in his memory.

"I met Kelly when I was twenty-two."

Laurel arched her brows again but didn't say anything. Then she laughed softly. "Gee, Jack. You're talking and we're not even naked."

He smiled, her words relaxing him. "Yeah, but I'm picturing you naked."

She waved a hand at him to continue.

"We met at Lake Tahoe. She… She needed me and I guess that felt good."

Her brow furrowed and she lowered her eyes.

"What are you thinking?" he asked.

That bright smile spread across her face, and he knew she was uncomfortable. "Jack to the rescue."

"Ah. Last Tuesday." That damsel-in-distress thing. But meeting Laurel was nothing like when he'd met Kelly. Kelly's reaction to him was very different than Laurel's, too. "Sort of like that," he said. "But…more. We got married about a year later."

"You were so young!"

"And stupid, it seems. Anyway, I couldn't make it work."

"*You* couldn't?" She shook her head. "Jack, marriage takes two."

He couldn't figure out how she'd come to that wrong conclusion. She'd seen Kelly. That woman couldn't handle more than picking out her wardrobe, which had to be something someone like Laurel couldn't understand. Laurel knew what she was doing, or seemed to. Not that he'd broached the subject of her plans past this Saturday.

"It was my job to make it work, Laurel. I asked her to marry me. I said, 'I do.'"

She stared at him for a long moment. "I won't pry."

"There's nothing to tell, really." His throat was tight for some stupid reason, and he swallowed. He studied the stem of his wineglass as he slowly twirled it. "I tried to make it work but Kelly wasn't happy. End of story."

She leaned toward him and placed her hand on his, stilling his fingers. "Kelly is a fool."

He looked up at her, at the cloud of golden curls around her face, at her wide eyes now filled with compassion. There was no pity there. "Yeah?"

She smiled, a genuine expression that lit those hazel eyes. "If I know one thing from this past week, Jack Butler, it's that you know how to make a woman happy."

That punch of desire struck him again, mixed with masculine pride at her simply-spoken statement. He stood and she did too. She padded over in her bare feet and raised up on her toes to fit perfectly in his arms.

He brought his lips to her ear. "Want me to make you happy?"

He pulled back to see her pupils were dilated, her lips parted, and he marveled that she could want him as much as he wanted her.

"Oh, yes," she breathed.

He saw a flush on her cheeks.

"Only you can look at me like you can eat me alive and still blush."

She lowered her lashes. "Jack."

He urged her ahead of him into the bedroom. They might not have anything past Saturday. But he would do his damnedest to make sure she would remember tonight for as long as he would.

Chapter 17

Laurel turned when the bell above the café door jingled, and her heart gave a little leap. But the big man framed in the doorway wasn't Jack. Bo Butler stood there, a sheepish grin on his face, and her heartbeat slowed to a normal rate.

"Hey, Laurel." He walked over to the table Jack usually occupied and sat. "Thought I'd stop by for lunch."

She heard a snort behind her and turned to find Chloe shaking her head.

"Clod," Chloe grumbled.

"What?" Laurel asked.

"I swear, the Butler men are clueless."

Chloe went back into the kitchen and Laurel walked over to Bo. She was almost relieved it hadn't been Jack there in the doorway. She still didn't know how she was going to face him after last night. Oh, the wicked things he'd said were enough to make her blush now. But what she'd said to him, what she'd begged him to do! And he'd done them. She'd never imagined... Well, let's just say it was on the growing list of things that she'd done with Jack Butler that she'd never before done in her life.

"What would you like, Bo?"

Bo shrugged and grabbed a menu. "Don't know. What's good?"

"Honestly, I've never brought out a plate from Tom's kitchen that didn't look good."

He nodded and closed the menu. "Tuna melt, then."

She jotted down his order. "And to drink?"

"A Coke."

He placed the menu in the holder and looked at her, his brows arched and his lips parted.

"Yes?" she asked.

His gaze skittered away toward the menus again. "The part still isn't in."

Ugh, the part. Her ticket out of Cloud Canyon. "Oh?"

"Yep."

He looked up at her, and she would swear his cheeks were red. What was going on?

"Seems to be some trouble with the distributor over in Sacramento," he said. "Maybe over the weekend."

"Okay." She just stared at him until he looked away again. "Huh."

When he didn't say anything more, she just shook her

head. Something was up. As she walked toward the back to place Bo's order, she caught a glimpse of something on Chloe's face. She was biting her lower lip, her brows drawn together. Was that guilt? Oh, yeah. Something was definitely up. Why would the Butlers care when her car would be fixed? Then it struck her. Oh. *Duh.*

She stuck the order up for Tom and face Chloe. "I'm staying through the weekend."

"Hmm?" Chloe's brow smoothed. "Oh, that's nice."

Laurel didn't buy her lack of interest for one minute. Let the Butlers conspire all they like. She was with Jack for the next few days and she wouldn't think past that.

As if she'd summoned him with her thoughts, the most handsome Butler walked into the café. She drank in her fill of the sight of him, not caring in the least that Chloe would read the interest on her face. His pressed green uniform might have been painted on. It wasn't tight but she knew how the body beneath was sculpted and ridged and so beautifully powerful. He swept off his ball cap and caught her eye, that big Jack grin curving his lips. She leaned against the counter and smiled back at him. What the heck? Bo and Chloe already sensed something between her and

Jack. Who cared if they saw the sparks now? Laurel imagined that anyone with eyes in their head would see the electricity flowing between the two of them.

Making herself take deliberate steps, she walked over to where Jack stood near Bo's table.

"Join me, Cuz?" she heard Bo ask.

Jack turned and settled across from Bo. "Thanks."

But he wasn't looking at Bo. No. Those Butler-blue eyes were running over her as she arrived at their table. "Hey, Laurel."

"Jack." She heard it in her voice, a low husky note that only this man had ever put there. "Lunch?"

"What's Tom got on special?"

"Turkey club."

He nodded. "Sounds good. And an iced tea?"

As she wrote down his order for Tom, she could sense his eyes on her face. Out of the corner of her eye she could see Bo's attention, too. It was focused squarely on Jack. Hurrying toward the kitchen, she took a breath. She felt bare and raw, like everyone could read every emotion swirling within her.

Her stomach churned, a physical reaction to the

turmoil in her mind. She was torn between the desire to stay with Jack as long as she could and the need to run as far away from him as she could get.

She was in very real danger of becoming the wimpy girl she'd left in San Francisco, so she made a conscious effort to rein in her emotions. Nothing but the physical mattered for the next few days. Yes, she was falling for Jack.

She was a fool if she thought it meant anything more to him.

* * *

Jack watched Laurel from across the café. How could he not? She was flustered and though he knew he should be a modern guy he couldn't ignore the certainty that it was what had happened between them last night that caused the pretty blush on her cheeks. He'd stayed in her bed for a while, and only when the sun started to peek through the lacy curtains to tease the crystal in the center of her dream catcher did he rouse himself. She'd slept so sweetly next to him, her face in the curve of his neck the way he liked, and he hadn't even cared if someone noticed his Jeep parked down on the street.

As she wiped a hand over her brow and turned, he stared at her slender neck. It was smooth and supple, teased by wisps of that golden hair.

"You got it bad, Cuz."

Jack jerked like he was dunked headfirst into Soda Springs. "What?"

"My only question is *how* bad."

Jack started to protest, then folded his arms on the table. "Yeah, I'm attracted to her. Who the hell wouldn't be?"

"True." Bo looked at Laurel for a bit longer than Jack liked. "She's hot."

"Yeah?"

Bo chuckled. "No worries, Jack. The girl only has eyes for you. And everything else, I'd guess."

Jack ran his fingers over the outside of his glass. "I'm not going to tell you anything."

Bo let out a low whistle. "So you've been—"

Jack pinned him with a glare and Bo grinned.

"Whoa there. I haven't seen you like this in… Well, I've never seen you like this."

"Like what?"

"In knots, Jacko."

"She's leaving in a few days. If you ever finish fixing her car, that is."

"Do you want me to finish fixing her car?"

Damn. Jack had known it all along, but for Bo to admit it? "You have the part."

"Maybe."

Jack's mouth thinned as he worked his mind around an idea. It wasn't honest, and that didn't sit well with him. But he wasn't the one holding her car hostage, right?

"Look, Bo." He leaned closer to his cousin. "Just give me this weekend."

"Yeah?" Bo arched a brow. "What's this weekend?"

"I'm taking her hiking."

"Another hickey in the woods?"

Jack felt his face grow hot and drank his iced tea.

"Laurel's not like that. That wasn't…"

"You got it real bad, then. Don't worry. I won't tell Chloe."

Jack opened his mouth to thank him but just then Chloe brought their sandwiches.

She stood with her hands on her hips. "What are you

two talking about?"

"No way," Bo said. "Never mind," Jack said at the same time.

Chloe smiled, then her eyes flicked to the door. Jack turned just as his mother stepped into the café. Could this day get more complicated?

"Hi, kids."

Josh was with her, and he hugged Chloe before clamoring up onto a chair. "Let's eat with Uncle Jack, Grandma."

He grabbed a potato chip from Jack's dish and folded his arms on the table in a mimic of Jack's posture.

"Jack?" his mother asked.

"Sure," he answered.

"I'll get you some chicken fingers, honey," Chloe said to Josh. "Mom?"

"That turkey club looks yummy."

"Who's watching the shop, Mom?" Jack asked.

She waved a hand. "Oh, I locked the doors. An hour won't kill business." Glancing toward the back of the café, she smiled. "Hi, Laurel!"

Laurel seemed to hold herself still for a moment

before coming over to their table. But she soon smiled and ruffled Josh's hair. "Hello. What are you two doing here?"

"We're here for lunch," Josh said. "With Uncle Jack."

Jack refrained from rolling his eyes. God only knew what his mother had said to the kid to explain this change in routine.

"What would you like to drink?" Laurel asked.

"Chocolate milk." Jack's mother clicked her tongue. "Please," the little boy added.

"And an iced tea for me, Laurel dear," his mother said.

Jack saw the glint in his mother's eye as Laurel left to get their drinks. "Stop it."

"What? Laurel looks very pretty today, doesn't she Bo?"

When Bo just shrugged, his eyes on the table, Jack could have hugged him. Laurel was pretty, the prettiest girl he'd ever seen. But the way she made him feel? That wasn't something he could think about right now.

He ate his sandwich in a rush, then stood. "Well, I have to get back to work."

All four Butlers stared at him, but it was Laurel he

wanted to see right now. She stood at the back counter, putting away glasses. He couldn't say good bye to her, not with his family watching. But he'd see her tonight. He had to. Nodding to his mother, he left the café.

* * *

Laurel watched the door shut behind Jack. He hadn't said good bye, but she didn't really mind. She couldn't exactly wrap her arms around his neck like she'd longed to. Not with his family watching. Her feelings for Jack were so new she felt all prickly. Imagine being so close to him while he was surrounded? It was too much.

"Laurel, sit for a minute," Jack's mother called.

"I don't—"

"Your boss won't mind," Bo laughed.

Chloe pushed at his shoulder. "Don't harass the help. Sit, Laurel."

So much for avoidance. "Sure."

She sat in the chair Jack had vacated, shifting as she found all their eyes on her. Bo seemed to take pity on her and he threw her a small smile. What had Jack said to him? Had Jack told Bo what's been going on? No. Jack didn't seem like a kiss-and-tell kind of guy.

"I haven't touched that design you made the other day, Laurel," Jack's mother said. "It's so pretty I couldn't bear to."

"What design?" Chloe asked.

"A mosaic. Laurel is an artist."

"Really?" Chloe asked. "What type of art do you do?"

"Stained glass," Laurel said.

"Wow. Do you show your work in San Francisco?" Chloe asked.

"Not yet."

"Why not?" Bo asked.

"I don't have a gallery," she said.

Jack's mother waved a hand. "Like I said before, if you had pieces to show I'd let you use my shop."

Laurel's mouth fell open. The woman barely knew her and she made such an offer? She was probably just being polite, but still.

"I don't have a studio," she said quickly.

The three older Butlers exchanged a look that was lost on Laurel.

Bo stood, placing his napkin over his empty plate. "Well, I'm finished. On my account, Chloe?"

Chloe smiled. "Yeah, yeah."

"See you, Laurel," Bo said.

With that, Bo left and Chloe went to get Josh and her mother's lunches. Laurel started to stand but Jack's mother placed her hand over hers.

"Tell me about your art," she said.

Laurel began to shake her head, then recalled how she'd felt arranging those pieces of china in the woman's shop. How she'd loved creating that design later in her sketchpad. She always got lost when she envisioned her pieces, but the nature scene she'd created in the antique store had captivated her. "It's something I've only toyed with."

"Nature scenes and such?"

"No. More Art Deco stuff."

"But you seem to enjoy the natural aspects, too."

Laurel smiled. "I'm surrounded here. How could I not?"

"True."

Chloe returned and as Josh started eating his chicken she sat down in Bo's empty chair. "Now what about this gallery?"

"I don't have a gallery. I don't even have a studio."

"What about your mother's store?"

The pain was less sharp than a few weeks ago, but the feeling of failure remained. "I had to close the store."

The other two women blinked at her and Laurel shrugged. "The rent was astronomical and the business just... Well, I couldn't make it work."

"That's a shame," Jack's mother said. "What about your mother's creations? Her beautiful clothes?"

"There wasn't much left, really. She didn't carry a lot of inventory, and then Brad said to let the store go."

"Who's Brad?"

"He's my ex-fiancé, actually."

"You have a past!" Chloe teased.

"Well I didn't just appear in Cloud Canyon out of nowhere, Chloe. Besides it's very 'past,' thank you very much."

"An artist. A woman with a past. Very interesting," Jack's mother said.

"Not very, I'm afraid," Laurel said. "My mother was the successful artist in the family. She was quirky and a little eccentric, but she was something."

271

"You must miss her terribly," Chloe said.

In an instant Laurel's eyes grew moist. "More than anything."

Again Jack's mother touched her hand. "She was lucky to have you. Any daughter who loved her mother as much as you obviously did? That's a treasure."

Silence fell on the table until Josh looked up. "What? Why's Laurel crying?"

"I'm not crying, honey," Laurel said with a sniff. "I just have something in my eye."

She got up and turned away from the table. She did miss her mother, and this time suspended in Cloud Canyon had given her the excuse to put her sorrow aside as well as her common sense.

Astrid Tanner would have liked Jack, though. She'd always had an eye for a good-looking guy. Maybe that's why she'd put up with Brad for so long. And maybe Laurel had taken her mother's acceptance of Brad as approval. But she'd asked Laurel more than once if she loved Brad. Laurel had thought so. But her heart had never raced when she'd seen him. Her body had never craved his touch. And how could her heart be involved if her body wasn't? She was certain now that her body couldn't be involved without her heart jumping into the mix.

The Butlers talked behind her, laughing and chatting with such closeness that Laurel was struck with a longing she hadn't felt since her mother's death. To belong to a family, to share a connection with people who loved you no matter what.

She lost herself in the mindless task of putting away the clean glasses. To keep her mind off of missing her mother. To forget about wanting a warm, close family like the Butlers. To convince herself that she had no business hoping a man like Jack would want her in his life for more than a couple of weeks.

Her lashes were damp and she blinked quickly. She glanced over at the Butlers. Maybe staying through the weekend was a really bad idea after all.

* * *

Maybe Laurel's staying for the weekend was a really bad idea after all.

Jack started the Jeep and pulled out of his parking space at the springs. Ever since he'd seen her at lunch, his gut had been telling him something wasn't right. Oh, she was as gorgeous as ever and when she'd looked at him her eyes had gotten all soft and deep. And when he'd looked back at her, he'd felt that odd shifting in his chest.

Last night was surprising, and he wasn't only thinking about the sex. Talking to her about Kelly, about his failure to be the man his ex-wife had needed, hadn't been the dentist-visit-without-Novocain he might have expected. But still, asking Bo to delay Laurel's car repairs? That was just low.

"Horny bastard." He cursed himself and headed the Jeep toward Cloud Canyon. There'd been something different about her this afternoon, and he couldn't lay all of it on his meddling family. She'd told him she had no one, and then the busybody Butlers had decided to show her precisely what they thought she was missing. If her car had been fixed she probably would have driven off without a backward glance, grateful for her narrow escape.

He smiled to himself. He couldn't help it. He was going to see Laurel this weekend, for the whole weekend, and he wouldn't think about anything else until the cold light of Monday morning.

Chapter 18

"So they're sleeping together?" Chloe asked, her voice low.

Bo leaned back in his chair. "Jack wouldn't say it out loud but, yeah. They've been going at it since her second night in town, I'd bet."

Chloe closed the office door and sat across from him. The mess on Bo's desk drew her eye for a second and she moved a few papers around. She took a breath. "I know Laurel, Bo. Even though she's only been here for a little while I know her. She doesn't seem the type for a fling."

"Yeah, I know." Bo scratched his chin. "Neither is Jack."

Chloe thought for a moment. Jack was about as impulsive and irresponsible as she was. Except for that brief period of insanity five years ago, their father's stubborn Butler steadfastness ran deep in her as well.

"Could it be something different, Bo?" she asked. "Do you think he's falling for her?"

"Damned if I know." Bo shook his head. "He gets all starry-eyed around her. And his eyes strip those pretty tops she wears right off of her." He winked. "Figuratively speaking, that is."

Chloe laughed. "I've seen those looks, too. It's embarrassing."

Bo barked out a laugh. "It's good to see Jack hot and bothered, Cuz. Kelly really screwed him over. We talked about this. He deserves to have a little bit of fun. Maybe even a little bit of happiness."

"Happiness? Bo Butler, are you becoming a romantic is your old age?"

Bo snorted. "Not any time soon. Believe me."

Chloe nibbled her bottom lip as she thought about the puzzle of Jack and Laurel. "Laurel is running from something, Bo." She held up a hand. "Someone, most likely. She's all closed up about it, though."

"Take her out to the Treetop, Chloe. Pour one of those frou-frou drinks they pour on ladies' night and get the truth out of her."

Chloe nodded. "Those Cloud Nines are like truth serum."

"Oh?" Bo arched a brow. "Spill your secrets there, do you?"

Chloe smiled. "Not even a little bit."

Bo's face grew serious. "What about Josh's father."

Anger swirled in her belly. "We've had the conversation."

Bo spread his arms wide. "Yeah, I know. I also know how torn up you were when you found out you were expecting the little guy."

Chloe thought back to that time. When she thought love would last and she would have her own miracle. She did, though. She had Josh.

"Josh's father hasn't been in my life for years, Bo."

"What about Josh's life?"

She gaped at him. "Are you seriously telling me to contact him and, what? Drag him on a show for a DNA test?"

Bo shuddered. "No. God, no. That, dear cousin, is one of my biggest fears."

"Says the best tracker in our part of the Forest."

"Yeah, I'm careful." Bo shrugged. "I'm not saying you have to do anything. But just look at Laurel. Coming into Jack's life when he least expected it. Stuff happens."

Chloe thought about how happy her brother looked when he was even just talking with Laurel in the café.

There was something more between them than a passionate affair. She would bet her life on it.

"Yeah, stuff happens. And sometimes that stuff can be wonderful." She took a breath. "And sometimes that stuff can turn your life upside down."

Bo leaned forward, his eyes so like hers and Jack's intent on her. "Is that what you're really afraid of? That your life won't be the same if you let Josh's dad into it?"

"I worked hard to make my life, Bo. With God's grace and the generous help of our crazy family, I managed to cobble out a pretty terrific life for me and my son. I work hard at it still. I won't give that up."

"Who says you would have to? Damn Cuz, you're so anal sometimes. You can't just let go."

She frowned at him, letting her frustration show for once. "Look. I don't have the luxury of breezing through life like you do. Bedding whatever tourist or townie I want and going on like nothing I do matters."

"Is that what you think of me?"

"Are you denying it?"

"Nope," he said simply. "But we weren't talking about me."

"And we're not talking about me anymore, Bo. We're talking about Jack."

Bo nodded his head in submission and leaned back in his chair. "I can't see him wanting another relationship right now."

"Or maybe ever," she agreed. "But Laurel is very different from Kelly."

"Night and day. But she's not staying. She was on her way to Reno when her little Beetle kissed that rock wall."

"Reno," she murmured. "Do we know why?"

"Why what?"

"Why was she going to Reno?"

Bo shrugged. "Why does anyone go to Reno?" Chloe jerked and Bo held up his hand. "Sorry."

Chloe swallowed as she shook her head. "Don't be. That lost weekend in Reno was eons ago. The place has its charms, even if I'm never going there again."

He leaned forward. "You have to face him sometime."

"Ugh, enough! I'll have to face him sometime, yes. But not anytime soon." She held out her hands. "Back to Jack. Please. What are we going to do?"

"Do? About what?"

"Look, I don't have a chance at a real relationship. Not for years, anyway. I won't let Josh get attached to some guy I'm just dating. And you..."

"What about me?"

"Bo, I love you but you're not a Steady Eddie kind of guy. We've established that fact."

He grinned. "You know it."

Chloe rolled her eyes. Bo sure had the bulk of the charm in the Butler clan.

"We can't let Jack's chance at happiness drive away from Cloud Canyon. Not to Reno, anyway."

"Look, uh... Jack asked me to put off fixing the car until after this weekend."

"Really? Whoa."

She thought for a minute. Jack was a by-the-book kind of guy. He didn't lie. He didn't shy from the tough truths and he didn't pull any punches.

"Jack wants you to keep her here," she said. It wasn't a question. "I knew he felt something for her."

Bo nodded and Chloe felt a flutter of excitement. Maybe Jack would succeed where she'd failed.

And she couldn't think of anyone better for him than Laurel.

"Laurel is good for him, Cuz. Jack looked after me after our dads passed and I owe him."

Chloe thought about that time when their dads died within months of each other. She'd had both Bo and her big brother to lean on but she realized now that Jack had taken care of their cousin, too.

"Jack wouldn't see it that way."

"Tough shit. I see it that way and I'm going to do what I can to make his life a little bit easier. And a whole lot better, unless I miss my guess."

"Then we'll just have to make sure they both have the time to figure out just how happy they could make each other."

Bo nodded. "I'll do my part. Just keep me posted."

Chloe stood, grinning down at her surprisingly sentimental cousin.

"Why Bo Butler, you're as bad as the Bennet sisters."

His mouth dropped open as his cheeks stained red. "I just want to know, that's all."

She waved a hand at him. "I'll see you later."

* * *

"You're going hiking?"

Laurel tried to keep her expression even as she faced Jack's sister. "Yes. If I'm going to be here for a little while I should see the sights."

Chloe propped a hip on the service counter. "And by the sights, you mean more than the café and the inside of my charming yet tiny apartment?"

"Your apartment is just perfect, Chloe. Very comfortable."

"And I'm glad you like it." Chloe straightened the straws in their holder, although they didn't seem to look a bit out of place to her. "You know, you can stay as long as you like."

"I'm leaving when my car is ready, Chloe. No ifs, ands or buts."

"Okay, okay." Chloe sighed and faced her again. "So hiking, huh? You won't find a better guide than Jack."

Laurel narrowed her eyes. "Is that a double-entendre?"

Chloe laughed. "Nope. In fact, you can borrow my hiking boots. God knows I haven't gotten out in the Forest in months."

Laurel gaped at her. "How can you be surrounded by all this and not want to get out and play in it?"

"You forget, I grew up here."

"Lucky."

"Come on. San Francisco is a terrific city."

Laurel nodded. "It is, for sure. But it doesn't have the raw beauty I see here."

"You really are an artist."

Laurel was once again seized with the desire to recreate the natural beauty of the Sierra Nevada in her art. The subtle differences of color and texture and soaring, sprawling vistas.

"This scenery just speaks to me."

"And yet, you're ignoring it."

"I'm going hiking in it, aren't I?"

"Yes." Chloe stared at her with those Butler-blue eyes. "And I'll just bet you'll find all sorts of inspiration out there."

Laurel laughed. "Chloe Butler, you're not fooling anybody."

"Neither are you."

Laurel waved a hand. "Never mind."

Tom called Chloe into the kitchen and Laurel took the escape for what it was. Chloe wasn't wrong. Not by a long shot. She wanted to explore the beauty around her. To experience it and recreate it. But more than that, she wanted to enjoy Jack Butler and his particular brand of nature. His forest. His mountains.

She would miss the scenery and the people of Cloud Canyon when she left, of course. The Butlers who took her to their breasts and made her feel at home. They made her miss her mother desperately too, though. Made her crave the family she could never have. She would find a way to have the art she wanted, though.

Pushing her dreams and wants aside for the moment, she decided to focus on this weekend. With Jack.

If she wanted more than this short time with him? That was just her too bad.

Chapter 19

Jack blew out a breath as he pulled the Jeep to a stop on the gravel drive, glancing at Laurel out of the corner of his eye. She sat beside him in the Jeep, a little stiff. He turned the key and shut off the engine.

"I thought I'd cook steaks on the grill," he said.

She offered him a smile. "Chloe loaned me her hiking boots," she said, grabbing her bag from the floor.

"If you don't want to stay tonight I can pick you up in the morning."

She stared at him, weighing his words. He didn't seem to be looking for a way out.

"I'm out of here come next week." She slid closer to him. "I'd be a fool to give up this last chance to spend time with you."

His shoulders relaxed a fraction. "Good." He got out of the Jeep and walked around to open her door. "I'll get started on those steaks."

As they entered the house, Smokey came running up to greet them. Snubbing his owner, he jumped up and down and danced at Laurel's feet. She laughed and scratched the dog's bushy head.

"Dinner, boy," Jack said, scooping some food into the dog's dish.

Smokey deserted Laurel for the kitchen and she laughed again. "So quickly forgotten, then."

"No way."

His words struck her. *If only.* She walked into the kitchen. "Would you like me to make a salad or something?"

"Sure. There's stuff in the fridge."

If he noticed how well they worked together, he didn't say anything about it. She wouldn't. Nope. She was out of there, probably on Monday. Why bring up something that didn't matter?

She sliced a big red onion, happy to have the excuse for her eyes watering. Jack was busy getting the steaks ready for the grill, and if she turned slightly to the left as she finished the salad she could watch him. This weekend was supposed to be her last fling with Jack Butler, and here she was getting all emotional.

Turning back toward the cutting board, she sniffed. Slice, shred, chop. She wiped the back of her hand over her cheek.

When he stepped outside onto the deck, Smokey following closely on his heels, she squeezed her eyes shut. For one foolish instant she wished to stay here with him. Wished she could share all her meals with him in this pretty house in the woods. Talk about a dream.

She chose a bottle of balsamic dressing from the fridge, then brought the salad bowl out to the table on the deck. Jack threw her a smile as he tended the steaks, and she felt that pull again. This definitely wasn't just lust.

Later that night, curled against him in the big bed, she knew for sure it was more than lust. Yes, her body still tingled with the memory of the delicious things he'd done to her. Yes, her mind was still fuzzy from her climax. Two of them, actually. But she couldn't deny it any longer. He made her feel wanted, desirable. And safe, from loneliness and the dull life stretching in front of her.

She couldn't think about that. About the dream deep inside that he would always make her feel wanted, desirable and safe. Not tonight.

* * *

"Wake up, baby."

Laurel shifted, smiling to herself as she caught the

delicious scent of Jack Butler.

His chuckle echoed against her cheek. "Not an early bird?"

She peeped one eye open and saw him grinning at her. His cheeks were dark with stubble and his glossy hair was mussed. He looked incredible.

"Someone wore me out last night," she said.

His eyes flickered with something then. "That right?"

She shifted on the bed, smoothing her hands over the buffalo plaid blanket. "You know what you do to me, Jack."

He sat up and braced his hands on the bed. The sheets slipped down to show his broad chest and flat belly. Yum.

"You don't usually talk about it," he teased.

She waved a hand. "Like I have to?"

"Nope." He tugged on his ear. "My ears are still ringing."

Her cheeks heated, but she wouldn't be embarrassed. She shrugged in what she hoped was a casual gesture. "Are you going to keep teasing me or are you going to cook breakfast?"

He arched a brow. "My pancakes?"

"Oh, no. I mean, maybe we can have something a little lighter?"

"I think that can be arranged." He got out of the bed and walked over to the bathroom. Jack from behind was as interesting as Jack from the front. Strong back, nice butt…

He stopped and glanced over his shoulder. "Join me in the shower?"

"I thought you said we have to get an early start?"

"Ah, you're too good." He continued into the bathroom. "I'll be out in five minutes, then."

She waited until he closed the door with a click then collapsed on the bed. Everything was so intense today. Razor sharp and clear. She was falling for him. Thank God she was leaving Monday.

Later, while Jack made some sort of "light" breakfast downstairs, she showered and dressed in khaki shorts and a T-shirt. She pulled on the thick socks Chloe had loaned her along with the boots and she was ready to go. Pulling her hair back into a high ponytail, she regarded herself in the mirror. She looked very different from the girl she'd been when she'd hit that rock wall. Older somehow, but in a good way. She didn't look like the wide-eyed wimp she'd been in San Francisco. It was definitely an improvement, if only on the outside.

She sat on the bed and tied her boot laces. Reaching into her purse, she pulled out her cell phone. She'd tossed it in there last night out of habit, but the display still read "no service." Still, she slipped it into the small backpack Chloe had insisted she would need and hooked her fingers through the little loop on top of the pack.

She would bring the sweatshirt Jack had bought her too, since he'd said it gets chilly in the woods. She tied the sleeves around her waist and went downstairs.

* * *

The scent of bacon and toast filled the kitchen as Jack piled food on the platters.

"That smells good," Laurel said as she entered the kitchen. She hung the pack on the back of the chair.

"Eggs light enough for you?" he asked.

"I didn't mean to—"

"I'm teasing you again." He scooped a pile of scrambled eggs onto a platter. "You're too easy."

"That's me."

He froze. "That's not what I meant."

"I know," she laughed. "I can give as good as I get, Jack."

He put the bacon out on the platter. "Grab the toast?"

She did and joined him at the table. "What's the game plan?"

"To take you on a guided tour of my woods."

"A Jack Butler patented excursion?"

"If that's all right?"

"That's great. I didn't get to see much last week."

"I promise to go easy on you." His words held a double meaning and his pulse jumped.

"Please don't."

Jack nearly swallowed his tongue. The possibilities boggled his mind. "We'll bring a blanket."

She caught his intent and smiled. Had he ever felt this comfortable with a woman? No friggin' way.

They finished breakfast and after he loaded the Jeep they were off for the woods.

"Where are we going?" she asked.

"One of my favorite spots. Not far from where I met you last week, actually."

"Maybe we'll see that deer."

"I'm sure your car is a distant memory for that guy."

"I was worried, I admit. And a little high strung." She glanced at him from the corner of her eye. "Though you did make me forget all about him."

"I'm flattered." His body flushed with the memory of that first kiss. "You made me forget everything else."

He caught her answering blush as she faced forward again. They approached the Old Mill Road turnoff, and Jack pulled the Jeep over the rutted road. It was a little overgrown, but the recent lack of rain made it passable. The service trailer wasn't occupied, as he knew it wouldn't be on a weekend. He made sure to stop here every couple of days during the week, but this area wasn't a favorite among tourists or locals. There was no water nearby, and no recreation to speak of except for narrow trails leading up to what he believed was the finest view in Yuma County.

He looked at Laurel again as he stopped the car. It was an ambitious hike for a first-timer, but he would take it easy on her despite what she'd said in his kitchen. As he grabbed his pack from the back of the Jeep, she stepped out of the Jeep and stared up at the trees.

"Wow, it's gorgeous out here." She turned and closed

her eyes. "It even smells amazing."

"Jefferson Pine, mostly," he said. "Crisp and lemony."

Her eyes opened and she faced him. "I remember the smell."

So did he. The long, soft needles on the forest floor beneath their feet had given up the same scent as they'd tangled together that first afternoon.

"Here." He handed her two bottles of water. "Put these in your pack."

"Oh, the dreaded dehydration. Gotcha."

"I've got some protein bars and stuff. I thought we'd go into Truckee for an early dinner later."

"Sounds good to me." She shifted and put on the pack. "Lead on, guide."

Jack watched her for a moment, staring at the front of her T-shirt stretched across her breasts. He hadn't been kidding about bringing a blanket. And he'd put those condoms in his backpack. A little foresight could certainly pay off.

"Come on, greenhorn," he teased.

She laughed. "Hey, I made no claims of hiking skills.

You're Mountain Man."

"All right, Mountain Laurel." He locked the Jeep and pocketed his keys. "Follow my lead."

"Always."

Something in her tone made him almost stumble, but he didn't look back. He hoped he covered his misstep well enough and they walked into the shaded woods.

"How long have you hiked this trail, Jack?"

"About ten years now, I guess."

"You spent your teens hiking, too?"

He glanced over his shoulder. "Not just hiking. Bo and I would hunt and fish with our dads. After they were gone, it was just the two of us."

"So Bo lost his Dad when he was young, too?"

"Younger than me. Uncle Paul had been an ace tracker. Bo gets that from him."

"A tracker?"

"That good old boy can track a mouse. I wouldn't go hunting without him."

She shuddered. "I wouldn't go hunting at all."

"There's a reason for hunting. The deer population would overrun the Forest if it wasn't controlled with hunting. They'd starve."

"I guess. So that deer I hit... He's being hunted?"

"Eventually. It's just about the start of the season soon, but we're in a restricted zone and on a designated trail."

She nodded absently. He wanted to ask her what she thought on the subject, but there was no way he was going to get into a philosophical debate on the subject. At least she hadn't called him a redneck, or any of the other names Kelly used to hurl at him.

The trail grew narrow and steep, and Jack waved Laurel in front of him. "Watch your step. It's been pretty dry and the path can start to crumble."

She slipped a bit, but balanced herself. Her legs seemed strong for being so slender, probably from climbing those crooked streets in San Francisco. After about a half hour, Jack called a halt.

"What?" She turned and smiled. "I was lost there."

He glanced up into the trees and could hear the bird song she'd obviously been listening to. "Yeah, I know. Sounds nice, doesn't it?"

"Very. I think I can hear the rustle of every leaf."

"The sounds of the woods are as big a part of them to me as the sights."

She sat on a fallen log and he folded his legs and settled on the brush in front of her.

"The colors out here, Jack. So many different shades of green, let alone the purple shadows and rich browns. I wish I had my sketchpad with me."

"You're definitely an artist." He took out a bottle of water from the larger store in his pack and cracked it open before handing it to her. "I like what you did with that broken china at my mother's shop."

She glanced down at her feet, her cheeks pink. "You saw that."

"You would do really well with those designs up here."

Her head shot up, her eyes wide. Then she shook her head and took a long drink of water. Fingering the cap as she twisted it back on, she shrugged. "No studio, no gallery."

Her voice was flat and resigned, like she'd said those words to herself over and over again. But he'd seen the excitement and hope on her face for that brief moment. He had no idea what opening a gallery or having a studio would entail, and anyway it was none of his business.

He finished his water and put the empty bottle in his pack.

She glanced over at him, her brows raised. "Are we going on?"

"Take your time." He folded his arms. "I don't want you overtired."

"Oh, really?" A smile lifted one corner of her mouth. "Hmm."

Jack felt a punch to his gut. Just like that, she could make him want her. He still didn't think she had any idea of her power, though. It seemed unconscious, and completely unpracticed. And sexy as hell.

They soon stood and Jack led the way up the path. It was nearing noon now, and the morning chill was giving way to August warmth. He felt sweat prick his brow, and swiped at it with his forearm. A glance back toward Laurel showed she was a little warm, too. Her cheeks were pink and her hair curled around her face and against her neck.

"Almost there," he said.

"I hope so," she said, her voice a little breathy. "I

don't want to get overtired."

He smiled to himself and stepped over a downed tree close to his favorite spot. "Watch your step."

She traced his steps and then gasped. Jack watched her face as she gazed out toward the vista spread below. It was a riot of greens and browns and blues, and he guessed the scene appealed to the artist in her. As for him, he liked the peace and quiet, the sense of solitude and isolation. Yet, amazingly, Laurel's presence wasn't intrusive at all.

"This is my spot," he said.

"Oh, Jack." She pushed a damp curl off her forehead. "It's beautiful."

He nodded and leaned against a tall pine. "Off the beaten path, anyway."

"That's what makes it so... Well, it's just perfect."

He watched her profile again, saw the awe on her face. She got it. Yes, she was beautiful. Yes, he wanted her constantly. But the look on her face as she took in the raw beauty of the nature around them called to a place inside himself that he'd thought could never be touched.

Like before, he supposed he should be scared of the feelings she caused inside him. But the smile on Laurel's face as she finally faced him killed any apprehension.

In two steps he had her in his arms, kissing her as he turned to pin her against the closest tree. She reached up to wrap her arms around his neck and he could smell the mingled scents of her and the Jefferson Pine, the dew evaporating off the brush beneath their booted feet, the crisp fresh air of the mountains.

"Baby," he said, running his lips over her throat. He could taste the tang of her perspiration, just a touch of salt to mix with the sweetness of her skin. "Mmm."

She leaned her head back and ran her fingers through his hair. "Jack." She tugged his shirt out of his jeans and clutched at his back. "Let's do it, Jack."

Simple words, yet immediately he was ready for her. Breaking away only long enough to spread the blanket he'd brought, he soon had her naked beneath him. Just a second or two to put on a condom and he was there. Deep inside her, her arms and legs wrapped around him as he buried himself with a groan.

"Yes!" she cried out. "Oh, yes!"

She murmured sweet words, throaty moans, until she arched tightly against him. He looked down into her eyes then, dark hazel and full of pleasure, and had to catch his breath. He could see down to her soul. He could see his reflection too. It was as if he could see the years stretch out before them, with the two of them linked completely.

It was too much, her body pulsing around him, her eyes pulling at his. Pleasure so sharp, sharper than their first time, cut into him as he moaned her name.

Afterward, she clung so sweetly to him. Her lips traced over his cheek when he moved to bury his face in her neck. He felt a connection to her that stunned him.

"Laurel, I…" He couldn't put it into words.

She nodded as she sucked in a breath. "I know."

What she knew, he wouldn't ask. But he couldn't let go of her, not yet. Rolling onto his side, he grabbed the edge of the blanket and managed to wrap it around the two of them. In the shade of the tree canopy above, he felt like they were the only people on the whole damn planet. And what they'd just shared was better than their first time. Better than all the times since. Deeper. More personal.

God help him, it felt so right.

Chapter 20

"Jack, I can barely breathe."

"Sorry." He shifted and she cuddled against him. That was better, just enough room between them to give them both some air.

"I could stay here all day, here in the woods." She kissed his chest. "Here with you."

Him. Not just some guy she'd picked up in the woods. Him. Jack Butler.

"So you like to do it in the woods," he said.

She moved to face him. "Who would have thought? Seriously, that first kiss was a real first for me."

"I think you said something like that."

She shook her head. "No. It was the first time I'd ever propositioned a guy."

"Really?"

Her lips quirked. "Thanks."

"No, I didn't mean that. It's just that you did it so well."

"Truth be told, you're only the second guy I've ever been with."

Whoa. He'd known there was something unpracticed

about her sensuality. Now it made sense. But if she'd never done anything like that before?

"And you picked me?"

"You're one hot mountain man." She trailed her fingers over his cheek, that warmth in her eyes again. "I couldn't resist."

"Huh."

She stared at him for a moment, then grinned. "Jack Butler, you're not a chatty guy."

He couldn't say anything. What would he say? That her admission made him feel like the luckiest guy on earth? That she'd picked him, that she chose to continue an affair with him, when she'd never done anything like that before? He could only shrug in answer.

"Gee, and we're even naked," she said. "I'll miss you, Jack."

She'd put her head back down on his chest so he couldn't see her expression.

"This doesn't have to end, Laurel."

Shaking her head, she sighed. "I'm not made for this."

His stomach clenched. "For what?" he asked, keeping

his voice even.

"For a once-in-a-while fling. This…" She waved a hand in front of her before settling it back down on his chest. "This is a total aberration for me."

His chest tightened and he realized he might never hold her so close to him again. He wouldn't say a word, though. Not on a bet.

"I'm sorry," she said.

"Don't be." He stroked her hair, as if he could memorize its silky texture. "This is a departure for me, too."

"But you were married. You have way more experience than I have."

"Not like this."

Her fingers wound through his chest hair and he could feel her smile against his skin. "Thanks for that."

He had to ask, although the question was a couple of weeks too late. "Do you have a boyfriend?"

"No. I had a fiancé, but that's over."

"And your mother's gone."

"Yes," she said.

He wanted to ask her just what was she going back

to? What was the appeal of San Francisco? Cloud Canyon had the mountains, the trees, the lakes and rivers. And him.

He just kept stroking her hair.

"I'm hoping to find space to do my art," she said. "I thought if I made enough money in commissions I could open a studio and gallery back in San Francisco. I wanted to get enough money to finance my dream."

"You don't have any opportunities in Frisco?"

"No. There's no one who believes in my art back there."

There was more to the story, but she clearly wasn't going to share it right now.

"So that's where you were headed."

"Silly, I know. But now most of my money is going to Bo." She faced him, her chin on her fist, and he could see the sparkle in her eyes. "I want to create big designs, Jack. I made sun catchers before, but only because I just didn't have the space to make larger pieces. If I could find a place to make panels, you know, window or even door sized, then I could open a gallery to feature my work and finally make something of my talent. It's a matter of money, though."

"What did your mother think about your art?"

"She loved it. My mom was a free spirit." Her voice was a little shaky, and he heard her swallow. "She loved me and encouraged me in everything. God rest her soul, she was no businesswoman, though."

"Did you manage the store for her?"

"Hardly. That was Brad's thing. My ex."

"You told me the store was closed."

"Uh huh. Brad gave it up as soon as the sales dipped. My mother wasn't gone two months when we had to close it because of the high rent." She blew out a breath. "He gave up on me just as quickly."

Brad sounded like a jerk, but Jack wasn't going to say anything about him. "So what will you do now?"

"I guess I can try San Francisco, but I don't hold out much hope. Everything is much more expensive there, and you really need a name or a patron and that's tough when you're just getting started. I really want this, though."

"You have the talent," he said. "From what I know about art, anyway."

She beamed, and the excitement on her face made his heart twist. "Thanks. Brad never thought much of my art. I don't know where I'm going to find the money now, though." She put her head back down and sighed. "But I was thinking about renting space in a studio, maybe making my sun catchers until I can save enough to open my gallery."

He nodded, but his heart turned cold on the edges. His experience with Kelly taught him that the city was expensive. Hell, San Francisco had to be even pricier than Sacramento.

If Laurel realized her dream, she would be out of his league.

* * *

Laurel's throat was suddenly tight with tears, sadness for her mother and anger at Brad's desertion. And here she was, pouring out her soul to the guy she just... Well, the guy she just slept with, although that's not quite what they just did.

"We weren't supposed to know anything about each other," she said softly.

He was quiet again, and she listened to the sounds in the woods around her. She'd heard nothing for a while there, lost in Jack's arms for what was probably one of the last times.

"That was your plan," he said. "I think we've moved past that."

She jerked her head up to find him looking up at the trees, the sky. She could see every angle of his face. A trace of stubble on his jaw where he'd missed shaving. The creases at the corners of his breathtaking Butler-blue eyes. The set of a mouth that amazed her, a blend of beauty and strength that was so much like Jack himself. She loved him.

"We should go," she said, scrambling to put some sort of distance between them. It was impossible, since they were still wrapped in the blanket.

He finally glanced over at her, his mouth set. "Yeah."

As he helped her to her feet, she felt a flash of embarrassment. Yes, he'd seen her naked. But she couldn't let him see the emotion she knew was in her eyes. Luckily, her clothes hadn't been tossed very far from the blanket. She dressed with her back to him, ignoring the sounds she knew would be etched on her mind. The birdsong, the stillness of the woods. The rustle of fabric over skin as he dressed. She touched her hair and scanned the ground for her ponytail holder.

"Laurel." She turned to find Jack holding the elastic out to her. "Here."

She nodded her thanks and pulled her tangled hair up off her neck. He watched her. She could see out the corner of her eye that he watched her. His mouth was still a thin line, his brows drawn together.

"You okay?" he asked.

She plastered on a smile and waved a hand. "A little winded, that's all. Maybe some water?"

He grabbed her pack and handed it to her.

"Thanks." Better to concentrate on drinking the water. She would cool herself off and keep her mouth occupied before she said something completely stupid. *I love you, Jack.* Yeah. That would qualify as stupid.

She heard a chirp from inside the pack and saw the tiny light on her cell phone flashing within. Drawing it out, she saw one bar indicating service. It flickered on and off, though.

"I think my phone is trying to work," she said.

Jack arched one brow and nodded as he drank his water.

Sliding the phone on, Laurel saw she had several

messages waiting. She tapped on voicemail to bring them up.

The first message was from Brad. The sound of his voice was jarring, tinny and off-pitch as the connection sputtered. She heard her mother's name mentioned, and something about the store. She couldn't really make it out. She tapped the button to play the next message and it was from Brad as well, asking her to call him. Something about a bank account. Her mother's, maybe? Without a sound, the phone cut out again.

"That's strange." She tapped the phone off and slipped it back into the pack. "I have two messages from Brad."

"Something wrong?"

"I don't know." At least this was a distraction from her feelings for Jack. She grabbed a bottle of water and opened it. "Can I use your land line when we get back?"

"Sure."

"Thanks." She drank from her water and shoved the bottle back into her pack. Concentration. That's what she needed to get through this weekend. And then she was out of here.

Bo was obviously stalling with her car. Chloe probably put him up to it. That was tough. She had to get out of Cloud Canyon before she made a fool of herself like she had with Brad.

"Where to?" she asked.

Jack shifted his pack and shrugged. "It's about an hour's hike back down. Then we can go back to the house and get cleaned up before heading into Truckee."

"Sounds good," she said.

The hike back down the mountain was as quiet as the one up it, but this silence was different. He was still "Quiet Jack." The Jack she'd come to know. Something had changed up there under that blanket, though. The sex was… Well, it was more than sex and she had to admit that at least to herself. When he'd looked down at her with such tenderness, she'd felt like crying. She shook her head. She was a fool.

Brad's voice echoed in her head, the horrible things he'd said before she left and the cryptic words she was able to glean today. Had he said something about her mother's store? Was there a chance they could reopen? She would call him tomorrow, though. Distraction would have to wait.

Tonight was her last night with Jack.

* * *

Dinner in Truckee was like before, but the drive back to his house was different. For Jack, anyway. This would probably be their last night together. And with the goals and dreams she had, he knew in his gut that he would never see her again after this weekend. He should be relieved. He didn't want another relationship, and he sure as hell didn't want to get married again.

Laurel didn't seem high maintenance like Kelly, but women change. Socializing with artists and collectors in San Francisco would surely make Laurel realize how much of a clod he was. She would get bored, once the thrill of great sex wore off. He might only be the second guy she'd slept with, but the girl was good. He, on the other hand… He'd had his share of women and they'd all seemed happy. But he'd never had the kind of response he got from Laurel. Not ever. He doubted he ever would again.

The Jeep ticked for a few seconds after he shut off the engine. Turning in his seat, he faced Laurel. She still stared ahead, as she had the whole drive back. He should offer to drive her to the apartment. He wouldn't, though. Maybe he was a selfish bastard, but he wouldn't give her an out.

"Let's go inside, baby."

She nodded, opening her door. Did she feel it? The tension strung between them so tight it practically hummed? Sexual tension, yeah. That was never far off when they were together. But there was something else there, something sweeter, that he'd seen in her eyes up on that mountain. And he wanted to see that again. If only for tonight.

Maybe Laurel felt the same way, maybe she just wanted something to remember him by, but when she stepped through the front door she stopped and stared at her hands for a moment.

Turning, she dropped her small pack on the chair near the window and faced him. The heat in her eyes had him hard in an instant.

"Upstairs, Jack. Please?"

Like she had to ask. He closed the front door and grabbed her hand as they climbed the stairs. It wasn't just sex that made his pulse jump now. At least not for him. Not anymore. But she intended to leave, and she would. So he would just keep his feelings to himself.

And then he would just let her go.

Chapter 21

They'd made love again, face to face like in the woods, and Laurel had slept like a rock afterwards. Thankfully, her subconscious hadn't entertained foolish dreams of forever and commitment with her mountain man.

Cracking one eye open, she saw Jack had left the bed, though her skin had missed the warm contact of his body as soon as she'd woken up. The slight groan of the pipes behind the closed bathroom door followed by the sputter of water told her Jack started the shower. She must have come awake as soon as he left her. So much for her subconscious giving her a break.

Letting out a yawn, she stretched and cuddled into his pillow. Mmm, spicy fresh Jack-smell. The nose was the quickest route to memory. She was grateful she'd never smelled this scent anywhere before because it would break her heart if she caught a sniff of it in the coming weeks. Months. Heck, years.

She rolled onto her back and stared up at the plastered ceiling. She would call Brad this morning and find out what was up with the bank account. Or maybe the store's accounts? She could hardly make out the voicemails he'd left. Funny, but his cultured voice had almost reached a whiny pitch there in the last message. Brad Covington, whining? She smiled. That she would pay to hear again. Maybe she would see if she could get a cell signal out on Jack's deck so she could hear the messages more clearly.

She turned into the pillow again, her gaze on the bathroom door. Jack was in there, soaping that incredible body. She would miss that almost as much as she would miss his smile. Last night had been such an eye-opener. Again she thought about the tenderness in his gorgeous eyes and squeezed her own eyes shut. Oh, she had to get the heck out of Dodge and fast.

The sound of the shower ceased and she steeled herself for the sight that would greet her when Jack opened the bathroom door. A minute later, she wasn't disappointed.

"The shower's all yours," he said.

She sat up and took a long look at him. His hair was tousled and damp, curling across his brow and against his neck. A towel wrapped his narrow waist, falling just to his knees. She was staring, she knew that. Heck, she was practically drooling.

"'kay," she said.

He took himself into the closet to dress and she closed her eyes again. She would commit that image of him to her memory forever. Swallowing a sigh, she went into the bathroom.

By the time she came out, Jack was downstairs. She dressed in shorts and a T-shirt, slipping on her sandals and setting Chloe's boots and socks into her overnight bag. Withdrawing her cell phone, she saw that once again there was no signal. She wouldn't bother trying to get one out on the deck. Jack's land line would have to suffice.

The edge of the nightstand drawer caught her eye. Jack must have left it open when he reached in for yet another condom last night. She stepped closer and caught the sight of something else in there. Her panties! The midnight blue panties she'd worn last weekend. How sweet and sexy was that?

She tucked the lace back into the drawer and slid it closed. Sure, maybe he'd just been tidying his room. He was pretty neat for a single guy. But she would let herself think this was just what she'd hoped. That he wanted a way to remember this as much as she did.

She went downstairs and found him making his heavy buckwheat pancakes. He threw her a smile over one broad shoulder. "Juice is in the fridge and the coffee should be ready soon."

"Great." She set the table and stood, gripping the back of her chair. "Can I use your phone?"

"Sure." He didn't turn to face her, didn't ask her why or who she'd be calling on a Sunday in a town where she didn't know anyone but him and his family. Of course she was returning Brad's calls. But Jack was curious. She could tell by the thinning of his lips that he wanted to ask her the specifics.

"Go ahead." He flipped a big pancake. "These will take a while."

Now? Did she really want to talk to Brad just now? "No. After breakfast will be fine."

She ate one of his pancakes, washing it down with juice, then grabbed the cordless phone on the counter. Walking over to the sofa, she dialed Brad's number and stood with her back to the kitchen.

"Brad Covington."

Only Brad would answer his personal line like that.

Pompous ass.

"Hi, Brad."

"Laurel?" His voice raised to an almost comedic pitch. "Is that you?"

"Yes."

"It's about time you returned my calls. Did you get my messages?"

There was the dictatorial tone she hadn't missed. "Yes. I didn't have service up here. What is this about an account?"

"Up where? Where are you?"

She glanced out the wide window at the riot of blues and greens and browns and nearly said it aloud. *Home.* "I'm in the Sierra Nevada."

"What the hell are you doing there?"

Just playing the fool again. "What's up with my mother's store?"

"Nothing. I thought you got my messages."

She sank down on the leather sofa. "They were breaking up. So what is this account?"

"Your mother had another bank account here, one that I can't find documentation on."

318

"What bank?"

"First Bank and Trust. Do you remember anything about it?"

There was something oily about his tone, and the hairs on her neck pricked to attention.

"Don't you know about this account?" she asked.

"It seems you're a signatory on the account and they won't release the information to me." She could almost see his finely-shaped brows furrowed with irritation as he blew out an audible breath. "I was her partner, for Christ's sake."

"Well, what do you want from me?"

"I need you to meet me at the bank."

Now the softly-pleading tone reached across the miles between them. It didn't affect her at all.

"I remember something my mother had me sign," she said. "But that had to be almost two years ago."

"That's got to be it! Come on, sweetheart. We can get to the bottom of this together."

She stood and glanced toward the kitchen. She really had no choice. She had to get out of Cloud Canyon. Yes, she was curious about this account. But this meeting would give her the excuse she needed to get away from Jack and her ridiculous feelings for him.

"All right," she said.

"Thank you, honey."

Brad's use of the endearment caused her lips to purse. "Where and when?"

"I'll call the bank manager and arrange it. Meet me tomorrow at three at the Market Street branch. Do you know where that is?"

What? She had been born and raised in San Francisco, after all. Had he always used this condescending, fatherly crap on her? The simple answer was yes.

"I'll be there." She pressed the off button.

* * *

Jack stood in the kitchen doorway, leaning against the jamb. "Everything okay?"

She walked over to him and handed him the phone. He cradled it as she went over to the kitchen table and sat. Lifting her coffee mug, she absently sipped. "That was really weird."

"What—?" Jack stopped himself. He wouldn't pry. He wasn't that kind of guy. He'd heard the irritation in her voice as she spoke to her ex-fiancé. When he'd heard her say the guy's name an alien feeling had punched him straight in the gut. Jealousy so sharp he'd sucked in a breath. That guy had her. That guy got her to commit to him. Jack couldn't get her to stay another day.

She set her mug back down and placed her chin in her hands. "My mother had another bank account. I'm apparently a signatory."

"And Brad needs you, right?"

She let out a soft laugh. "I don't think he ever needed me."

This confirmed for Jack that Brad was an idiot. She told him about the meeting set for tomorrow, and Jack started to shake his head.

"What?" With an arch of her brows, she crossed her arms and leaned toward him. "What are you trying not to say?"

"Look. I don't know this guy. But I'll tell you this. From what little you've told me, he's a real shit."

"That's very astute of you."

"Do you think you should go meet him?"

"Brad poses no threat to me. He always chose to hurt

me with words."

That said it all to Jack. She'd loved the lucky bastard.

"I don't think you should go."

She stared at him, hard. What did she see? That he wanted to beg her to forget about everything she wanted? That he wanted her to stay with him forever and let go of her dreams? He held his emotions in check as always and kept his gaze even to meet hers.

"Look, Jack." She stood, the chair scraping softly on the wood floor. "I don't need some man telling me what to do and what not to do. I've had that and I'll never put up with it again."

"Laurel, I—"

"I'm going." She brushed past him and got halfway across the living room before coming to an abrupt stop. "Crap. How am I going to get there?"

"I'll take you." The words flew out of his mouth, but they seemed right. "I don't trust that guy, anyway."

She faced him. "I don't need some mountain man to protect me, either. I do, however, need a ride."

He nearly crowed with triumph, but managed to simply nod. "We should probably get there early."

Thankfully she agreed to that statement with a nod. "I guess I'll have to tell Chloe I have to leave after the breakfast rush tomorrow. But you're not coming into the meeting. I can take care of myself."

The way she said that last sentence almost sounded like she was surprised. He wasn't. She was smart and capable, even if she didn't see it.

"I'll be there if you need me."

Her eyes went soft again, but he saw she also clenched her fists at her sides. Determination creased her brow and he marveled that he could know so much about a person after so short a time. Yes, she was capable. And complicated. And someone he wanted to get to know for the next fifty years.

That thought hit him out of nowhere. "Let me clean up in here and I'll take you back to the apartment."

"Jack, wait."

"Why postpone the inevitable?"

Her eyes sparkled now, green and gold. "Because if I only have one more Sunday in Cloud Canyon, I'm sure as heck going to spend it with you."

It wasn't a commitment, but damn if it didn't feel like

something close to it.

"Good."

She beamed that smile he'd only seen a few times over the past weeks, and he welcomed the longing that curled in his belly. Yeah, he would take her to San Francisco tomorrow. But she had to come back to Cloud Canyon to get her car, right? Maybe he could convince her to stay longer than just a few more days.

Feeling like whistling, he walked back into the kitchen.

Chapter 22

Jack scratched Smokey behind the ears as the dog devoured his breakfast. The Deputy Regional Forester's office made note of Jack's taking a personal day off, a first for him, so that was taken care of. Laurel hadn't talked about today's trip again after their disagreement yesterday morning. Disagreement? He guessed it could be called an argument. It had certainly felt like one. But there had been none of the hurtful name-calling Kelly had always seemed to delight in.

Laurel's mood had cleared and the rest of their day together had been as good as last Sunday. Barbequing on the deck, rolling around in his bed and finally taking a shower together had given him plenty to reflect on when she left Cloud Canyon for good. And she would. If he'd harbored any doubts before, he didn't now.

Smokey slammed through the dog door and Jack poured himself another mug of coffee. The place seemed so empty to him. That was amazing, as he used to crave his solitude above all else. But that had been before Laurel.

When Kelly had been here, she'd filled the place with her complaints. It was little wonder he'd wanted the house to himself after the divorce, a decision that was still costing him in the form of a second mortgage.

Maybe Laurel was right. Maybe it hadn't been all his fault Kelly was unhappy. Maybe he could let some of the guilt go.

When Smokey returned a few minutes later, Jack still stood at the counter. He hadn't made breakfast today. His heart wasn't in it and he had no place to go this morning. A smile teased his mouth as the obvious stuck him between the eyes.

He would have breakfast at the café. He would see Laurel, always a plus, and make sure she hadn't changed her mind about letting him drive her to San Francisco. It would be too easy for her to ask Chloe if she could borrow her car.

"Boy, I'm outta here," he said to the dog.

Smokey glanced at him as he trotted toward Jack's study, his domain during the day, as if to say "see ya'."

Jack grabbed his keys off the counter and headed out the door.

* * *

Laurel wiped down the counter and turned to Chloe.

"I'm sorry to leave you stranded for lunch."

Chloe shrugged. "Wouldn't be the first time I've worked it myself. And it probably won't be the last."

Laurel's gaze skittered away as she fingered the ties of her apron.

"You are coming back, right?" Chloe asked.

Laurel met her gaze. "Of course. If for nothing else than to make sure that cousin of yours finishes with my car once and for all."

"And then you're…what? Gone for good?"

Laurel chewed her bottom lip. "I'm going back to San Francisco." She looked straight into her friend's blue eyes. "When my car is fixed, I'm outta here."

"What about Jack?"

"What about him? This…" She waved her hand. "Whatever it is means the same to him as it does to me. A diversion. An affair. In short, nothing."

"Yeah, right."

Chloe's gaze shifted toward the door, and the smile on her face told Laurel who had just walked in. Jack. Laurel's breath seized.

She picked up the coffee pot and headed for the

closest occupied table. She saw her mistake in the next instant. The Bennet sisters sat there, their identical eyes wide open as they glanced between her and the doorway. She impressed herself as she refilled Charlotte Bennet's cup with a steady hand before turning toward the door. Jack stood there, yummy in chinos and a golf shirt, and just looked at her. His face was perfectly still, his Butler-blue eyes steady, and she tried to mirror his expression.

Giving him a nod of greeting, she turned back to the ladies at the table.

"Seems Ranger Jack needs breakfast, Laurel," Charlotte Bennet said.

"He does look hungry, doesn't he?" Betty Bennet put in.

"And the way he's looking at our Laurel makes me think it might not be for anything Tom could cook up!" Jane Bennet said.

The ladies were their usual loud, tittering selves and Laurel didn't have to wonder if Jack heard them. She straightened and headed for the relative safety of the service counter. Chloe's ear-to-ear grin caused her to gnash her teeth in frustration. So she had no secrets, then?

"I'll take him," Chloe said as she walked toward her brother. "Gracing us with your presence at breakfast, Jack?"

"Thought I might as well, since I'm taking…"

Laurel started and glanced over to find him looking at her in question. She gave him a tiny nod.

"I know you're driving her to San Francisco," Chloe said.

"Jack's driving Laurel to San Francisco, Charlotte," Jane Bennet said.

The other two Bennet sisters murmured their opinions on the arrangement as they continued to glance between Laurel and Jack.

"And as long as you bring her back," Chloe went on, "it's none of my business."

"Yeah, right," Jack said, echoing Laurel's thoughts on the subject.

Laurel hid her smile, her breath at last coming easier. By the time the Bennet sisters left, the rest of the place was empty except for Jack. It was nearly ten-thirty, and if they were going to get to the bank early she had to hurry and get ready.

She went over to where he sat, untying her apron as she walked. "Let me go change and I'll be right down."

"Sure."

Those eyes of his ran over her T-shirt and she felt herself react as she usually did. Heat infused her and she crumpled the apron in her hands. "I'll be right down," she said again.

He nodded and wiped his mouth. Mmm, she could look at his mouth all day. Shaking her head, she turned and went through the back of the café and up the stairs to the apartment.

She changed into one of her mother's creations and a pair of Capris. She'd chosen a shirt in shades of pink and red, the colors coordinating with the dream catcher hanging in the window. Again the little crystal bead in the center winked at her and caught her eye. She rubbed the soft suede strips dangling down from it, tracing her fingers over the beads at the ends. "Dream new dreams," the Native American woman had told her. Tears pricked her eyes and she released the dream catcher to let it swing gently in the window. She'd been living a dream these past weeks, acting against character and having the best time of her life.

Jack was the best time of her life and she would never forget him. But to dream of a future with him? It wasn't what he wanted. And it wasn't what she needed, really.

She could only hope the money in this mysterious bank account would be enough to reopen her mother's store and start planning for her own future. In San Francisco. Without Brad.

And without Jack.

* * *

Jack didn't try to hold the door open for Laurel when they got to the Jeep parked at the curb. After she'd gone upstairs to change, Chloe had continued to pester him about their trip. He didn't know what Laurel had told his sister, and it wasn't his story to tell. Chloe would have to get over her obvious disappointment at being left out. Yeah, he would bring Laurel back to Cloud Canyon. But he couldn't make any promises about keeping her here.

"The Jeep will probably make better time than my Beetle did." She clicked her seatbelt and glanced at her watch. "When do you think we'll get there?"

Jack turned the key. "Probably a little before two."

She nodded and he pulled out onto the main road.

After about fifteen minutes of silence, she placed her hand on his thigh. He managed not to jump.

"Thank you for taking me."

She didn't say it, but he could imagine an apology in her tone. There was no need for one. "No problem."

"I'm serious about the meeting, though."

"I know."

He felt her gaze on him but kept his eyes focused forward.

"You'll wait outside the office?"

Glancing over at her, he saw flicker of doubt in her eyes. "Of course."

She smiled at him and faced forward again. That jerk Brad must have ordered her around and ignored what she wanted all the time. Just another reason not to like him. This confident Laurel Tanner must be very different from the one that had given her heart to Brad. And she had it handed back to her so soon after her mother's death. The guy was a jerk.

They didn't speak much on the two and a half hour drive, but that was fine by Jack. He really didn't want to know what she was thinking about her upcoming meeting with her ex, and Jack was all too happy to keep from arguing with her about it. He'd given his word that he'd stay out of it and he would keep it. He was a man of his word. Laurel didn't know that, not yet. But maybe when she came back to Cloud Canyon he could prove that to her.

"What exit?" he finally asked as they neared the city.

"Market Street," she said. "Two more exits and that's the one."

She directed him to the bank and Jack found a parking space one door down. Pulling the emergency brake up with a loud creak, he set the Jeep on the steeply slanted road and shut off the engine. He glanced over at Laurel and saw she had her eyes closed. Steeling herself to face her ex, then. Good.

His watch showed two ten. "I'll wait in the lobby, if that's okay."

She opened her eyes and nodded. "Thanks."

Jack climbed out of the Jeep and closed the door, purposely waiting for her to get out. She needed to do this on her own, and he knew how highly she valued her independence.

She stepped out of the car and he followed her into

the bank, grabbing a magazine he wouldn't read as he entered the waiting area.

* * *

Laurel left Jack in the lobby and walked up to the wide receptionist's desk. "Hi, I'm Laurel Tanner. I have an appointment with the manager, but I'm early. The appointment is set for three."

The woman blinked at her through her glasses. "But I thought… Well, you're already here."

"What?"

The receptionist quickly tapped on her keyboard and nodded, her brow furrowed. "Mr. Brockhurst's two o'clock appointment with Brad Covington and Laurel Tanner. They're in Mr. Brockhurst's office right now."

Laurel felt the floor tip beneath her feet. "Wait. I'm Laurel Tanner." She withdrew her driver's license and showed it to the woman. "See?"

"Yes, you are." The receptionist stood, her lips pursed. "Come with me. I'll show you to Mr. Brockhurst's office."

Laurel looked over at Jack, who's eyes were intent on her. He'd set aside his magazine and leaned forward, his

elbows braced on his thighs. She gave him points for
staying in his chair and not rushing to her aid.

She followed the receptionist down a short hallway
and, when the woman rapped sharply on the mahogany
door, she heard the unmistakable sound of Brad's cajoling
voice.

"This is Laurel Tanner," he insisted. "She doesn't
have I.D. because her purse was stolen last week."

The receptionist knocked again.

"Come," another man, the manager probably, called.

The door swung open and Laurel saw Brad standing
in front of the bank manager's desk. A woman sat in one of
the two chairs facing the desk, her hands folded in her lap.

Brad turned toward the doorway and froze, his well-
shaped mouth gaping. "Laurel?"

"What's going on?" she asked. It was the first
question that popped into her head, and seemed as good a
place as any to start.

She ran her gaze over the woman sitting in the chair.
Her hair was blond, obviously a bad dye job by the brown
roots visible, and she wore some tan shapeless skirt and
top. A look of fright was on her face, and her brown eyes

were wide. Brad had to be the one behind all of this.

"Let me explain," Brad rushed out

"Someone had better," the manager said.

Laurel smiled at him. "I'm Laurel Tanner, Mr. Brockhurst." She held out her hand and he took it. "I believe my mother had an account here?"

"Yes, she did." He shook her hand and released it. He looked over at Brad, who was whispering to Blondie. "I don't know who this woman is."

Brad straightened as the woman came to her feet. "May I have a few minutes alone with my fiancé?"

"Ex-fiancé," Laurel said.

"This was a mistake," Blondie said in a quavering voice as she edged toward the door. "Good bye, Mr. Covington."

Brad didn't watch the other woman leave. "Laurel, sweetheart. I can explain everything."

Laurel put her hands on her hips. "Start."

"I didn't want you to have to bother with the signature card, or any of it. You know you never had a head for business. You're like your mother that way."

She sucked in a breath. "Look, something's going on

here and it just might be illegal." She turned to Mr. Brockhurst. "Am I right?"

The manager shook his head. "In truth, he'd only attempted to present that woman as Laurel Tanner. I didn't receive any false documents claiming her identity."

"I know we have to go over the specifics, but is it fair to say my mother's account is substantial?"

The banker smiled. "Yes."

Laurel's heart tripped with excitement. And anger at Brad. "Explain yourself."

"Mr. Brockhurst, may I speak with Ms. Tanner alone?"

Mr. Brockhurst looked at her and she gave a curt nod.

"You may use the small conference room just down the hall," he said.

Brad held the door open and waved Laurel in front of him. Laurel snorted as she stepped past him. Now he played the gentleman. Jerk.

When they reached the conference room she turned and crossed her arms over her chest. "Well?"

Brad swallowed. "Your mother had this account, sweetheart."

"Cut out the 'sweetheart' crap."

"Okay." He looked at her uneasily, from the tips of her toes to the top of her head. "You've changed."

His voice sounded odd, like he was surprised and a little pissed.

"The account?"

"I found the bank statements. Just a few of them, actually. Apparently she'd been selling her designs on the Internet."

"Really? The Internet?" She was stunned by the savvy business move her mother had made. "What an inspired idea."

"Yes. The products, shirts and skirts mostly, are made back east and drop-shipped to customers all over the world."

"Whoa."

"And if the bank statements are any indication of the contents of this account, we can be back in business."

She narrowed her eyes on him. "We?"

"Yes, Laurel." He edged closer, his green eyes holding that false affection she'd fallen for too many times. "We can reopen the shop. Maybe expand."

She leaned against the doorjamb. "Expand?"

"Maybe you could even open that little studio you wanted to. Make those trinkets."

"You don't get it." She straightened and shook her head. "You never did."

"What?" Now his eyes ran over her in appreciation, and her skin crawled in response. "I have to say, I like the changes I see. You seem more confident. And you look hot. Maybe I was too hasty to break our engagement."

Ugh, had she ever craved this man? His heart? No. Not the way she longed to lose herself in what she'd shared with Jack these past weeks. She hadn't known what she was missing.

"Your breaking our engagement was the best thing that ever happened to me. Well, that and wrecking my car in the Sierra Nevada."

"Come on, Laurel. Say you'll sign the account over to me and we can share it. Everything. The store. Your studio."

She let the anger that had been simmering in her belly bubble forth. "I don't need you to access my mother's account or anything else. What's more, I've discovered that

I have resources of my own. Strengths I didn't know I had when I was stuck here with you."

He pulled back. "Laurel—"

"And now with my mother's bank account and Internet business, I can finally think about opening my gallery."

She turned and left the conference room.

"Come on." Brad trailed after her. "Don't let it end like this."

She stopped in front of Mr. Brockhurst's door. "I don't need you, Brad. I don't need any man to fulfill my dreams. I can do that quite nicely on my own."

She was aware that the bank lobby grew quiet and turned to find everyone staring at her. Including Jack. She faced her ex again. "Good bye, Brad."

She knocked on the manager's door, turning her back on Brad and her past. She heard him stomp his expensive oxfords on the carpet as he strode away.

She thought about that mousy woman Brad had brought with him, that fake Laurel. Did he really see her like that? Tentative and drab? Maybe she was like that, before. Before Cloud Canyon. Before Jack.

Mr. Brockhurst opened the door with a smile. "Ms. Tanner, I presume?"

"Yes," she laughed. "I believe we have the matter of my mother's account to discuss?"

She sat down facing his desk, and was grateful for the support when he told her the contents of the bank account as well as info on the company making the clothes. Her mother's Internet business had put over half a million dollars in the account, with more coming in every day. This was hers now. Her mother's business and success. Brad would never get his fingers on any of it. Of that, she was very sure.

Brad would never take anything from her again.

Chapter 23

Jack sat in the lobby, his hands clenched against his thighs. Laurel remained in the bank manager's office. Her words still rang in Jack's ears. She didn't need a man to make her dreams come true. That was painfully obvious to him. Brad was all smooth charm, but Laurel had been able to get rid of him. A reluctant smile curved Jack's lips. The girl was something.

The office door opened with a click and Jack stood as Laurel entered the lobby.

She caught his gaze for a moment, her steps faltering, and turned to shake the manager's hand. "I'll be in touch, Mr. Brockhurst."

The manager gave a nod, and Jack didn't miss the smile curving one side of his mouth. "Anything you need, Ms. Tanner. Anything at all. My staff is at your disposal."

Laurel nodded and turned toward Jack again. Her eyes sparkled with excitement, and Jack felt a jump in his pulse that had nothing to do with his usual physical response to her. It was as if he could feel what she felt, could gauge her emotions as if they were his own.

"Jack, you won't believe it!" She grabbed his hand

and squeezed. "You just... Well, it's unbelievable, that's all."

"What?"

"My mother—" She glanced around the lobby and tilted her head toward the front door of the bank. "Let's go?"

"Sure." He waved her in front of him and they walked toward the Jeep.

She almost vibrated with excitement beside him as they pulled out onto the highway. "Jack, it's incredible. My mother had an Internet business. Well, the business is still intact and still making money. So much money!"

Jack gripped the wheel and nodded. "What kind of business?"

"She arranged for a company in Massachusetts to manufacture her designs and set up an account online to manage sales and drop-shipping. She was very successful, Jack. Very successful."

He heard the awe in her voice, the amazement. "You sound surprised."

She turned in her seat to face him. "Stunned is more like it. I thought she was just this flighty, artistic spirit.

Brad called her a flake, and I admit I thought she was a little flaky. But this business of hers. Wow." She was quiet for a minute. "You know, I remember her taking a trip to Boston back when this account was apparently opened. I should have asked for the particulars, but now I know she didn't want Brad to get his hands on her business."

He could guess how Laurel felt. He was amazed by how much more Laurel was to him now. "She was more than you thought."

"She was." Laurel nodded. "Savvy and so much more. And the business has already earned almost five hundred thousand dollars."

Jack's stomach flipped. *Whoa.* With that kind of money, she could open her gallery and realize her dream away from Cloud Canyon. Away from him.

He couldn't say anything more, his throat was so tight. This was it, then. This was probably the last time he would be this close to her again. He was losing the best thing that ever happened to him. Kelly had accused him of having no emotions? Well, she would laugh if she could see him now. He was on the verge of telling Laurel to stay, of begging her to give up everything she'd dreamed of to make a life with him in the mountains. He couldn't do it.

He would just have to let her go and take his heart with her.

* * *

Laurel settled back and let the hum of the road beneath the Jeep soothe her nerves as they headed back to Cloud Canyon. Her mind was still spinning from everything Mr. Brockhurst had disclosed. Her mother, a business mastermind? Unbelievable. Astrid Tanner, savvy businesswoman. And she'd been smart enough to leave Brad completely out of the mix. That made her mother much smarter than Laurel. Because of her mother's foresight, Laurel would be able to see both their dreams through.

Using her phone, she pulled up the website. It was called Chasing Dreams and it was bright and fun and so much like her mother her eyes grew misty again. She put her phone in her purse and let out a breath.

She glanced over at Jack, so silent and still at the wheel. No big surprise there. He was the quietest man she'd ever met. No wasted words, no wasted movements. Maybe that was what made his compliments, his sweet and naughty words, so much more precious. She was so grateful for it. For Jack giving her something that had exceeded any expectations she'd ever imagined.

"Thank you, Jack."

He grunted in answer, an economic sound accompanied by a short nod. Did he know she was thanking him for so much more than the ride to San Francisco? Brad had said she'd changed. Well, he was right. He thought she was hot now? It was amazing that she couldn't care less about Brad's opinion of her after so many years of longing for one measly compliment from him.

She'd been such a fool. Shame churned within her now when she thought of it. But she had changed, and if it took Brad's off-handed comment to make her realize that, maybe she could manage to be thankful to him for this one small favor.

So now she and Jack were headed back to Cloud Canyon. For how long, she didn't know. Do would undoubtedly fix her car this week, since she suspected he'd had the part for some time now.

What would Jack say when she left? She couldn't read him. He was stoic and kept his emotions in check at all times. She could guess that his clingy ex-wife hadn't been able to deal with that. Well, Laurel wasn't clingy, not anymore. She didn't need constant contact and reassurance like she used to.

Jack would no doubt be relieved when she left. No connections, no strings. Just like she'd made him promise weeks ago. She stared out the window. *Be careful what you wish for.*

The studio, the gallery. Independence. Well, she would have all that and more. Her mother's business too, and now she had the confidence that she could run it.

A glance at a passing sign showed they probably had another hour or so before they would reach Cloud Canyon. The confines of the Jeep might be close, but they might as well already have hundreds of miles between them.

She'd better get used to missing him. She would miss him for the rest of her life.

* * *

"What will Laurel do now?" Jack's mother asked him.

"She'll go back to San Francisco."

"And you're going to just let her leave? Just like

347

that?"

Jack's hand tightened on the phone and he forced himself to relax. "Laurel has a plan, Mom. Her own dreams that have nothing to do with me or Cloud Canyon."

"They could. I've seen you with her. The two of you have something that doesn't come around every day."

"Mom—"

"She's nothing like Kelly."

As if he needed her to point that out to him. "Look, Smokey needs to eat and I need to get some work done for tomorrow."

His mother was quiet for a moment, finally letting out a soft sigh. "All right. Why don't you bring her to Aunt Beth's tomorrow night?"

"I'll ask her if I see her."

It was all he would allow tonight and his mother would just have to accept that.

"Good night."

"Good night, Mom."

Jack cradled the phone and cracked open the beer he'd set on the counter when the phone had rung. Laurel's dreams were none of his business. He'd read the excitement all over her beautiful face as she'd talked about her mother and the amazing change of events. As she'd explored her mother's website on the drive home. There was nothing to hold her back now. Well, he wouldn't be the big stupid Mule Deer standing in her way.

As he drank his beer his gaze slowly went around the cozy living room. Everywhere he looked there was something that reminded him of their time together in this house. They'd had such a short time together, really. But memorable. And it wasn't just the sex he remembered, either. The easy talks, the long silences as they just enjoyed each other's company. He would never forget her. And maybe, when she wasn't so busy with her mother's business and her art, she would think about him.

Laurel was nothing like Kelly. His mother had never spoken truer words. Kelly was clingy and whiney and always out for herself. Laurel was kind and sweet, but she was also determined and independent. Jack could barely speak in the Jeep for that last hour of their trip back from San Francisco. He'd had nothing to say to her. And he had nothing to say to her now.

She would leave Cloud Canyon, but he wanted to

keep her with him. Forever. He would get used to sharing his life with her. To having a person who wanted to be with him. But she was successful now, with a world of possibilities spread out in front of her. Her studio, her gallery, her mother's business.

His eyes burned as he let his head fall against the back of the couch.

What the hell did he have to offer her?

* * *

"A half a million dollars?"

Chloe's voice squeaked on the last word and Laurel nodded with a grin.

"Yep. Imagine my mother, a savvy business woman. I'm so proud of her I could burst."

"You should be."

She'd found Chloe in the café when Jack dropped her off, getting the place ready for tomorrow's breakfast rush.

"So tell me about Brad," Chloe asked.

Chloe sat and Laurel settled in the chair across from her. "Nothing to tell, really. Though I have to say I don't know what I ever saw in him."

"Ah, you'd just never been with a Butler before."

How right she was! Jack made Brad look like every other metro-sexual she'd seen in San Francisco. Polished to reflect so much light they practically disappeared.

"I was a fool to let Brad get to me. You should have seen the girl he brought to impersonate me."

Chloe crossed her arms and leaned on the table. "Hmm, let me guess. Meek and mousy?"

Laurel arched her brows, then gave Chloe a half smile. "Thanks."

Chloe laughed. "That's how he'd have to see you, right? To walk all over you? The difference between then-Laurel and now-Laurel must have floored him."

"He thought I would take him back. He offered to take *me* back, actually."

"Prick."

"So you know him?" Laurel teased. "Needless to say, he's not a happy camper right now."

"How about you? It had to feel strange to see him again."

Laurel hadn't told Chloe much about Brad's breakup, but obviously it was enough for Jack's sister to get a pretty clear picture of their uneven relationship.

"You know, I expected to feel something. Shame for what he'd said to me that last day. Maybe regret that I hadn't been able to keep him. But today I felt nothing but irritation that he thought he could trick me out of my mother's business."

Chloe gave her hand a squeeze. "Good for you. I wish I could be that strong. At least I doubt I'll see Josh's father in the near future."

It was one of the rare times Chloe broached the subject and Laurel couldn't resist learning something more about her friend. "Does he ever see Josh?"

"No."

"Wow. I can't imagine a guy not wanting that. I'm sorry. It's not my business."

"Don't worry about it. He's never seen Josh. I tried to contact him when I was pregnant but I never heard back from him. Now, what are you going to do about Jack?"

Laurel blinked at the swift change of subject. She wouldn't press Chloe to talk more about what was obviously painful.

"I'm not going to do anything about Jack. Once Bo fixes my car, I'm out of here."

Chloe opened her mouth, then pressed her lips closed. "Nope. Not my business." She stood and walked toward the back of the café, flicking off the lights before turning back to Laurel. "If you two want to be foolish and throw away something special, who am I to argue?"

Laurel followed her, keeping her thoughts to herself as she turned toward the staircase to the apartment. She knew what she felt for Jack was special. She was also sure his heart was completely out of it.

"Thanks, Chloe. I'll see you tomorrow."

"Hey, I'm going up to the Treetop Inn for ladies' night tonight. Nothing fancy, just a few friends getting together in a relatively testosterone-free zone. Why don't you stop by?"

Laurel wasn't in the mood to make the acquaintance of more people that would most likely end up to be related to the Butlers. She wanted to go and have a good sulk.

"I don't think so. Thanks, though."

Chloe just nodded. "If you change your mind, we'll be in the lounge around eight."

Laurel nodded and slowly climbed the stairs.

Tomorrow, Tuesday, she would spend a few hours working

in the café and then head over to Bo's to get a definitive answer on the status of her car. Not more screwing around, and no more phony delays. She had to take charge of her life, and she couldn't use the excuse of car troubles to keep her in Cloud Canyon living a fool's dream.

She opened the fridge and found some leftover Chinese takeout. Cold lo mein noodles. Great. Kicking off her sandals, she sat at the kitchen table and nibbled at the food. She wouldn't think about the first time she'd had Chinese food here in the apartment. She wouldn't think about that first time here with Jack, either. Passion, attraction… A lump formed at the base of her throat and suddenly she couldn't swallow.

Her appetite gone, she folded the food box shut and dropped it into the garbage can. It was still light out, but the day was waning. She would take a long, hot soak and get into bed. Alone.

Jack hadn't offered to stop over when he'd pulled the Jeep up to the curb outside the café. Well she hadn't brought it up, either. She was a coward, but after the tumultuous day she'd had an excuse. What his was, she wouldn't guess. That would lead to the inevitable conclusion that he was more than ready to end their affair.

When she finally emerged from the steamy bathroom almost an hour later, she blessedly felt nothing but tired. No more anger at Brad's machinations. No more pining for a relationship with Jack that would last beyond the physical.

The damn dream catcher in the window caught her eye and she scowled at it. "New dreams, huh? Oh, shut up."

She tried not to think about Jack or his absence in the bed beside her. She really did. She had no claim on him and that was how he wanted it. That had been her preference, too.

And if her heart suddenly wanted something else, that was just her bad luck. Chloe's invitation niggled at the back of her mind. Why the heck not?

Going through her favorite things her mother had made, she chose an outfit and got ready to meet Chloe and her friends. And put Jack Butler out of her mind.

Chapter 24

Laurel had seen the Treetop Inn on her treks to Bo's garage but she'd never stepped inside. It wasn't very far from the café actually, so she would just walk there tonight. She'd chosen one of her favorite tops, this one in shades of buttery yellow, and paired it with a pair of khaki capris. Nothing fancy, but her hair had curled while she'd soaked and sulked in the tub so it was full and thick. She'd put on a little more makeup than she normally wore, too. Why the heck not? It felt good to dress up a little bit and just go out and have fun.

Jeez, it had been so long since she'd had fun. She didn't count the sexy fun she'd shared with Jack over these past weeks. That was so far from her normal realm of experience it was almost surreal.

Brad was never one for impromptu evenings out. Or any evenings out, actually. Ugh, she'd wasted so much time on that worm. And to think that all that time he was trying to rip her mother off. She suspected that he'd been skimming money from the store, but she had no proof. And now, she couldn't care less. She took a breath and blew it out, dispelling Brad from her consciousness just as brusquely.

She reached the Treetop and stared up at it. She'd heard from the Bennet sisters that the inn, a three-story Victorian-era structure, was once the largest house in town. The Bennets had apparently been a wealthy family and, even though they used their maiden names now, town lore had it that all three sisters had married well. Nothing like well-married women to pry and peer into everybody else's lives in Cloud Canyon. Laurel couldn't rouse anger at them, though. They were adorable.

Chloe had told her that the house, clapboard and uncluttered with hardly any of the gingerbread trim that smothered most Victorian homes in San Francisco, had been left to only son Fred Bennet. Fred, the beleaguered and put-upon brother of the three sisters. She couldn't help wondering what he was like.

Grabbing the ornate brass door handle, she pulled opened one of the thick oak double doors. She walked into the lobby and stood in the foyer, her eyes on the Oriental rug beneath her feet. She had no idea where the lounge was. Crossing to the stand holding ads and brochures, she idly glanced at the colorful flyers. She really hadn't seen much of the area since that deer forced her hand and stranded her here. And now she was leaving.

"Hello, there," a man said from behind her.

She froze, then turned a smile on the elderly man behind the desk. He could only be Fred Bennet. The family resemblance was striking, although his silver hair was a little thin on top. She suspected he never missed a thing from his post behind the desk, either. Those baby-blues peering through his wire-rimmed glasses looked to be as sharp as his sisters'.

"Hello."

"Fred Bennet." He leaned forward, a smile wreathing his round face. "And you must be Laurel Tanner."

She smiled at him. "Must I?"

He nodded. "My sisters talk so often of you I feel like we're good friends."

Laurel would just bet they did. She gave a quick nod. "I don't think I've seen you in the café. You should come by and join them sometime."

"Those three?" The old man snorted. "I get enough of those magpies at our weekly dinners."

She laughed. "So big, inquisitive families are quite

common here in Cloud Canyon?"

"Very, my dear. The difference between my sisters and me, though? I've learned to keep my secrets close." He winked. "Purely a defense mechanism."

"Well, I envy you."

"Oh? The secrets? Or the family?"

Laurel felt herself warming to this kinder, gentler Bennet. "The family. I'm afraid I'm the only one left in mine."

He tipped his head. "I heard the Butlers took you into their fold."

"They've been very kind." Her eyes pricked. "I'll miss them when I go back home."

"To San Francisco."

She blinked at him.

"My sisters, Laurel. There's little that gets past them."

"Yes, San Francisco."

He glanced over tall French doors that were closed tight and dressed with gathered curtains on their windows. "You're here for ladies' night, I take it?"

"I am."

"The lounge is through those doors." He smiled. "You won't find Cloud Canyon to have anything by way of a bustling night life, Laurel. But the inn serves good drinks and great conversations." He winked again. "And not just on ladies' night."

Her smile widened. "That's sounds just perfect, Mr. Bennet."

"Fred, dear. Please."

"Fred, then." She nodded her head. "Thank you, Fred."

Laurel made her way across the carpet and as she neared the French doors she could hear the murmur of voices just beyond. She turned the knob and entered, taking in the room for a minute.

It was decorated much like the lobby, with red velvet and globe lights and lots of fringe. An ornately-carved bar done in dark wood stretched across the left side of the room and the scrolled-iron backed stools were almost all occupied by women of various sizes, shapes and ages. Several round tables filled the rest of the lounge, draped with moiré fabrics in jewel tones. They all sported a globe lamp in the center and there were groups of two and three women around nearly each one. The lounge was delightfully gaudy and old-fashioned and she loved it. She half-expected to hear a tinny piano plunking out a tune instead of the softly-playing pop standards, and to see Miss Kitty sauntering around with one of her girls.

Smiling, she made her way toward the bar. Chloe was seated on one of the stools, holding a martini glass and talking to a woman to her right.

"Hey, Chloe," Laurel said.

Chloe swiveled as she looked at her, then her eyes went wide. "Laurel!" She put down the glass and grabbed her in a hug. "I'm so glad you decided to come."

Laurel hugged her back, then shrugged. "I wasn't doing myself any good sitting in the apartment brooding."

"Nope." Chloe released her. "Nothing good ever comes from brooding. Sit."

Laurel settled on the stool to Chloe's left. She eyed the light blue drink in Chloe's martini glass. "What are you drinking?"

"This, Laurel, is a Cloud Nine."

"What's in it?"

"Heaven," the woman to Chloe's right answered. "Hi,

I'm Josie."

"Oh, I'm sorry!" Chloe placed a hand on Josie's.

"Laurel, this is Josie. She recently moved here from Tahoe."

Josie looked to be about twenty-five. She had long, shining black hair and a very pretty heart-shaped face.

"It's nice to meet you, Josie."

"It's nice to meet you too, Laurel. Chloe said you've been working at the café?"

Laurel arched a brow at Jack's sister, who laughingly shrugged. "Hey, not much going on in my own life. I told her about your car and how you're staying in the apartment."

Chloe took a minute to order a Cloud Nine for Laurel. "Josie doesn't have much family, either." She sighed. "I love my crazy bunch but sometimes I wouldn't mind some time away from them."

"Your family is hot," Josie said. "At least, that cousin of yours is."

Laurel nodded her thanks to the slim and handsome bartender when he brought her drink, then took a tentative sip. Ooh, it was sweet and tart with a kick she knew she could use tonight. "Mmm. Heaven is right."

Josie nodded. "So Bo Butler is fixing your car?"

"So he says."

Josie's blue eyes widened. "Huh?"

Laurel shook her head. "I'm sure he's a great mechanic. And a great guy, too. But I'm also sure he's been stalling to keep me hanging around Cloud Canyon."

Chloe choked on her drink, then set the glass down.

"Do you have something to say, Chloe?" Laurel asked her. "A confession, perhaps?"

"I don't know."

"Hmm." Laurel wasn't buying it. "Seems like you know more than a little bit about that?"

"I'm not saying there isn't a dot of truth in that statement."

Laurel laughed. "Yeah, right. If Bo's holding my Beetle hostage you're the one writing the ransom notes."

Josie laughed, too. "I know there's a story there. Bo is hot, though."

She'd said that before. "Have you been seeing Bo?" Laurel asked her.

Josie's cheeks turned a little bit pink. "Not seeing,

exactly."

Chloe shook her head. "Yeah, cousin Bo is usually one for a booty call. Not so much on the dating, though."

"Jeez, tell all my secrets why don't you?"

"Josie, I've known you for a sum total of twenty minutes. What secrets could I possibly know?"

Josie sipped her drink, a thoughtful expression on her face. "Well, you could guess I was dumb enough to fall into bed with a guy I hardly know."

That struck a little close to home for Laurel. She'd never had close female friends, but between the subtle lighting and lush furnishings, not to mention the pleasant way her Cloud Nine had disappeared and been replaced with its twin, she was suddenly longing to spill her guts.

"I did the same thing," she blurted.

"No!" Josie said, leaning closer. "Tell me it wasn't with Bo."

That earned her a shaky laugh from Laurel. "No. I found my own mess to fall into with a completely different Butler."

Josie opened her mouth, then shut it. "Chloe's brother."

Laurel's cheeks were hot now. "I'm afraid so."

Josie let out a low whistle. "He's hot, too."

Chloe rolled her eyes. "This was supposed to be a testosterone-free zone, girls. The last thing I want to think about is how hot the men in my family are. Ick."

"It can't be helped," Josie said. "Hotness cannot be denied."

Laurel agreed. "Besides, I'll be leaving in a few days. Then you can go back to the blissful ignorance of thinking of both Butlers as annoying relatives and nothing else."

Chloe's face grew serious. "Then you're still leaving."

It wasn't a question. Not from Chloe's tone and not from the sadness stamped on her face. "Yes."

Chloe sighed. "Jack will be crushed."

"Hardly that. Jack is his own man. With his own life. It's time I got on with mine."

Chloe was quiet, so Josie perked up. "Where are you going?"

"Back to San Francisco."

"Oh, I love San Francisco," Josie said.

Laurel couldn't muster up the enthusiasm for the

place right now. "Yes. It's nice."

"What's there for you, Laurel?" Chloe folded her arms on the bar. "What's there that you can't have here?"

Laurel met her Butler-blue eyes with a steady stare. "I need to start my own life, Chloe. I have to make my mother proud."

Chloe covered her hand. "She's gone."

Laurel's throat grew thick. "I know. I've loved getting to know your family but I have to stand on my own two feet now. Thankfully, my mother left me the means to do just that."

"I don't know the particulars but I'm with you on the two-feet thing," Josie said. "My last boyfriend was a prick of the first order. Told me what to do. How to dress. Where to work." She picked up her drink and threw it back, placing the delicate stem back on the bar as she licked her bottom lip. "Prick."

"My old boyfriend was like that. He was almost criminal as well, so there is that."

Josie nodded. "Yep."

Chloe let out the whisper of a breath. "I don't even have an ex to complain about."

Laurel had to have heard her wrong. There was so a guy in her past. The one she never liked to talk about.

"Really? So where did you get Josh? From under a cabbage leaf?"

Chloe swatted her arm. "Never mind."

"Is Josh your boyfriend?" Josie asked.

"No." Chloe sighed. "Josh is my son. He's four." She threw a look in Laurel's direction. "And his father was never my boyfriend."

Laurel just shrugged and sipped her drink. She'd tried to get Chloe to open up about this before. She was so not going to do it tonight.

"Ooh, there's a story there," Josie said.

"Yeah, there is," Laurel said. "But don't try to get it out of her, Josie. She's like a Pismo Beach clam."

Chloe waved a hand. "It's not that I don't want to talk about him."

Laurel and Josie made sounds of disagreement to that.

"It's not," Chloe insisted. "He was part of my life for such a short time and that's the way I like it."

Laurel knew she needed to talk about the guy but this wasn't going to be the venue. No, she guessed it would take a lot more than a couple of Cloud Nines and a lot less people around to get Chloe to finally open up about Josh's father.

"Did you love him?" Josie asked.

Laurel held her breath as she waited for the answer to that particular question. It sure was nice having another woman here to ask the questions that were on the tip of Laurel's tongue.

"Yes," came Chloe's soft answer. "But I don't love him now and he has nothing to do with Josh."

"What a deadbeat," Josie said.

Laurel knew there was more to the story than Josh's father being a deadbeat dad. Chloe looked like she wanted to let that statement just lay there but she finally shook her head.

"No. He's not. He never knew Josh. We don't have any contact now and never did."

"That's too bad, then. I bet your Josh is a little cutie."

"He is," Laurel said, her breath catching in her throat. "I'll miss him."

Chloe's eyes widened. "Don't start that! You're going to make me cry and there's nothing more pitiful than a grown woman crying into her Cloud Nine at the Treetop."

Laurel sniffled, then smiled. "That's very specific."

"Let's just put a pin in the subject of your leaving, okay? Josie here is looking for a job and I don't think she'll be foolish enough to come and work for me so put on your thinking cap."

Josie smiled encouragement and the three of them talked and laughed and drank until Laurel could almost forget the troubles she'd shoved under the rug tonight.

Almost.

Chapter 25

Jack nursed his beer as Bo went on about some kind of new car he'd had in the shop. They sat in Jack's living room with Smokey curled up at their feet as the flat screen TV played an episode of American Pickers on the History Channel.

"Cuz, you're not even listening."

"Yes, I am." No, he wasn't.

"Yeah? Then what was I talking about?"

Jack shrugged. "Something about an electric car."

"A Tesla, Cuz. A friggin' Tesla this guy brings in."

"Tesla? Like the inventor? The lightbulb guy?"

Bo grinned. "I told you, you watch too much History Channel. Yeah, like the inventor. This car was a beauty, man. All smooth lines with a gorgeous body."

As Bo went on about the guy's expensive car and Bo's lust for it, Laurel popped into Jack's mind. Her supple curves. Her sweet lips. The way she cried out her pleasure and cuddled so close to him after.

"Damn, I don't know what you're thinking about with that sappy look on your face but it sure isn't a car."

Jack ran a hand over his face. "It's nothing."

Bo snorted. "Right."

Jack cursed softly. "Okay, it's Laurel. I'm thinking about Laurel. Are you happy now?"

Bo grinned. "I am, but you're sure as hell not. What happened today in Frisco?"

Jack shook his head. How could he tell his cousin how inadequate he felt now that Laurel didn't need him for anything? Not that she had before, but he'd considered them on a pretty even playing field before she became so friggin' rich.

"Her old boyfriend was trying to swindle her but he didn't get away with it."

"That's good, right?"

Jack made a sound of agreement.

"Then why do you look so miserable?"

"Because she inherited enough from her mother to go back to San Francisco and start her gallery. She can practice her art and have her own life."

"Her own life. Without you, you mean."

"Yeah, without me."

"Did she say that's what she wants?"

"She didn't have to."

Bo's brows furrowed, then he shook his head. "Look, Cuz. I don't do relationships so I'm the last guy you should be taking advice from. But I've seen you and Laurel together. You have something. Yeah, sparks." He smiled. "I saw those the first day. Sparks, and that hickey. But there's something more."

Jack smiled a little at the memory of the day he'd met Laurel. She'd been amazing and her kisses had been the sweetest he'd ever tasted. Still, that was all they'd had. Hot sex and a few close talks. That was it.

He shook his head. "I don't think so."

"Do you love her?"

Jack's mouth thinned. "I can't talk about this."

Bo shifted on the couch. "Yeah, this is a little bit too touchy-feely for me too."

They grew quiet and watched as one of the guys on the show went ape-shit over a rusty bike he'd found. The guy had a bike gasm every time. Each and every time.

"Speaking of touchy-feely, did I tell you about the girl I met last week?"

Jack arched a brow. "No."

"She's a hottie. From Tahoe."

"Jeez, not Tahoe."

Bo chuckled. "No, I know you met Kelly there but she's nothing like your ex-wife. Believe me. This girl is a free-spirit."

"Not into entanglements, I take it?"

"Nope. She might be sticking around Cloud Canyon, though. So that puts an end to the poke and tickle."

"That's a shame. For you." He took a long sip of his beer. "Where did you meet her?"

"At the garage. Pretty thing with long black hair. It can't go anywhere, though."

"Why not?"

"Because if she stays in Cloud Canyon it'll get too complicated."

"Then you agree with Laurel? Things got too complicated? That she should go back to San Francisco?"

"I didn't say any of that."

"Then, what? She didn't end up staying here, did she?"

"She should, though."

"Why?" Jack straightened. "Why is my case different than yours?"

"Because you're different, Jack." Bo shoved him with his shoulder. "Come on. You're the marrying kind. A family kind of guy. Not me."

Jack wouldn't talk about marriage or Laurel with Bo right now. It had been like a knife in his gut, the pain of losing her this afternoon.

"Chloe said she was going out tonight," Jack said, eager to change the subject.

"Yeah, to the Treetop. They do a ladies' night every couple of weeks." Bo winked. "Wanna head over there and see what's going on?"

Jack sipped his beer. "No, thanks."

"Hey, I'd be game to buzz the place. See if my latest is there."

"It's ladies' night, Bo. Fred Bennet would never let you in there."

"That's true. That guy is a tough one. I remember when this one girl was staying there, I think she was a pharmacy sales rep or something, and I had to sneak past old Fred to go upstairs and get my prescription filled, if you get my meaning."

Jack laughed. "Bo, I always get your meaning."

"What's Laurel up to tonight?"

"I don't know."

"I thought you said you brought her back from Frisco with you."

"I did. And I dropped her at the apartment and came home."

"Why?"

"Why, what?"

"Why did you just drop her off?"

"Because she didn't seem like she was up for my company."

"Your company?" Bo snorted. "You sound like one of the Bennet sisters."

Jack rolled his eyes. "Okay, I didn't think she would go for one more fling before leaving for good."

"And she will be leaving. Her car is ready."

"I know."

"So what are you going to do?"

"Nothing to do."

He thought about what Bo had said earlier. About Jack being the marrying kind.

"I don't know if I'll ever get married again."

Bo was quiet for a minute. "With an ex like Kelly, I don't blame you. But Laurel is nothing like her."

"No. She's not. But she's also not sticking around so there's no point in arguing."

"Did you ask her to stick around?"

"What?"

"Did you ask her?" Bo asked deliberately.

Jack just stared at him, his expression flat.

"Jesus, you're an idiot," Bo said. "How's the girl supposed to know you want her to stay if you don't ask her to?"

"I won't do that, Bo. I won't ask her to put her dreams aside to stay here. What can I give her that she can't give herself?"

"What do you mean?"

"I have no money. My salary is decent but nothing to write home about. Besides that, Kelly takes a bite out of me every month. I'm just a ranger with a nice house and a shaggy dog. That's it."

Bo slowly shook his head. "What does any of that shit matter?"

"It matters, Bo. To someone from the city, it matters.

Big time."

"You've never been one to give up, Cuz. Not when your dad died. Not when mine did. Not when Kelly chewed you up and spit you out."

"What are you saying?"

"Nothing. I'm not saying anything you don't already know."

Jack stood. "Another beer?"

"Sure."

Jack went into the kitchen to get the beer. And to get away from Bo and his questions. The guy might look like a dumb hick but Jack knew there was a sharp mind behind those laughing eyes and easy grin. He'd gotten too close to the truth. Jack did want to get married again but only to Laurel.

He leaned back against the counter and thought back to that night after their dinner in Truckee. He hadn't been able to resist taking Laurel right there on his granite counter, he'd been so wild for her. He'd never had that before in his life. That passion that seemed to burn hotter than any forest fire.

She was sweet, too. He liked talking with her and just

being around her. Watching her smile at Chloe's customers and work with people she'd only known for a short time. She was great with his family too, and he knew that she missed her mom. That she missed having a family of her own. She was one of a kind, and he had to let her go. He'd never met a woman like her before. He knew he never would again. He'd never have that passion, that connection. Not with her. That was for sure. And not with another woman. There would never be another woman in his life like Laurel.

"Where's my beer?" Bo called from the living room.

Jack swiped at his burning eyes, taking a breath. "Coming. Keep your pants on."

"Yeah, yeah." Bo was smiling when he joined him again. "Sadly, my pants are on. You're the one who didn't want to go to the Treetop."

Jack shook his head and sank back down on the couch next to the cousin.

"You're a piece of work. You know that?"

"I'm a charmer, Cuz. And don't you forget it."

Jack chuckled and drank his beer.

"So, tell me about this girl with the long black hair."

Chapter 26

"Hello?" Laurel let the door wheeze shut behind her as she approached the service counter. "Is anyone here?"

Bo stuck his head out of his office, his brows raised. Then he smiled that Butler grin at her. "Hey, Laurel."

She returned the expression. "Hey. I'm here about my car, which you can probably guess."

Bo stepped out of his office, nodding his head. "Yep. I, uh…"

"I guess you have the part?"

A flash of red showed on his cheeks. "Yep. The car can be ready in a few days."

Laurel shook her head without anger. "I know about the delays, Bo. I have to get back to San Francisco."

"You're leaving, then?"

"I'm sure Chloe told you."

"Well, yeah. But I figured that maybe you and Jack…"

She ignored the stab of pain the mention of Jack caused. "There is no 'me and Jack.' There never really was."

He stared at her for a long moment. "If you say so.

I'll get the car finished by tomorrow. I'll bring it by the café in the afternoon and we can settle things."

That was it, then. That was what she'd wanted.

"Great. Thanks, Bo."

She turned to go.

"Hey, Laurel?"

She stopped and faced him. "Yes?"

He gazed at her evenly, looking more like Jack in that instant than she'd ever seen. "You know, sometimes there can be more to something than anybody can figure."

She wouldn't let herself hope that was true. It was what she'd struggled with all last night alone under the faded quilt. "Are you turning into a philosopher, Bo Butler?"

"Jack's the deep thinker in the family." Bo grinned then, bright and sunny and totally Bo. "Me? I'm just the charmer."

She laughed and left the garage. As she passed the Native American shop where she'd found the dream catcher, she let herself linger over the items on display. The colors of the small plaques, handmade key chains and dangling ornaments were rich and deep, and the motifs of nature spoke to her. She thought about the mosaic she'd played with in Jack's mother's shop. Maybe she'd found new dreams after all, at least where her art was concerned.

Hiking in the mountains with Jack, seeing the amazing vistas of the Sierra Nevada everywhere she turned in town, had put her more in tune with natural designs. And with the money from her mother's business, she could afford to indulge her newfound inspiration and create pieces large enough to encompass all she'd seen here in Cloud Canyon.

Another lonely evening stretched out in front of her, and tomorrow would give her the freedom to return to her former life. Well, her new life in her former home. She should be grateful, but the hollow beat in her chest told her she would leave her heart here in the mountains.

As maudlin and melodramatic as that seemed, she had to admit it to herself. She was in love with Jack Butler, and what they'd shared had meant more to her than she would admit to Bo. True, there was no "her and Jack," but not as far as her own heart was concerned. She would just have to learn to live with it.

As she made her way back toward the apartment, she

passed Jack's mother's antique store. When the woman saw her through the window, a smiled wreathed her face. Laurel felt another pang in the vicinity of that hollow in her chest. Oh, she was so emotional today. Maybe it was all this business with her mother that made her long for that connection again.

Steeling herself, she pulled open the door and set off the jingling of the bell.

"Laurel, honey!" Mrs. Butler beamed. "How nice to see you."

"Hello, Mrs. Butler." She weaved through the items on display, old furniture, stunning beaded lamps, and chipped enamel metal serving pieces which any tourist would find charming. "You have some new things."

Jack's mother shrugged. "My inventory changes daily, thank goodness."

As if to prove the point, a shopper made her way toward the purchase counter with several items in her arms. Laurel occupied herself with rearranging a display on a nearby table, moving slender graceful hand-blown bottles to flank chunkier pressed glass ones in pleasing contrast. She heard Jack's mother total and ring the purchases and the shopper passed Laurel with a smile on her way out the door.

They were alone in the shop now, and Jack's mother walked up to her. "That's interesting." She flicked a tiny piece of lint from the mouth of one of the pressed bottles. "Very eye catching."

"Sorry, but I tend to rearrange things."

"You have a flair. I saw that when you put my mismatched dishes into sets. And of course the broken dish told me you had an artist's eyes."

"Thanks. I admit the colors are some I'd never considered before. Greens and blues and browns, all the colors of the surrounding woods."

Jack's mother stared at her, one corner of her mouth lifting.

Laurel stopped, her cheeks warm, and shook her head. "Sorry again."

"You're an artist, Laurel. You have a gift, and when you talk about it your whole face lights up. Don't ever apologize for that."

Before she could stop herself, Laurel hugged her. "Thank you. You've been very kind."

Jack's mother hugged her back. "We're going to miss you."

Laurel pulled back and swiped a hand over her damp cheek. "I didn't mean to... I'll be leaving tomorrow, and I wanted to say good bye."

"Tomorrow?" Her brow furrowed. "So soon?"

Laurel laughed softly. "I think I've overstayed any sort of welcome in Cloud Canyon. Besides, I have to get back and put things in order."

"Yes, your mother's business. Chloe told me. You must be very proud."

"I loved my mother. But now I find there's so much I didn't know about her, things I'm so proud of I could burst."

"Do we ever really know someone?"

Laurel thought about Jack, and his deep-running still waters. "No. I guess not."

She bade Jack's mother good bye, accepted another hug, and left the shop.

* * *

Jack walked into the café, hungrier to see Laurel than to eat lunch. Last night had nearly killed him. He'd longed to go to the apartment, to ask her to stay with him, but in the end he'd known what he had to do all along. Laurel wasn't meant for him and he wasn't meant for her. Then why the hell was he here today?

She hadn't seen him yet. She was busy fussing and cleaning behind the service counter with her head down. Chloe caught his eye, though. She stared at him, one of her patented probing expressions she'd learned from their mother. He nodded in her direction and sat, earning a snort from her that he could hear from three tables away.

She came up to his table. "What will you have, Bro?"

"A burger, I guess." He took off his ball cap. "And fries."

"Iced tea?"

"Yep."

Chloe still stood there, an expectant look on her face.

"What do you want from me, Chloe?"

"Nothing you're going to give me, obviously."

His sister turned and stalked toward the back of the café. Laurel looked up then, her hazel eyes fixed directly on him. He felt his chest tighten in response. He couldn't look away, damn his weakness. Her hair was in a low ponytail, silky curls brushing her cheeks. Those cheeks were flushed, the color pink and delicate and soft. He knew how soft her skin was, too. He would never forget. She licked her lips, probably from nervousness, and turned from him. Just like that, the connection was broken and she went into the kitchen.

Chloe brought him his iced tea and he focused on nothing more than the cold glass in his hands. Before she could bring him his burger, he heard a horn honk. A glance out the window showed him the shiny front bumper of Laurel's little blue Beetle. Damn.

A few seconds later, Bo pulled open the door to the café. "Hey, Cuz."

"Hey."

"Got Laurel's car. All ready to go."

"Looks like."

"Hey, Bo!" Chloe called. "You've got Laurel's car, I scc."

"Yep. She around?"

Chloe pushed the kitchen door open and called to Laurel. She stepped out and froze, her eyes on Bo and the keys dangling in his hands.

"The car," she said softly.

"Your baby's all ready." Bo walked over to her and handed her the keys. "I have to get back to the shop. Pete's in the truck waiting for me."

"Okay." Laurel stared at the keys in her palm. "Wait! What do I owe you?"

"Leave your email address with Chloe and I'll get you the bill." Bo winked as he opened the front door. "I know you're good for it."

Thanks for that, Bo. So everyone knew Laurel was rich and needed nothing. Jack sipped at his tea, his appetite gone. He felt Laurel come closer, the pull of her, the scent of her, as she neared his table. He couldn't look at her. If he did, he'd say something stupid. *I love you, Laurel. Stay with me.* He was a fool.

"Jack."

He steeled himself and looked at her. "Your car's fixed."

"Yes. I wanted to tell you I'm leaving."

"I figured."

"I also wanted to say good bye."

There was so much he wanted to say to her, but he

didn't have any right to spoil her plans. He offered her a small smile. "Good bye."

He stood as Chloe brought his lunch to the table.

"Where are you going?" Chloe asked.

Jack stood and put on his cap. "I have to get back to work."

He ignored his sister's shocked expression and couldn't look at Laurel. He just couldn't. He wasn't strong enough to keep from begging her to stay. If Bo was still here he would've gotten a kick out of this. He'd urged him to do that very thing just last night.

He walked past the Beetle, which bore no evidence of its battle with the deer or the rock wall. Bo was a master.

Too bad he couldn't straighten and buff out the marks Laurel left on Jack's heart.

* * *

"What a moron," Chloe said.

Laurel watched Jack's retreating back, then turned to her. "That's it, then."

She walked on numb legs to the service counter, her fingers fumbling as she tried to untie her apron. She heard the door latch and lock and glanced over to see Chloe pulling the shades down.

"My brother's an idiot." Chloe picked up Jack's untouched food and walked toward her. "But I figured you for a smart cookie. Guess I was wrong."

Laurel finally pulled the damn apron ties apart and whipped off the thing. "What do you want me to say? We talked round and round about this Monday night, Chloe. I have to go back. There's nothing for me here."

"I just don't get it." Chloe dumped Jack's food and put the plate on the counter for Ricky. Her eyes grew round. "Oh my God, you're in love with him!"

Laurel started to argue, then just sank into the nearest chair. "Yes, I love him." She sniffed and blinked rapidly to hold off the tears. "I love him and I'm a fool for it. Thank goodness my car is fixed and I can get the heck out of here."

"That's it? That's all you have to say?"

"I'm sorry to leave you without help."

"You're as big an idiot as Jack is!"

"What?"

"Tell me you can just leave. Tell me you can just go back to your life in San Francisco and never see my brother again."

Laurel shook her head. "Look, I've learned a lot about Jack in the short time we were together. He's a man of few words and he says what he means."

"So he's a clod. So what?"

"He's never said he loves me. He's never said he'd like me to stay."

"Again I ask, so what?"

"Oh, you're hopeless."

"*I'm* hopeless?" Chloe sat across from Laurel and took her hands in hers. "You're in love with my brother, and you're afraid to tell him because he hasn't told you first?"

Realization hit Laurel right between the eyes. "I am an idiot."

Chloe stood and hugged her.

Laurel was too stunned to do more than pat her arm in return. "I have to talk to Jack."

Chloe pulled her to her feet. "Yeah, you do."

Laurel felt like crying and laughing and shouting. Her heart raced and she bounced on the balls of her feet. "I was just going to leave. Even if he doesn't say anything, there's no way I can go without telling him how I feel."

"Now, that's my girl."

Laurel hugged Chloe then, tight. "Thank you."

She went upstairs to pack. And to get ready for the scariest, bravest, stupidest thing she would ever do. She fingered the dream catcher hanging in the window and nodded.

She was going to tell Jack she loved him.

* * *

Jack pulled down the drive toward his house. He'd taken his time today, finishing up paperwork at the station long after the rec area closed at dusk. What was he rushing home to? There was Smokey, but lying around the house was making the dog pudgy and missing a meal wouldn't hurt him.

The Jeep rocked as he banked it down the last turn. So what if the house was empty? It was his and he'd learn to live in it alone again. The first thing he noticed were the lights. The house's windows were all lit. The place looked welcome after the hell of a day he'd put himself through. Then he saw Laurel's Beetle.

His heart did this silly flip thing and he spun the tires

of Jeep as he pulled to a stop. He cranked the brake and hurried out of the car and up the steps to the front door. "Laurel?"

She pulled the door open. "Hi."

"Hi." He walked in and she shut the door behind him.

"Chloe gave me your spare key." There was a softness in her eyes but there was something else there, too. Uncertainty?

"Um, what's up?" He put his keys on the table and didn't know what to do with his hands so he put them in his pockets. "I thought you were leaving."

"I was."

She swallowed and he watched the motion.

"And?"

"Jack, I love you."

His heart fell to his feet as the breath left his body. There was a rushing in his ears and he felt the room tilt beneath his boots. "You what?"

She lifted her chin and said it again. "I love you. I don't want to leave."

He grabbed her then, everything coming completely into focus as he held her close. The smell of her, the feel of her. The way she fit, up against him and in his heart. "I don't want you to go."

Laurel let out a laugh, a light beautiful sound that made him want to shout out his own happiness. Then he kissed her, tasting those lips he would never forget and now wouldn't have to. When he pulled back, she still clung to him.

"Let's sit down, baby. Before I fall down." They settled on the couch and he took her hands in his. "These past weeks. I never expected anything like this."

"Me either."

"I'm not cut out for 'no strings.'"

She blinked at him. "What are you saying? We can't be together?"

"No! Look, you have everything you need. And I wouldn't take that from you. But I only have one thing to offer. Me."

"That's convenient." She smiled. "You're all I want."

"God, I love you. Marry me?"

She gently pulled her hands out of his. "Jack, I…"

"Marry me, Laurel. Stay here and open your gallery and studio. You can run your mother's business from here.

We'll make it work, I swear."

"You've thought about this." Slowly, excitement lit her eyes. "Yes, Jack. I'll marry you."

Epilogue

Six months later

Laurel clicked the mouse to close the account spreadsheet, a smile on her lips. Her mother's business, renamed Astrid's Dreams, was doing well under Laurel's direction. Keeping the inventory narrow and deep—only a few styles with plenty of stock in most sizes—made management easier. Every few weeks she played with a new design to feature but for the most part the business took care of itself, leaving her time to focus on her own art and business.

She leaned back in her desk chair and fingered the white gold wedding band on her left ring finger, watching as the diamonds encircling it caught the late afternoon sun through the window behind her. She'd worn the ring for a little over a month, since marrying Jack on New Year's Eve.

Her studio and gallery was just down the road from the Butlers' shops and the café, in an oversized shed that Jack had made over to her specifications. It suited her, just like her new life.

The bell jingled above the door as Laurel stepped out

of the back office/studio. Chloe and Josh entered the gallery. "Hey, guys."

Josh stomped the snow off his little boots. "Hey, Aunt Laurel!"

"Don't touch anything," Chloe said to the little boy, as she did every time they came into the place. "That's a beautiful panel in the window."

Laurel glanced at the three-by-eight-foot panel she'd completed three days ago, one depicting the view from her and Jack's favorite spot. Greens and blues and browns caught the light and made the piece come alive. "I got another offer for it this morning. A ridiculous offer, actually."

"Are you going to take it?"

"Nope. But I'll make another one." Not exactly like it, though. This panel had a touch of color in the lower right corner, a representation of the blanket she and Jack had taken with them on their first hike. The day she'd realized she loved him.

She hugged Josh. "Josh, I picked up a few more books for you. They're on the table in the back."

"Thanks."

The little boy hurried toward his makeshift play area, carefully keeping his arms close to his sides. Laurel faced Chloe. "You need to call him. He should know what a terrific kid Josh is."

As usual, Laurel only touched on the subject of Josh's father. Chloe was always closed-mouthed about him, but that only confirmed the fact that she needed to talk about him sometime. She needed to see him too, but Laurel wasn't going to give her that particular opinion. She wasn't one of the Bennet sisters.

"I will, I promise," Chloe said at last. "Someday."

Jack walked into the gallery then, big and strong and wearing that crooked smile she'd seen just that morning in their bed. "Hey, baby."

She'd learned that every winter since his divorce he grew a beard that looked wonderful on him. She'd also learned that the beard tickled in all the best places. He'd shaved it for their wedding, against her protests. But by the end of their week-long honeymoon in Lake Tahoe he'd grown back a very nice bristly stubble.

"Hey, Jack," she said, hearing the low notes of love and want in her voice.

"Let me go get Josh," Chloe said.

Chloe grabbed Josh and they said their good byes. "Will we see you at Aunt Beth's?"

"Maybe," Jack said, his eyes still on Laurel.

Chloe laughed as she tugged her son out of the studio. "Newlyweds."

Jack pulled Laurel close. "You ready to go home?"

The heat in those Butler-blue eyes never failed to set her pulse racing. "Oh, yeah."

Home. Amazing. Altitude and attitude had shifted, and the thin air of Cloud Canyon proved as heady as Jack himself. Laurel had met her mountain man by accident, and tumbled into the best romance of her life. She'd let her passion guide her but it was her heart that found a home.

She had her feet on the ground and her head in the clouds, and she wouldn't want it any other way.

About the Author

JoMarie DeGioia is a bestselling author of Historical and Contemporary Romance. She's known Mickey Mouse from the "inside," has been a copyeditor for her tiny town's newspaper, and a bookseller. She is the author of over 40 Romances, and writes Young Adult Fantasy/Adventure stories and Paranormal Romance too. She gets lost in DIY projects around the house and works out plot ideas during long runs. She divides her time between Central Florida and New England.

Discover other books by JoMarie DeGioia

The Bridgewater Brides series, including
The Heir's Treasure
The Viscount's Vixen
The Earl's Beauty
The Gentlemen Undercover series, including
A Hero and a Gentleman
A Hero and a Rogue
The Shopgirls of Bond Street series, including
That Determined Mister Latham

The Dashing Nobles series, including

More Than Passion

Pride and Fire

Just Perfect

More Than Charming

The Cypress Corners series, including

Cypress Corners Boxed Set

Finding Harmony

Taming Jake

Loving Cassie

Winning Ben

Showing Jessie

Seeing Shannon (Barefoot Bay World novella)

Dreaming Eli

Giving Chase (Barefoot Bay World novella)

Kissing Bree

Wishing Joy

Bugging Nate

The Gifted YA Fantasy/Adventure Trilogy, including

Gifted

Braunachs of the Dell series, including

Luke's Gold

Patrick's Promise

The In the Castle series of Historical Novellas, including

In the Lady's Heart

In the Baron's Bed

In the Knight's Chamber

Connect with me online

Twitter: https://twitter.com/JoMarieDeGioia

Facebook: https://www.facebook.com/JoMarie.DeGioia.Author

Website: www.jomariedegioia.com

www.ingramcontent.com/pod-product-compliance
Lightning Source LLC
Chambersburg PA
CBHW072109250626
47159CB00007B/2362